Fall Into Fantasy 2021 Edition

A Cloaked Press Anthology

All stories in this collection are the creation of the author's imagination and are intended for entertainment purposes only. Any resemblance to person, places, events, etc. - living or dead - Is purely coincidental, or used in a fictitious manner.

Published by:
Cloaked Press, LLC
PO Box 341
Suring, WI 54174
https://www.cloakedpress.com

Cover Design by:
Fantasy & Coffee Design
https://www.fantasyandcoffee.com/SPDesign/

Copyright 2021 Cloaked Press, LLC
All Rights Reserved
ASIN: B09CGCCTDS
ISBN: 978-1-952796-05-0 (Paperback)

Cloaked Press is proud to present:

Shane Porteous
Barend Nieuwstraten III
Alex Minns
Andrew P. McGregor
Joanne Blondin
James Pyles
Anstice Brown
J.C. Pillard
Linda M. Crate
Matthew McKiernan
Jabe Stafford
Clarissa Gosling
R. A. Clarke
R. A. Meenan
Marsheila Rockwell

Contents

Gathering Genocide by Shane Porteous 1

Hearthshare by Barend Nieuwstraten III 19

The Concealed Witness by Alex Minns 41

Demon Dave: Dinner Time by Andrew P. McGregor 61

Astounding Performances by Joanne Blondin 75

Theo Klaaggorn, Private Eye by James Pyles 87

Beneath the Roots by Anstice Brown 107

Three Drops in the Snow by J.C. Pillard 119

Flight of the Fae by Linda M. Crate 135

The Each-Uisge by Matthew McKiernan 145

Dead Next Door by Jabe Stafford 157

The Genie of the Ring by Clarissa Gosling 173

The Brightening by R.A. Clarke 183

Some Things Remain by R. A. Meenan 193

Play it Again, Sem by Marsheila Rockwell 211

Gathering Genocide
by Shane Porteous

Galvreed was a giant amongst men, such size normally served him well. It had given him the brawn to out brawl a bear once, when the beast had gotten between him and his blade, he had to rely on his hands to stop the animal's attack. Considering he had crushed its skull, his hands had accomplished more than simple stoppage. He was strong enough to carry three barrels when most men barely could carry one, allowing him to finish his labours before lunch, this meant he often ate alone. His size had allowed him to wield a weapon that was weighty enough to cleave off the heads of soldier or stallion alike, all with a single swing. It also allowed him to wear armour that was thick enough to withstand blows from blades, bows, battle axes, bolts, even a battering ram a time or two. But such armour wouldn't keep him safe now, just like his size simply made him an easier target, this didn't serve him well.

By some freakish fluke the attack had taken off his helmet but not his head. He had hit the forest floor almost as fast as the dead that had been felled around him. He hadn't been slaughtered but that didn't mean he was unscathed, he could feel the blood, billowing from his brow, staining the strands of his grizzly brown hair and sideburns. Lying on his belly, his bourbon coloured eyes, became so big they seemed to claim a third of his face.

The war was supposed to be over, the enemy exiled from these lands, now more than ever this seemed a lie. Hence why they had never seen the attack coming, even if they had, he doubted they could've done anything to dodge it, the hellish hail of an attack had happened too swiftly, too successfully. One second, they were walking and whistling, the next they were down and dead.

Galvreed couldn't bring himself to believe it had been the work of bandits, whatever these weapons were, they surely could be sold for more money than whatever could be stolen from slain soldiers. Such things were too crude and capable to simply be spears, they stuck out from the slain, dark orange lengths that radiated a hellish heat, like these lengths were some freakish leeches sucking the warmth out of the bodies they had wrecked. Galvreed was gutted by the fact he had failed to keep his men safe, hence why they wore beige armour and he wore dark blue, such shading signified his command and rule number one about being a commander was keeping your companions alive.

He felt that wouldn't be his only failure today.

He stayed on his belly as his eyes shifted all across the forest before him, searching for whoever had launched the hellish lengths. He could see nothing but the trees, barks and bushes, he also couldn't see either bug or bird, the animals were smart enough to stay away from whatever had launched the assault; how dumb he felt.

Galvreed crawled forward, ensuring that a big tree stayed as a shield as his hand slowly moved to his waist. Despite still having a sword that could send a tree into splinters with a single strike, it wasn't his weapon he reached for. Instead his hand went to a pouch positioned on his belt, where he plucked out a pipe and pinched out some sort of weed, placing it into said pipe all with one hand. He kept his eyes before him as he did so, despite the fact they were filled with the sight of the tree, his instincts told him to keep contact with his substitute shield.

His eyes only moved away when his fingers failed in their search to find a striker. As did his eyes, before he could continue silently cursing himself his sight was swayed towards the closest corpse of his companions. Brekkor was the name that had once belonged to the body. The length had lacerated his chest, pinning him to the ground like he was a leaflet. Galvreed had let him borrow his striker, for reasons that were no longer relevant. Galvreed crawled slightly towards his dead friend, assured he would find the striker in Brekkor's bag. Although he moved only slightly out of the shielding of the tree, he held his breath, unsure of how that would save him from a second attack, it wouldn't, but he did so anyway.

As he got closer to the corpse, he could feel something other than sanguine stain his face, the feeling made him freeze for a second, before he realised it was sweat. The hellish length that had left Brekkor lying in death, remained radiating with wicked warmth, its dark orange was an omen he couldn't decipher, but still dreaded all the same. Instead of searching the bags of a dead body Galvreed placed his pipe upon the length and within a second smoke began billowing from the pipe. He removed it, placing it in his mouth as he moved back towards the tree, crawling to keep concealed. With three puffs the emerald smoke had enlarged and before long had engulfed the entire forest like fog. Galvreed kept the lit pipe in his mouth, watching as the air was all consumed by the smoky colour. Only putting out the pipe with his red gauntlet covered pinky when he was certain the smoke weighed too much for the wind to wash away.

He had used this tactic many times before during the war, had trained his men to march and move within this mist as masterfully as rain moves through a storm cloud. It wasn't so much that he could see through this mist, but Galvreed had gazed through it enough times to tell the difference between shadows, which were still, or stirring, which needed to be slain. More importantly the mist would make him an almost impossible target. Hence why he slowly moved to full height, hence why his hand no longer held the pipe but the hilt of his sword. He couldn't save his companions, but he could possibly make their attackers meet them in the afterlife.

Galvreed had taken two steps before his belly bashed into the ground again. He was amazed that he had seen it in time, the onslaught of orange that moved through the mist and the trail of trees before him, sending them all into sawdust, shrinking the once oak shield into little more than a stump. The mist hadn't been a burden to his attacker any more than the sea was to a shark. The attack had been so devastating that, not only did it destroy the line of trees directly before him, it had caused the mist to disappear completely, as if even the fog was so fear filled it had fled the forest. Galvreed scrambled to place his back upon the stump, putting himself in a seated position as his breaths became like a bellow. He couldn't stifle such sounds, not after what he had seen, not after what he had barely survived. He still held his sword, but it made him feel as safe as a leaf in a lightning strike. He kept as much of his head behind the stump as possible as he peered around it.

The sawdust the slain trees had become had settled and the air was now free of any fog, he finally could see his attacker, in the short distance just outside the line of destroyed trees. Lengths of iron surrounded her, but there was nothing messy about their mass gathering. What struck him the most about such a sight, was not her striking appearance, even a blind man could tell she was beautiful. It wasn't her hair, long lengths of lavender no flower could make, with a fringe that fell across her right eye, but left the amethyst that was her left to be seen clearly. It wasn't her dress, single shouldered, as simple as it was spectacular, that reached right down to her feet. It wasn't the colour of her skin, as dark and dreamy as dawn. Nor was it the ring of silver that sat around her neck. It wasn't even her lips, even though they were the colour of larva. It was the gathering of small blue circles that had collected near her left elbow. He knew such shading and shapes of said terrain weren't tattoos. Just like he knew there was only one kind of creature that could see through smoke so clearly.

"Lady dragon," he called out, his voice was both elegant and enormous, decimals so dignified and distinguished even the deaf could hear them. But not the dead, hence why he stayed hidden behind the stump.

"Do you know what that item around your neck is known as?" he asked, pausing just to catch his breath. "It isn't a necklace," he added, hoping to halt any oncoming attack.

It seemed to work, considering he was still alive. But that didn't stop him from keeping both his head and sight behind the stump.

"It is called a hound shoe," something in the air silently told him to stop speaking for a moment, something he listened to. "It is called that because whoever is cuffed by it must follow out whatever command they were given by whoever placed it upon them. The cuff only removes itself once the order has been complete, like a hunter commanding a hound, only freeing the animal from such service when it has fetched what the hunter shot. Why it is called a shoe is because of its u shape, like what a horse would wear on its feet." He paused again, just to gather his thoughts; it didn't take a wise man to know just how carefully he needed to choose his words.

"That's what those blue circles on your arm are, scales, whoever placed the horseshoe on you, forced you into your restrained form, commanded you to kill my countrymen, every death brings back a single scale."

He sensed her looking at such circles, he was sure of it, even though he continued to keep his head shielded by the stump.

"That's why you chose this place to come to, an iron mine, because you know what makes the most death during war, or rather the aftermath of it." Galvreed shook his head slightly as new thoughts travelled through it.

"Appalling," he began. "We won the war and instead of accepting defeat they decided to get a dragon to do their dirty work. How did the bastard get a hound shoe on you? I fought them long enough to know they're too cowardly to face you head on, sneaky scum, they must have placed it on you while you were sleeping, just sneaked right up and shackled you."

Galvreed became wordless as he waited for a response, he just hoped it would be with words and not weapons.

"You're lucky," she replied, her voice a melody no mortal nor music could make.

Galvreed clenched his jaw, containing a laugh from being let out. Of all the emotions engulfing him, luck wasn't among them.

"You can't have survived two of my assaults because of skill or smarts, you must know how dumb it is to taunt a dragon." her words were slow, surreal and striking.

"My lady," Galvreed was quick to say, as he held his sword ever tighter. "You misunderstand me, I was not mocking you at all. I just know how much your kind values knowledge, that's what the tales of your breed always get wrong, when they say you horde wealth, that doesn't mean dollars, it means wisdom."

He held his breath as if hell itself was hovering over him.

"What else do you know?" she asked, the strength of her speech couldn't be measured in muscles.

"As I said before, I know the reason why you chose to come to the iron mine. Because that is what actually kills the most people during war times, it isn't the fighting, it is the famine." He paused, to allow her time to disagree, she did no such thing.

"During the war every ounce of iron and steel is needed for weapons, but when the war is over, the time comes to turn metal into tools. If you can't harvest from the hard ground, hunger will haunt you more than the sight of a million marching men ever could. A sword is good for stabbing stomachs but not soils, in such times a pick is worth far more than any pike. The empire of bastards knew that better than most enemies we've faced before, hence why they butchered so many of our blacksmiths. Far easier to forge tools from raw iron than reshape weapons. A fact they unfortunately never forgot. The war went far too long, as most wars do, our food stocks have been picked bare, a new harvest is needed. That's why you're here, to stop iron from being mined, there will not be enough tools to take food from the ground, meaning thousands will be torn apart by starvation, meaning scales would sprout on you in far greater numbers." Galvreed, couldn't bring himself to say it was clever, even though it was. Just like he couldn't stop thinking about cruelty, because it was.

"That's what we were doing here," he said, pausing as his stare was stained by the sight of the slaughtered around him. "My battalion was sent to stop bandits from breaking into the mines."

He lowered his head in mourning for both his lost friends and for his failures.

He raised his head when his ears were hacked by the sound of something smacking the ground right next to him. His eyes were directed to the dead man's face, stuck within a silent scream. The body didn't belong to any of his battalion, nor was this man someone he would ever call brother. She had thrown the body of a bandit like it had weighed no more than a whisk, showing him her sheer strength.

"That's the other scourge of war times, it isn't just starvation, it's also stealing," he paused, finding it hard to look away from the horrified face of the bandit, not wanting to share the same fate.

"That's where it comes from," he began pulling his stare away from the dead bandit. "Scorched earth policy, burn the crops of your enemy and simply let starvation slay them instead of swords, save yourself the steel."

He couldn't stop himself from looking back at the bandit before he continued. "That's where humans got the idea from, inspired by your kind." He paused, again infected by the sight of the dead bandit, not to mention the one who murdered him.

"You seem the kind of man that would try to tell a bird about flight, next are you going to tell me the reason why my lips in this form are the colour of larva?"

"Because restrained as you are, you do not have the strength to breathe fire, but you can breathe such heat from your lungs into lengths of steel or iron, driving them forth like darts."

Something told him he shouldn't have said something so obvious; he could feel his head sink towards his shoulders as if fearing she was going to direct said dart his way.

"Every dragon knows that humans got the scorched earth tactic from my kind," she replied, and he was relieved her response wasn't the removal of his head.

"But have you ever met a man that knows your kind was inspired to do such a thing because of a practice performed by certain villages long ago?"

Her silence said things speech simply couldn't. He didn't laugh at this, but he let something out of his lungs that sounded similar as he found her soundlessness most impressive.

"You're intrigued?" he said, unsure if it was a statement or a question.

"I'm more intrigued by how you used the leaf of the gegem, I must admit you are the first man I've ever found that smokes the leaf rather than simply chewing it."

Her words seemed to fill his mind the way waves fill the mouth of a thirsty man. He raised his head and closed his eyes as if seeing a second long dream. It wasn't quite a smile that his mouth widened into, but it was something close.

"It has been hundreds of years since I've heard someone call that tree by its proper name," his words were so heavy they sounded hushed. "Most men simply call it the gentleman's god. You chew its leaves and you'll have fresh breath for life."

"So why did you smoke it? At least originally, it is clear you smoked it today to try and conceal yourself from me."

There was nothing taunting about her question or clarification, and yet for a moment Galvreed seemed gutted by the statement.

"I just wanted something that would make me unique, I never saw anyone try to smoke gegem leaves before, I just wanted to stand out." He stopped as he stared at the slain soldiers all around him, ravaged by how their armour was beige and his was uniquely dark blue.

"It was a simple mistake," such dread filled decimals were meant more for his ears than hers. But she heard him all the same.

"What do you know about the practices of certain villages long ago?" she asked.

Hearing this question Galvreed took a breath so heavy his chest was heaved towards his chin. He leaned his sword back from his forehead seeing how the sunlight was captured within the steel, making it into a mirror and as he stared at it, he found himself looking at a man he didn't like.

"That they were simpler times," he said, still staring at his reflection. "Times when a simple snowball could save an entire village from starvation." he stopped again, still staring at his own reflection, it wasn't the sight of his own blood that bothered him.

"Back then," he began after talking a long languishing breath. "It was up to the elders of the village to decide when it was time to eat, when it was time to harvest. Those winters were wicked things, within a day or so they could descend and make the ground too hard to harvest, meaning there wouldn't be more meals for months. So often during the dying days of autumn the children were sent to find snowflakes, they would spend hours searching and collecting them, because the snow would be so scarce before the cold came. If they could gather enough to make a snowball than that would be enough to convince the elders the time for harvest had come, before the snows gathered and forced starvation to set in."

He simply stared at the steel of his blade, haunted by the sight of himself.

"Witnessing those practices gave your kind the inspiration to burn any crops around your caves, keeping many simply seeking a meal away. Amazing is it not, how something as simple as a snowball saved so many from starving." His last sentence was spoken with a long low voice, more like a thought escaping than intended speech as he simply continued to look at the man he didn't like.

"That's correct," she replied slowly, surprise staining her speech, which was a sound as rare of a red leaf in spring. "How did you know that?"

"Probably the same way you do," he replied, still staring at his reflection. "I saw it." He paused again, peering at his own eyes in the reflection, their bronze seemed to bruise him. He placed the hilt back on his forehead, leaning against it and stopping the mirror the sunlight had made.

"That's not entirely true, my lady," he said, not forgetting his manners. "I did see it, but I didn't know that is why the children gathered snowballs...I just wanted to be different."

Before he said the last part the sword leaned back into the sunlight to show him his face once more, so he could see the sentence leave his lips, he still didn't like who he saw.

If words were water than the silence that followed was a sea, one too dark and deep for him to swim in.

"The mystic that placed the hound shoe upon you, do you know who he is?" Galvreed asked, raising his head so he wasn't staring at his own reflection.

"Yes," she replied, the word rippling through the forest like the shimmering that comes before a storm.

"Do you know how to find him?" Galvreed asked, keeping his head raised.

"Yes," she replied, the air rippling more severely.

"If you found him again, would you be strong enough to bypass his spells and slay him." Galvreed asked, keeping his glance away from his sword.

"Not in my current form," the dragon answered, disappoint designing her tone.

"In your released form?" Galvreed asked.

"Yes," she replied, her certainty cutting through the air like a claymore through a cloth. Galvreed nodded at this, although there was no approval in his gaze.

"You seem to be a man that enjoys stating the obvious," the dragon began. "Why are you asking me this?"

"Because I know of a way of releasing you from the hound shoe right here and now," Galvreed answered, staring back at his own reflection.

He watched as shadows seemed to darken the blade, as if the sunlight could see into his mind and was now scurrying away. He could almost feel the frenzy of questions flashing through her mind and so he simply waited wordlessly for her to speak again.

"How?" she said, a question as simple as it was suffocating. "How could you possibly know how to release me?" she added when he hadn't said anything.

"Because," he began finally, staring at the steel that no longer shone. "I'm wearing one to."

If words were indeed water than the silence that followed was not a sea, but a flood, one that could drown men and dragons alike.

"And what was the command your mystic gave you, to defend this land until your dying breath?" The dragon asked, the intrigue in her voice infecting him.

"No," he replied. "The reason why I've fought for this land for so long is because I owe it, far more than my life could ever give." He paused, no longer peering at his blade, no longer peering at anything, despite his eyes being opened he was blind to the world, as thoughts too terrible to ever speak trampled through his mind.

"Strictly speaking," he said as he slowly saw the world again. "It's not a hound shoe," Galvreed then added. "But I am wearing a shackle of my own."

Again he could fathom the frenzy of thoughts in her mind, so again he waited wordlessly.

"How would having a shackle of your own help me be released?" she finally asked, her words moving through the forest like wind.

"Forgive me, my lady," Galvreed began. "I know your kind values wisdom, but I am not wise enough to explain the reason in its entirety. But think of it like the connection between a shout and an echo. I release my shackle and in doing so yours will also open."

He watched as his sword continued to darken, the sunlight stirring even further away and for a moment his blade appeared entirely black.

"Do you not value the lost lives of the men that now lay around you?" she asked, the question straightening his spine.

He looked away from his blade but couldn't bring himself to look beyond the stump.

"I ask because I find it strange that a man would want to help someone who had slain his companions?"

"I value each and every one of them," he said, his own certainty cutting the air like it was a curtain. "But I cannot allow my fury to allow me to forget the very reason why these men fought, they didn't suffer through a decade of death and destruction only to allow their loved ones to be slain through starvation." He paused, peering at the sky as he did so, sunlight seemed more and more to be staying away from him.

"I am simply not strong enough to slay you," *in my current form*, he added in thought, but not words. "I am surely not the wisest man you will ever meet, but I am smart enough to know that my sword could never reach your heart before I was decapitated by one of your darts. Besides," he began after pausing. "Even if I managed to kill you, then the mystic who put the restraint on you will just send something else to cause starvation in this country. Not only that," he continued. "Who should the hawk hate, the hound sent to retrieve its corpse or the hunter that caused its death in the first place."

Again he waited wordlessly.

"I must admit," the dragon began, causing him to hold his breath. "You're wiser than I first thought."

While clearly a compliment it wasn't happiness that haunted his expression while hearing it.

"I don't feel that way," he began. "Considering what I am comprehending isn't something smart."

"How so?" the dragon asked, little worry in her words.

"Because there's a very good reason why I am wearing this shackle."

"Which is," she said with more than a little worry in her words.

Galvreed's head grew heavy once more and as he leaned it against his sword again, he could feel his hands slightly trying to shift it, so its edge would enter his head, anything to stab out the thoughts in his mind.

"That, my lady, isn't easy to explain."

His eyes closed then, not seeing slumber so much as seeking something slumber could never provide. Hence why he opened them again. Before he spoke once more, he moved his hands off the hilt of his blade, his fingers lowering upon the steel length as he moved it back and forth, trying to make a mirror once more. He wanted to see his expression as he spoke, but the sunlight stayed far away.

"Perhaps this question will answer it," he paused, giving himself one more pointless attempt to make a mirror.

He failed.

"Do you know how the moon was made?"

The soundlessness that followed was severe, the kind of silence created by strangulation. But amongst the appalling noiselessness he noticed the subtle sound of the dragon clutching a length of iron. As he heard this sound his fingers loosened on the sword, allowing it to lean to the side beyond the stump. This made a mirror, not for his reflection but hers, he could see that she kept the iron close to her lips, just in case she needed a dart driven right towards him.

Clearly, she had heard his question.

"Forgive me..." he began, and his mind made thoughts that tore through him like teeth.

"Lady Dragon," he managed to continue. "Your actions are justified, but I am quite a cynical person. In order for me to believe that you know how the moon was made. I must ask another question."

It wasn't so much that he held his breath as his breath felt trapped in his throat, as if his subconscious had stuck it there, and with good reason.

"What colour was the night before it became black?" he could breathe again, but didn't feel better about this fact.

He watched the reflection of her and for a fleeting moment he was convinced she was going to bring the length to her lips.

"Lavender," she answered and his hands seized the sword murdering the mirror it had made and bringing the hilt of the blade back to his forehead. He paused in a strange kind of prayer, not to any god, but to nothingness, which for him in that moment was something worth worshipping.

Galvreed couldn't bring himself to speak, not just yet, he needed to stare at the blue sky in silence and he was sure she knew why.

"Please," he began with a brittle breath. "My lady, if you know tell me what is it that I gathered into a globe that day."

The weight of his words could be felt even on her shoulders, considering the creature she was, that said something speech simply couldn't.

"I know it wasn't snow," she replied.

It wasn't a smile his mouth made, simply a shape that let out a breath that didn't belong in his body. Galvreed's head rose back as his tongue turned itself over and over again as if conjuring a truth too terrible to tell.

He told it anyway.

"For hundreds of years what happened that day has haunted me. The half dozen times I've managed to find someone or something that knows how the moon was made, that is always their answer, it wasn't snow."

Once again, his sword leaned from his hands, showing him her reflection once more.

"With as much respect as I can muster, my lady," he began, unaware he was baring his teeth. "But you seem to be quite the hypocrite. You accused me of mocking you once and clearly didn't care for it. Yet you have no problem mocking a man willing to help you, despite the deaths you have delivered to those he held dear."

There was no threat to his tone, but it seemed more tremendous than a thousand thunderstorms.

It was not intimidation that infected her eyes, but inflexion.

"You're mistaken," she began. "I did not mean to mock you," she added with a sincerity that should've soothed him, but didn't. "I do not know what you gathered that day, or why it has let you live for hundreds of years passed a mortals perish, all I know truthfully was that it wasn't snow."

Despite the care in her voice, Galvreed took the same breath someone took upon being stabbed. Despite the sword keeping her reflection Galvreed didn't look towards it, with continued stabbed breaths he just stared at the sky for several severe seconds. His head then lowered, nodding in a way that could wound the world. He then leaned out from the stump, turning his head towards her, the mirror of the sword no longer satisfactory. Even the lady dragon was dominated by the look in his stare as it began trembling, like an earthquake had emerged behind his eyes.

"But you can see how a boy could mistake it for snow, how a young child, abandoned and alone, who just wanted to be accepted, just wanted to be acknowledged, would look at these cold flakes of green, believing them simply to be a special kind of snow, you can understand how a child, who had only known the cruelty of others, just wanted for one bloody day in his dreary life to be special."

There was a dignity to his tear drops, a maturity that most, even if they lived for a million years could never make. And yet in those moments, for all of his size, strength and gravitas, Galvreed looked like a little boy, lost and languishing. His gaze was of one that had seen genocide, a look that would linger for a long time even in a dragon's mind.

"Yes," she said in a whisper that wove around him like a whirlwind.

He turned back around, taking breaths that still sounded affected by a blade. For several moments he sat in a soundlessness even the sky seemed to listen to. He didn't wipe his eyes, but no more tears formed or fell, as if his subconscious knew such things couldn't scrub his sadness away.

"Do you know my name?" he finally asked, bringing the blade back before him, although he used it neither as a mirror or something to lean on.

"Galvreed," she replied, keeping the iron length in her hand, but no longer close to her lips.

To this he nodded, although it wasn't approval aiming his gaze.

"So," he began, his breaths seemingly sheaving the blade that had once broken it. "I remove my restraint, which will cause yours to be removed, you then take on your true form and then you will kill the mystic that placed the hound shoe on you, you'll spend your time attacking and living in the empire of bastards and you will leave these lands alone?"

"Yes," she said with a sincerity that satisfied him.

"And you know what you need to do once both of our restraints are removed?"

"Yes," she replied, bringing the length of iron closer to her lips.

"Forgive my cynicism again my lady, but in order to know you are going to do the right thing, I need to hear you say it specifically, what do you need to do directly after our restraints have been removed."

"Drown you in flame," she said, her words filling the forest despite the fact she hadn't raised her voice.

To this Galvreed nodded, a gesture that wasn't grand but it was genuine. He rose slowly, but didn't grunt or groan, despite the breath he took as did so, sounding like an old dog, one that should've been put down decades ago. Despite both believing the other, Galvreed and the lady dragon kept their lengths of metal in their hands. Clearly neither forgot whose presence they were in. They simply stood staring at one another for several long silent moments, both realising the rarity of each other.

"Please speak true, my lady," Galvreed began. "I've heard it said that the bodies of those burned away by dragon fire are purged of their sins, that those whose mortal shells are made into ash by your flames are forged a path to paradise? One that even a man without feet could've walked across?"

"It is true," she said soothingly.

Hearing this Galvreed's head lowered as he glanced around at the extinct expressions of his butchered brethren. His eyes came to rest on the sight of the dead bandit and after a second of thought he seized the dead man's arm and dragged the corpse with him as he moved into the centre of the collection of corpses. Galvreed was feeling generous, while he had no sympathy for stealing, perhaps this bandit had seen one of the heated lengths of iron and simply wanted to be special. He didn't ask the lady dragon if this was true, the time for conversation was quite quickly coming to an end. As he stood surrounded by the slain, there was only one more thing to ask.

"Are you ready, my lady?" he asked, watching and waiting as she nodded, a motion as simple as it was sincere.

She dropped the length of iron a second before he dropped his sword. The biggest difference between their two actions was things continued to descend from him. His movements were minimal yet oddly marvellous, enough to make the dark blue protective plates of his armour drop from his anatomy, one after another. Before long, his skin was bare of all steel, the only clothing he now wore was a simple set of slacks, too faded to form a colour, and something that sat on the entirety of his left forearm like a second skin.

The same something both warrior and dragon were now staring at. There was no circles or scales amongst it, in fact it looked deceptively simple, a length of brown leather that an archer might wear to stop the string from scratching his skin. It certainly looked like something no bandit would bother to steal, but they both knew better than that. Galvreed glanced back towards the lady dragon as if determined to ensure that she was still there. She was, and her glare told him she was well aware of the gravity of what he was about to do.

He could feel his body bulking, his muscles moving, making themselves harder than stone. It was as if his subconscious was trying to shift them into shields, but he was well aware they wouldn't be any more successful than the stump had been. He flexed his hand several times, the movement reminiscent of stones flickering together hoping to form a spark. As his muscles continued to tense the length of leather on his arm began rolling at its end, shifting like a snake shedding his skin. Underneath the leather they both could see lines bulging under his skin as if his blood was becoming as thick as syrup. Seconds passed and such lines began pulsating with something that didn't seem to be blood. They began becoming different colours, both yellow and silver, but it wasn't metal moving under his skin. Such pulsating surely seemed painful but all expression seemed to have evaporated from his face as if there was no emotion eternal enough to reveal what he was feeling.

His fingers slowly stopped flexing, staying still as if they were holding some sort of sphere. They both knew it would be holding something before long. The deceptively simple length of leather had scrolled down to his wrist now, revealing the powerful bulging lines of silver and yellow swelling his entire forearm. In that moment everything around him seemed to freeze, not with frost but fear, as if even the foliage could feel the frightening power, he was about to unleash. He looked back towards the lady dragon, seeing how her head was lowered the way a beast does when danger drew near. She didn't return his gaze, she kept it upon his palm, he didn't need to wonder why this was so.

Galvreed's gaze stayed on her, partly to ensure she wouldn't evaporate out of his presence, but mostly because he couldn't bring himself to see it again, the appearance of that which had caused such atrocity so long ago. The length of leather, which now appeared little more than a wrist band separated in a simple snapping sound that stung the air more than a million stabs ever could. Much like the iron length and the sword, the shackle around her neck descended just after his restraint had.

Before the second was over scales were spreading across her body like strangely beautiful boils. There was nothing strangely beautiful about the sphere of energy enlarging and hovering just above Galvreed's hand. The globe was a greyish yellow, the colour of sunlight shining on a gravestone. Such a colour cast no shadow, as if the sun was still smart enough to stay well away from him. Galvreed's glance stayed on the lady dragon as like a leaf in autumn her dress descended off her, before any bit of her womanly frame could be witnessed, her body had begun to shift, not just in scales but in size and shape.

Before the moment was over the maiden had moved into something the size of a mountain. Gone was her purple hair, replaced by lavender spikes, longer than lances and far sharper. Wings wider than walls had woven out from her back, seeing them stretch out was a spectacular sight. They were so huge they could hurl hurricanes with a single flap. They showed their strength as they lifted her into the heavens with an inescapable ease, causing a wind that carried itself across the forest, making everything from blades of grass to strands of Galvreed's hair shake. The sole exception was the sphere, it stayed undisturbed by the wind, perhaps even the air was aware of the appalling power it possessed and couldn't be driven upon it even by a dragon.

Her beauty remained, although it was no longer that of a lady. Seeing her transformation complete was intimidatingly impressive, more so than a billion flowers blooming at once. The one thing that stayed the same about her, was the lavender of her eyes, her sight remained just as stirring, just as special. A sympathetic sorrow could be seen in them. So much so Galvreed's glance stayed upon them as her tail, longer than a tower was tall, whipped across the ground, in one smooth strong motion seizing the lengths of iron and placing them into a pile far behind her. With the restraint removed she fortunately saw no need to allow the people of this land to starve.

She soon opened her mouth, revealing teeth that could bite through bridges like they were biscuits. Before long a burning ball of flame formed before her mouth, rivalling the size and intensity of what hovered over Galvreed's hand. As like a comet her flames came crashing towards him, he didn't smile, but his mouth moved into a satisfied shape.

The lady dragon had kept her word.

When Galvreed regained consciousness, he was completely naked, face down with a mouthful of a foul taste. The first thing he turned his head to was his hand, to ensure nothing was hauntingly still hovering over it. Nothing was there, only he didn't completely fathom this until his fingers could touch each other again. The second thing he turned his head to was the restraint, it sat, still intact, having come back together again, on the burnt black terrain. Quickly he seized it slipping it back upon his forearm as fast as he could, despite the power of the dragon's flame, not even an inch of it was flaked. He had awakened alone, accompanied only by ash and air abandoned by the wind. The dragon's fire had burnt away every body, whether bandit or brethren, the earth all around him so scorched no seed would ever sprout for several centuries. It was even powerful enough to make the sphere's energy seep back into his body, but he knew not even a dragon was strong enough to destroy it entirely. If he removed his restraint again, he was sure it would return, as certain of this as a corpse was of death.

He knelt upwards, taking a breath big enough to shake the ashes from his anatomy, revealing the deluge of dragon's fire hadn't damaged his skin.

Some sins couldn't be scorched away, the thought turned in his head like a torturer's screw. His head rose to the night sky, only now realising the flames had forced him to faint for several hours.

How black the night was.

As much as he wanted to, he couldn't look away from the nocturnal heavens, any more than he wanted the memories of that day massacring his mind.

He was able to shift his eyes, ever so slightly, just enough to look upon the moon. It was the most marvellous thing he had ever made, but the memory of its creation still maimed him. When he had gathered those green flakes on that day, they didn't start to change colour or grow in size until he had made his way into the village, until it was too late to stop the sphere, as it grew and grew goring through everything in its path.

While the wails of the villages he heard that day still haunted his head, still made him lose sleep. It was the sound of the sky screaming that stained him the most, it was a noise not even nightmares would dare create. The only thing more terrible than the sound was the sight of the purple plunging out of heavens, like the sky was skinning itself, trying to save itself from the infection of the growing sphere.

It didn't work.

He remembered seeing a dragon, drawn by the destruction, a second before it sent down a deluge of flame upon him and the sphere. He remembered waking up in a world greatly wounded by what he had made. He remembered shuddering, he remembered being scorched, he remembered being the sole survivor. He remembered being appalled by the atrocities all around him, he remembered seeing the specks of silver on the ground, the only things that hadn't been swallowed by the sphere or scorched by the fire. He remembered thinking how snowballs were meant to make everything better, so he gathered the silver into a sphere, hoping that would somehow reverse the ruin.

It didn't work.

He later learned what the silver was, the corpse-crumbs of what was left of the lavender. Placed together they were strong enough to return to the sky, but too crippled to claim their correct colour, too weak to widen beyond a simple sphere. The stars were the specks he found as he walked further and further trying to find another survivor, he stopped collecting them when he remembered what had made the sky black in the first place.

As he sat there now, an anomaly amongst the ashes, he tried to take solace in the fact the full moon hadn't increased in size over the centuries.

It didn't work.

Shane Porteous is the master of the legendary 77 donut devouring technique. He lives in a place of strange dreams and an even stranger reality. A lifelong writer with over 50 publications, he has an immense passion for imaginative and if possible original storytelling.

Hearthshare

by Barend Nieuwstraten III

"Hurry," Ewen yelled to his lagging companion, releasing a breath cloud of white vapour that dispersed into the cold evening air.

Snow fell fast as the sun fell slow. An orange glow followed the sun west as it withdrew its heat from the lands around the Middle Sea, taking it to the lands beyond the great western ocean, while darkness filled the eastern sky.

A small cluster of wooden buildings with thatched roofs lay ahead of the southbound pair, trudging in their thick brown furs. A small town with no sign of life, save for a single yellow glow atop the one building producing smoke from its chimneys. Ewen looked back to Wenbry and pointed to the small inviting beacon of light. "You see that?"

Wenbry nodded, too exhausted to talk and struggling to keep up.

"I'm not going to die a quarter-mile from a fire. You catch up or I'm leaving you out here," Ewen teased his sluggish companion, encouraging a quicker pace. "I might even lock the door behind me out of spite."

As they approached, Ewen saw another figure on the road, well past the town. It wasn't till the pair were within the settlement that they could see the distant traveller was approaching from the other direction, wrapped in grey fur. Ewen threw his well-covered arm up in a friendly greeting and got one in return. As he smiled, he could feel the moisture, he was breathing into his short black beard, start to stiffen it in the cold accosting his face. He waited at the corner of the building for his friend to catch him up, then pushed him through the door.

They stepped inside a cosy inn with a high roof lit by a suspended chandelier made of large interlocked antlers. A railed wooden loft provided a partial second floor that ran along three of the inn's walls.

"Welcome friends," a middle-aged man said through his big bushy light-brown beard, while a short stocky woman leant on the bar beside him, giving them a warm inviting smile.

"There's another on his way from the south," Ewen announced, in the local tongue, as he brushed his gloved fingers through his short black hair to shake out the snow.

"All are welcome here," the innkeeper said, giving him a curious look and pointing to hooks upon the wall for their thick brown cloaks. "My name's Bjoric, this is my wife Urala. Welcome to Hearthshare Inn."

Ewen hung his cloak, while Wenbry tucked his gloves into his belt and rubbed his hands together to heat his fingers. Resting them on his hairless red cheeks, he crept towards the fire. Ewen slowly made his way towards the innkeeper, as he looked about the inn.

There was a man in a hooded cloak, seated in a large red padded armchair by the hearth, hunched forward as he warmed his wrinkled skinny hands on a stone goblet, releasing a warm thin vapour. He had his back to most of the room, with the only person close to facing him in a similar chair by the fire, asleep. A young burly man.

"Something warm to drink?" the innkeeper offered. "Hot spiced mead, gluhwein, soup?"

"Two hot meads, then two hot soups," Ewen said, looking back at Wenbry, pacing around the inn like a mute. Still too cold to stand still, but not venturing far from the hearth.

"Little quiet tonight?" Ewen observed, tapping his fingers on the bar.

"Don't expect many. But then, I never am. Not this time of year."

"I'm not surprised. This feels like the only inhabited place in town."

"That's because it is," Bjoric confirmed. "Aside from my wife, children, myself, and Sverol, having a little nap over there, this town's deserted every winter."

"Seasonal desertion?" Ewen asked, frowning curious. "So, where do they all go?"

"Up north, to the city of Giants Rest," the innkeeper said, ladling hot liquid for his latest guests. "The jarl houses them in the city for winter."

"That would be the place to be I suppose. Wasn't terribly keen about leaving when we passed through," Ewan said. "I must say that's very accommodating of the jarl."

"Well much of the food the city lives on through winter is grown here during the merciful months."

"I see," Ewen said, accepting two small steins from the innkeeper. "Wenbry," he called out, summoning his wandering friend to the hot drink he held out for him. "He had a little too much to drink last night," Ewen explained to the innkeeper, "and stayed up far too late with a girl in Giants Rest who, as luck would have it, was also quite accommodating."

Wenbry collected his drink and raised the stein with a silent thankful nod to Bjoric. His shoulder length wavy brown hair dangled around the stein, as he sniffed, deeply inhaling the spiced vapour rising from his drink.

"Not that I blame him," Ewen shrugged. "We've a mundane task ahead. He'll probably be napping like your young friend by the fire, soon enough."

"Ah, is that why he's so quiet?" the amused innkeeper asked. "A little tender today?"

"That, and he doesn't understand a word we're saying."

"Ah, I was starting to wonder where you're from. I mean, I can understand you, you know the Crag tongue. But while it varies, east to west, it's almost as if you've taken words from very old songs and rearranged them to suit your meaning. Where did you learn our language?"

"Hjaanmar."

"Oh, you're a long way from home," the innkeeper remarked.

Before Ewen could respond, an icy chill swept through the inn. It overtook the traveller from the south as he finally arrived, despite his best efforts to open and close the door as quickly as possible. He rested his back against the door, staying in his grey fur a little longer as he caught his breath. "Wind's picked up," he puffed. "Snowing bloody sideways out there."

"Then you best come get something warm inside you," the innkeeper offered. The newcomer raised a thankful but also hedging hand, needing a moment before any action could be taken. Bjoric gave him an understanding nod.

"Actually, we're not from Hjaanmar," Ewen said, resuming the conversation. "I just learned the language there."

"Well, that explains it then. Even *they* call it the old tongue when *they* speak it," the innkeeper said, pouring a warm mead into another stein for himself as he waited for the latest arrival to hang his coat and approach. "At least that's what the passing Hjanmaarians, I've met, have told me. So, where do you hail from, then?"

"Cliffguard, of Umberdale," he said.

"Umberdale?" an old man's voice asked, from the fire. "Do you not mean the Umberlands?"

"Not for nearly twenty years," Ewen scoffed amused, turning to face the shrouded elderly man who had his back to him, nestled in his comfortable red chair. "I take it you missed news of the unification."

"Hmmm, sounds like I *did*," the old man said, as if the old news left a bitter taste on his tongue. "I'll wager the Citadel of Light was behind that. They didn't make House Rosendor the kings of this unified Umberdale, did they?"

"House Wyndes rule from the capital of Ironcrest in…"

"Densdale. Yes, I remember House Wyndes," the old man said, "but I can't imagine House Aeligis of Southmarch going along with that. Nor House Belethon of your kingdom, or whatever it is now. Province?"

"They did not," Ewen said, blowing on his hot drink. "At least from what I heard. I was only a lad at the time." Intrigued, he took a few steps closer. "You know much of my homeland."

"I lived in Southmarch a very long time ago," the old man said, as Wenbry gave a curious look, hearing the mention of names and places more familiar to him amidst a tongue he didn't know.

"How's the mead?" Bjoric asked, from behind the bar.

"Good, good," Ewen said, turning back to the innkeeper, taking an obligatory premature sip that burned his lips. "So, yes, I was going to ask, if the town is deserted, why stay behind?"

"Tradition," the innkeeper said, shrugging. "Mostly because the local townsfolk kept returning every spring to find travellers had snuck into their barns and homes to shelter from the harsh winter, only to die huddled in some corner. Dead folk don't make for the most pleasant homecoming, so a long time ago, someone decided to keep this place open and running through winter as a refuge in the cold, to keep you all alive and stop you rotting in the homes of locals like Sverol." He pointed to the young burly blond man sleeping by the fire, failing to keep the old Umber company.

"Appreciated," Ewen said, raising his stein and clinking it with the innkeeper's.

"If we just waited for you to turn up dead in someone's home, we wouldn't get to ask you why you'd want to travel south so late in the year?"

"*Want,* would be a strong word for it," Ewen replied. "We were hired for fetching and gathering. Nothing exciting. We just thought we'd have more time before winter took hold."

"Seasons don't read calendars, as my father used to say," the innkeeper jovially recalled. "I hope whoever sent you is paying you generously."

"Well, as you say, we wouldn't have jumped on a southbound ship this late in the year if they weren't. Just wish your winter had given us a few more days."

The whiskery dark-blond stranger, they had seen on the road, pointed to the gluhwein as he reached the bar. "Perhaps you should hold off till the spring," he suggested, joining the conversation. "You could join me, heading back north in the morning. Unless there's some urgency to your task."

"I think spring is far later than our current employer was hoping we'd return, but the real urgency is the arrangement of payment on delivery," Ewen confessed.

"Ah, well," the stranger said, with a sympathetic grin. Sipping his gluhwein from his ceramic goblet, he eyed Ewen and Wenbry's sheathed swords. "I've *been* there. What was it my old mentor used to say? Your stack of coin is a pillar that keeps up the stone roof of starvation. If you let it get too low, you'll be crushed."

Ewen huffed, amused. "Well, we're keeping our knees bent and heads low at the moment, but by winter's end we'll be crawling on our bellies in your old mentor's house of coin and hunger."

The northbound stranger winced. "Then brave the cold you must," he suggested. A dozen or so years his senior, he patted Ewen on the shoulder, before making his way to the fire. He stood between the red chairs, looking to the sleeping man then the old hooded patron. "That must have been quite some story you were telling him, old man."

The old man gave a dismissive wave and shook his head.

"So, who is everyone?" the stranger asked, turning to face the room. "I'm Ulfrem, from Hrenmar."

"I'm Ewen and that's Wenbry," Ewen said, pointing to his companion, who lifted his head at the mention of his name. "Though, as we're from Umberdale, he only speaks the Kestrian tongue."

"Winter's blessing upon you, Wenbry," the old man said, in the language spoken across their home continent.

Realising he could actually converse with someone, Ewen's pacing companion gravitated towards the fire, collecting a wooden chair from one of the tables on his way.

"And you, old man?" Ulfrem asked. "You have a name?"

"Old man," the old man gave, as a bitterly sarcastic response. "But you can call me… Old Man."

"Suits me," Ulfrem said, shrugging with an awkward grimace as he pointed to the sleeping man. "And this one, off wandering Solondil's restful forest?"

"Sverol," the innkeeper reminded him, amused by the colourful description.

"Ah yes, of course," he said, gently clinking his goblet with Sverol's neglected one on a small side table. Finding little entertainment there, Ulfrem began to wander back towards the bar as Wenbry pulled up by the old man's large soft red throne, on a far humbler wooden seat, introducing himself in the only tongue he knew.

"So, it sounds like you're in a similar line of work to us," Ewen said, pointing to Wenbry and himself as Ulfrem reapproached. "What dragged you away from warmer places to go venturing to the cold lands south?"

"Coin, as always," Ulfrem said, biting his lip before raising his goblet for another sip.

Ewen waited with a raised brow, anticipating a more elaborate explanation that never came. "Well… that thrilling tale of adventure ate up far less of the night than I had hoped." Ewen chuckled, glancing at Bjoric.

Behind the bar, the innkeep rolled his eyes, sipping his own self-served mead.

Ulfrem smiled, "I didn't realise I was the night's entertainment. Sorry," he said, as if retracting his earlier extroversion. "What of you? What sends you so far south?"

"Arcticite," Ewen said. "Weather permitting."

"I don't know what that is," Ulfrem confessed. "Some kind of metal?"

"Ice crystals that form when frostdrakes or white dragons breathe frost on any naturally occurring moisture," he explained.

"Longfrost," the old man by the hearth said, without looking away from the fire, interrupting his own conversation with Wenbry to assist Ewen. "That's what they call it down this way."

"Heard of longfrost, but I didn't know that's what it was," Ulfrem admitted. "Who's asking you for *that* then?"

"A sorcerer back home. It's a material they use in some of their alchemy. Not something local herbalists seem to carry, I guess. At least not lately, or they wouldn't be sending a pair of fetch-and-carriers like us, I suppose," Ewen reasoned. "But then, like you, I'm doing it for the coin. I'm not all that interested in the application. I just know what it looks like and have a fairly good idea where to look for it. Whereas you seem so focused on the coin you've earned, you don't even seem to remember what you already did to collect it," he teased Ulfrem's elusiveness.

"Alright, alright. Look, it's not much of a story," he assured Ewen and the listening innkeeper. "It's just a job like any other. Someone with coin wanted me to fetch something they wanted. So, I fetched it from the place they said it would be and, come morning, I'll resume that delivery. Then I should have enough money to stay somewhere warm for the rest of the year. Until the spring brings in the new one, when I'll see who wants what from where."

Bjoric whistled, impressed. "They're paying you enough to put your feet up for three months?" the innkeep asked, leaning on his bar.

"That must be quite a *thing* they wanted fetched," Ewen added.

"Yeah, see, well, this was just the kind of conversation I was hoping to avoid with strangers." Ulfrem shook his head, again eyeing the sword by Ewen's side. "It's not a valuable item to you or anyone other than the person who sent me to fetch it. It's not useful to anyone else."

Ewen pulled his head back, surprised, raising a reassuring hand. "Oh, I think you've got the wrong idea," he assured him. "Just looking for conversation, friend. No one here's going to rob you. We all just want to be somewhere warm for the night, and the night's barely begun. I plan to have some hot food, more hot drink, and relax for the night, before marching through that horrible weather in the morning. In the opposite direction, I might add, to your collector of things of no value to anyone but him. Not even of fireside conversational value, it would seem. So just relax, friend."

"Aye," Bjoric agreed, pointing at the man with his stein, "the only thing anyone here's interested in stealing from you is some banter."

Ulfrem looked the Umber over, considering his words and those of the innkeep. "You're right. Of course, you're both right," he apologised. "I'm a friendly man by nature. I've just had a few past experiences that have tainted my desire to share *too* much with strangers."

"So, perhaps tell us of some adventure from some other time, where the item is long safe delivered, and the coin long safe spent," Ewen suggested, while the innkeeper nodded in agreement.

Ulfrem smiled apologetically. "That I can do."

Sometime later, as Ulfrem was telling a story in an exchange of many, a crack came from the wooden loft above, heralding footsteps as someone walked upon the landing above. Ulfrem whipped his head up, startled, looking concerned.

"Ah, sounds like the nightshift is up and about," the innkeeper said to his wife.

Urala gave her husband a single upward nod with a smile.

"The nightshift?" Ewen asked.

"Aye, my children. They run the tavern at night while my wife and I sleep. Though all four of us do together in the late evening and early morning," he said, looking up to a young man slowly descending the stairs, caught in a long yawn as he buttoned a leather vest over his thick brown woollen shirt. "You're going to suck the fire out of the hearth if you yawn any harder, Edvin."

His son gave him a dismissive wave as he continued down towards them. Ewen looked back to Ulfrem, curious about his jumpiness, as the innkeeper's son passed them to fetch himself a bowl and fill it with soup.

Ewen raised his stein in a polite silent greeting, matched by the young man who raised his bowl in a similar gesture. Looking up from him, Ewen was startled as he noticed, for the first time, an enormous bear's head mounted high above the bar. "Good gods. Is that how big the bears get down here?" he asked, disturbed by the grey-furred head of the creature that must have once been the size of a carriage.

"Ah, that's Gjallarbjorn," the innkeeper said, as his son looked back to it and smiled. "He watches over the place."

"He looks like he could bite a man in half," Ewen said. "Or at least could have, in his day."

"It's a dire bear," the old man by the fire said. "Couldn't believe them myself when I first saw one."

"Don't worry, they normally don't wander this far north," the innkeeper suggested. "Sometimes, during the bitterest of winters, when the *real* cold comes up from the Everwinter Wastelands, it can bring some of the things that live down in it."

"Aye, the cold tide," the innkeeper's wife added, as she began setting a table. "The cold winds can wash up stuff, like the sea does sometimes."

"The cold tide?" Ewen asked, pulling his head back. "At least when the ocean leaves stuff on the shore it's either dead or stranded. I don't imagine you'd be able to just walk around one of these fellows like you might a beached fish." He pointed up at Gjallarbjorn.

"They're not the worst things that live down that way, either," Ulfrem said, with a tone of knowing dread.

"Though beyond dire bears, I suppose I don't really care if there's worse," Ewen reasoned. "Shark infested waters are hardly the place to worry about seadrakes and blue dragons if you're overboard."

"Until you're back on the ship, I suppose," Ulfrem suggested.

"Well, this old fellow came up long before my time, and no one's seen one around these parts since, so I wouldn't worry too much," the innkeep reassured Ewen.

Ulfrem and Ewen continued to exchange tales over drinks and food for the next few hours, as the old man continued chatting in the Kestrian tongue to Wenbry by the fire, discussing some long history and politics of the Umberlands, while the local man, Sverol, continued to sleep in the chair opposite them.

The innkeeper and his wife saw everyone fed, then sat relaxed at a table while their son, Edvin, and daughter, Hedvig, took over the bar and periodically fed the fire.

Sverol finally kicked awake, startled by the main door suddenly opening and slamming shut, and the cold rush that accompanied it. A shorter figure, buried in furs, stood with their back to the room, leaning against the door with both small gloved hands pressed against it. They took a few breaths and muttered under their breath as a handful of snowflakes that followed them in fell to the floor.

Without surrendering their cloak, or several as it appeared, the figure made for the heat of the hearth.

"Something hot, friend?" the innkeeper's son called across the small inn. "Spiced mead, gluhwein, soup?"

"I think a gluhwein to start, please," a woman's voice answered, from under the hulking layers of fur. "And I hope it's hotter than the Burning Pools of Azuhl's hellish realm."

The room went silent, as few would be so bold as to make such a troublingly dark reference so flippantly. Only the old man stirred after an awkward lull, in which the crackling of the fire had replaced all conversation. He hummed a low gravelly growl of amusement. "You'll be there soon enough, if you stand any closer to that fire under that pack of wolf pelts," he warned.

She turned back, revealing only a dimpled chin under a devious smile. "Good point," she said, and returned to the door to hang her coat. Once removed, it seemed to have made up the bulk of her initially perceived frame, now revealing a petite one underneath it all. "Still, a tempting alternative to out there," she said, pointing to the door.

Her skin was a little too tanned to be local, as if it had once been darker but had since been starved of sun this far south of wherever she was born. Her thick black hair sat in a short puffy bob and she wore layers of brown leather with draped black cloth that fell and looped in an elegant pattern about her hips and legs with a short cape that hung from her shoulders. Her feet stepped inline as every man in the inn watched her move across the room with cat-like grace towards the bar. With thick pouty lips, slow blinking dark eyes, and high cheekbones, she was a rare exotic beauty in a place where her kind lived only in tales.

Seemingly immune to her natural allure, or aged beyond caring, the old man turned back to Wenbry. "So, who now are the lords of the two southern kingdoms of the... well, of this new Umberdale?" the old man asked his fireside companion in the Kestrian tongue.

"Oh, uh, House Rosendor rule the *region* of Southmarch from the new capital of Stormbeach while House Aeligis rule the city of Whiteborough, which they renamed Aeligfall after the unification," Wenbry said, still watching the woman approach the bar. "And, uh… Cliffguard had similar changes. House Belethon was reduced from kings of the region to lords of the city of Hillspear while Fleetwatch was made the new capital on the high southern peninsular, ruled by House Eeburn."

Ewen couldn't help but listen to the old man and Wenbry's conversation though his eyes remained with the recently arrived woman approaching the bar where Edvin handed her a goblet steaming with gluhwein.

"Ah, the lords of Wardenfort," the old man scoffed bitterly. "So, it *was* the Citadel's work after all. Supplanting the kings of the Umberlands with obedient puppets of the faith," he said, humming disapprovingly. "Again."

"Again?" Wenbry repeated intrigued, leaning back in towards the old man. Their conversation was in a tongue that less than half the room understood, but it had become the only one taking place while the attractive dark woman sipped slowly and seductively at her goblet of hot spiced wine without even attempting to cool the dark red liquid by first blowing on it.

"Yes," the old man continued, "they tried to make Orland Rosendor the king of Southmarch when King Garaug Alegis ruled. The Knights of Paliodor went from lord to lord in the north to instigate a rebellion but ultimately failed."

"That's going back a few centuries. You really know your history," Wenbry said, impressed. "Garaug... I know that name. Wasn't he the first king of House Aeligis? Garaug the conqueror or something."

The old man nodded, "That's right."

"But the knights of Paliodor? Who were they? Wait... you don't mean the paladins, do you?"

"So called holy knights of the Citadel of Light?"

"That's them," Wenbry confirmed, between sips of his mead. "Doesn't sound like you're too fond of them."

"Men who use the first gods as an excuse for their own ambition deserve no reverence."

"Their own ambition?" Wenbry said, shocked by the old man's candour. "I don't think there are many who would share that assessment of the paladins."

"Their own ambition, the order's ambition, its much the same thing. To see more coin funnelled back to the citadel by controlling every kingdom-turned-region with a puppet lord warden in place of their rightful kings," the old man said.

"Well, I think there *was* a paladin involved in the unification," Ewen leaned back from the bar and joined in, grimacing as he reluctantly vindicated the old man.

"There you have it. See?" the old man said, with the tone of someone telling a cautionary children's tale, "Everyone dropped their guard, and look what happened."

Ewen smiled, amused as he watched his companion slowly dragged step by step through their kingdom's history by the old man and his heretical and impossibly outdated view. If only he'd learned another language instead of relying on Ewen, Wenbry might be standing by the bar with the dark beauty instead of the bitter old separatist by the fire.

"Let me try some of this soup then," the woman asked Edvin. The Innkeeper's son nodded, smiling as he reached for a bowl without looking away from her as he backed towards the pot.

She removed her soft leather gloves with her teeth, as Edvin's sister, Hedvig, took the bowl with an amused smirk and scooped the soup for the latest patron. "Here you are," she said, wiping the outside of the bowl with a cloth.

"Thank you," the woman said, putting her gloves on the bar, so she could take the bowl in both hands to warm her fingers.

As Ewen looked around, he realised Ulfrem looked at her more with suspicion than with the same interest shared by the other men within the inn. The woman looked up to Gjallarbjorn's big furry head on the wall and raised an eyebrow before bringing the bowl to her mouth, sensually humming as she took the steamy broth in. "That's quite good," she said to the brother and sister behind the bar.

"Hello, I'm Ewen," Ewen introduced himself.

"Hello, Ewen," she said, with a friendly smile. "A pleasure to meet you. I'm Silana."

"What brings you out in such hostile weather?" he asked her, as Ulfrem quietly retreated to a table nearer the fire and sat down.

"I was sent out from my cosy, comfortable confines into this harsh nightmare of an early winter eve, to fetch something for my master," she said. "Most inconvenient."

"Beyond inconvenient," Ewen agreed. "Your master sounds rather callous."

"Oh, yes, he certainly can be," she said, with a flirtatious smile. "Sometimes I think he has a heart of ice."

"And he sent you out alone?" Edvin asked, in disbelief, as he pretended to clean the bar.

"Well the thing I have to fetch isn't all that big, you see. So, it's not as if I need help carrying it."

"Well, I don't think anyone's leaving this place until morning," Ewen said. "But when we do, if there's anything I can do to help…"

"Oh, that's so kind of you," she said, looking about the small inn. "I do believe that one of you *could* really help me." She took another sip of her soup as the old man leaned out of his chair for a moment to get a brief look at her, again. He huffed quietly to himself and began drumming his wrinkled fingers on the arm of his chair, leaning over to Wenbry, whispering something in the young Umber's ear.

Wenbry seemed amused but then the old man pulled him back in and quietly said more, leading to a confused look from Ewen's companion.

Silana took another slow sip of her soup from the bowl. "So, are you just returning from the south?" she asked Ewen.

"Actually no. We're still planning to head down that way, but the sun fell and the snow with it, so hopefully in the morning we'll be able to continue down and get back to our task," Ewen said, pointing to Wenbry.

Silana raised her brow and looked back at the other Umber, weathered by his previous night's inebriation, raising his second stein of mead, as he leaned out from the other side of the old man.

Ewen thought the response was surprisingly intuitive, considering they were speaking a language he didn't understand, and he'd not mentioned Wenbry by name.

"Your task must be dangerous if you carry swords with you," she said, tapping a fingernail on the pommel of his longsword as she moved quite close to him. "Expecting some resistance?"

"Shouldn't have thought so," Ewen said, "Just gathering longfrost, but you never know what you might cross paths with," he said, tilting his head towards the giant bear head on the wall above as he confidently leaned back on the bar. "It's not always gathering jobs, though. Sometimes we escort folk for protection. Escorted enough herbalists in my time to know what to look for myself on jobs like this one."

"Longfrost?" she said, nodding politely as she slowly retreated from the intimate distance. Somehow, somewhere in his brag, he seemed to have lost her interest. She turned to face the recently woken Sverol, approaching the bar yawning. "What about you?" she asked him.

"What about me?" the hefty young farmer asked, seemingly immune to her charms.

"What brings you to this place?"

"I pulled most of your dinner out of the ground and put it into barrels to see us through the rest of the year," he said, pointing to her bowl.

"Oh, well, thank you," she said, raising her bowl and bowing her head.

"Oh, well, my honour," he said, pointing to the pot. "And time I tried some myself."

Hedvig gave him an affectionate smile and fetched a bowl.

"So, that means you've been in town for at least...?" Silana waited for him to finish her sentence.

"My whole life," Sverol said, taking a bowl of soup from the innkeeper's daughter.

"Oh, I see," Silana said, turning to the older couple sitting at the nearest table, then back to their children serving from under the great dire bear head on the wall. "Mother, father," she said, pointing to the innkeep and his wife before turning back to the young pair behind the bar, "son, and daughter."

"Yes," Urala said, smiling proudly, "we run the place as a family, my husband and I."

"So, five of you are local, two of you are travellers who've yet to travel a step further south than where you stand this very moment..." Silana pondered aloud, slowly stepping towards the fire with her bowl in both hands. "That just leaves two."

"Well, you just missed a few stories before you got here," Ewen said, hoping to recapture Silana's attention as she stood between the old man by the fire and Ulfrem, hunched at his table, clenching a fist around the stem of his goblet of gluhwein.

"Oh, what a shame," she said, swapping her gaze between the two men. "I think I might take the scenic route," she said, seemingly to herself as she stepped around the other padded armchair. "May I?" she asked Sverol across the inn.

"Oh please," he said, gesturing to it. "You're more a guest than I am. I'll spend half the winter in it anyway."

"I can see why," she said, humming pleased as she leant back into it. "Very comfortable."

Wenbry sighed at his wooden chair, beside the old man, realising he'd missed the opportunity to seize the grander seat.

Ewen shrugged and looked to Sverol, "Good morning," he joked.

The young farmer smiled. "Aye, bloody naps. Don't know where or when I am after nodding off like that."

"Sun's only been down a few hours," the young woman behind the bar informed him, reaching over to brush his shoulder with a smile. "You worked pretty hard this morning, earning yourself a good nap."

Observing the affection of the young pair's shared gaze, Ewen slipped away, leaving them be. He wandered towards the fire and sat at Ulfrem's table.

The elegant woman finished her soup. "So, what of you, sir?" she asked the old man, placing her empty bowl on the small table with Sverol's cold neglected drink.

"Strike you as a knight, do I?" the old man asked.

"Just a courtesy, but something about the way you sit tells me you once carried a sword," she said, crossing her legs and leaning forward as she playfully bounced her upper shin. "Though I see no sword about you, now."

"Fewer pounds to carry while dragging my bones through the cold," he said. "Over time, I've lost the muscles that afforded me the strength to swing such weapons, gaining knowledge and wisdom in their place."

"Indeed," she mused. "Are you a local also?"

"No, just passing through," he said, looking at his own hands. "Have to expose myself to a hearth from time to time, so my skin doesn't freeze and rot off."

"An undesirable outcome," she agreed, delighting at his frankness. "So, what makes you travel in such inclement weather? Considering the harsh consequence of your exposure to it."

"Debt," he said.

"Debt requiring such urgent resolution, you ventured out into winter at your own peril?" she asked. "The consequences of defaulting on this debt must be dire indeed."

"No," he said, sounding burdened by regret. "This debt has seen far too many winters and its payment requires knowledge I've failed to accumulate despite the many years spent acquiring what I *do* know."

"A debt that can be paid in knowledge?" she said, reclining with a hum of curiosity. "Consider me intrigued. Please continue."

Ewen found himself drawn in, briefly glancing back at Ulfrem with a playful frown and raised brow, to share a wordless exchange. However, his table partner was eyeing the door, the walkways above, and the hanging cloaks. Ulfrem, it seemed, was distracted by other concerns, returning to the jumpiness and caginess he'd exhibited earlier.

"A friend and mentor who's responsible for many of the things I achieved in my youth and what I would later become," the old man continued. "He once granted me the ultimate gift. I promised him I would return the favour. But when the time came, my skill was insufficient to complete the task. I failed him," the old man said, despondently. "I've read every book I can find, practiced and honed my skills, but failure haunts me as time slips away. I've travelled for more knowledge, seeking it abroad. But only a single ancient legend truly caught my attention. Mentioned merely as a footnote, in a tome I once found. Almost dismissing it at first, but now I must find-"

"An ancient holy relic," she finished his sentence for him.

"That's trimming a lot of fat from my tale, but ultimately yes, I suspect," the old man said, with a suspicious tone. "How do you know of this?"

"Do you think you can just walk right into a holy place and take what doesn't belong to you without repercussions? Without retribution?" She angrily demanded.

He leaned forward. "A holy place?"

"The place of worship for even the darkest of gods is a holy place," she rebuked in a retaliatory tone, as if taking his last words as derision. "You dare mock what you don't understand?" She stood.

"What know you of this?" the old man demanded. "Who are you? Who sent you?"

"One who has come to reclaim what you thought you could steal." She grabbed his garments about the chest and lifted the old man, effortlessly, out of his chair.

"Release me, you mind-rotted zealot," he insisted.

Wenbry stood quickly with his hand on the hilt of his sword. "What's happening?" he called out in the Kestrian tongue, understanding nothing of the sudden escalation.

"Is it zealotry to protect sacred artefacts from thieves?" she demanded, shaking the old man.

Chairs scraped against the inn's wooden floor as all hastily stood.

"This a friendly place," the innkeeper yelled, from the across the room. "There is no fighting in here. This is a sanctuary."

"You leave that elder be," Sverol demanded, pointing at her threateningly from the bar as he began to approach.

Ewen also now stood with his hand on the hilt of his own half-drawn sword. "Come now," he said, attempting to calm her. "There's nowhere to go. Surely we can resolve whatever this is peacefully."

"There will be peace when I leave with what I came for," she insisted, as Ulfrem abandoned his table, hiding behind Ewen. "There will be peace," she continued, "when this old fool relents and what I seek is safely in my hands."

"Do you have any idea who I am?" the old man asked. "Who I was?" he yelled, grabbing her hands with his bony fingers to pry them off his person.

She released her grip on his garments and instead turned her wrists to grab his hands. There was a high screeching crackling sound between them as the old man looked startled at his fingers.

"What have you done?" he demanded, grimacing.

"I've frozen your thieving fingers," she said, sneering wildly.

Snatching back his hands from her, the old man held is blue fingers towards the fire, while she grinned defiantly at the small crowd of seven gathered about her.

"Bloody crazy wench," the old man cried out, crouching by the fire, desperately attempting to thaw his fingers. "You've ruined them."

"For those of you unfamiliar with magic, you might want take a step back and consider sheathing your swords," Silana warned, stepping behind the hunched over old man, rubbing his fingers by the hearth. "Take another step and see what happens," she threatened.

The innkeeper tried again to assert his authority, "Listen to me, woman. You do not come into my place-"

"You harbour thieves from justice," she accusingly interrupted.

"No, I harbour folk from the cold," Bjoric yelled, pointing to the door. "Resolve whatever grievance you have with my patrons in a civilized manner or you may return to that cold."

"You would send *me* into the cold instead of this thief?" she bitterly hissed. "Fine, then, let him have *all* the fire." Turning back, she kicked the crouching old man, sending him face first into the burning hearth.

Everyone took a step to help him, but his hair caught alight as did his hood. Skidding his feet out as he pushed his hands into the burning wood, he tried to lift himself out, but was unable to control his icy fingers. He yelled in anguish before Sverol quickly pulled him out of the fire, getting burnt himself as the burning man's cloak went up in flames.

The old man collapsed in a burning pile, hissing angrily as he thrashed about on the floor. Edvin and his father scrambled, getting towels to beat out the flames while Wenbry and Ewen pointed their now drawn swords threateningly at Silana, who laughed mockingly and fearless.

It was at that moment, that movement caught Ewen's eye. A cloaked figure by the door attempting to leave. He recognised the grey furry cloak from when he first saw it enter the inn. "Ulfrem?" he called confused.

The cagey man looked back, "I'd rather take my chances out there than deal with this madness," he said.

"I don't blame you," Silana said, as the old man burned in the corner. "But you won't be leaving anytime soon. I froze the door shut when I first came in."

Ulfrem's shoulders sank defeated as he stepped away from the door. "Hells," he simply sighed with dread.

The men who ran the inn were beating the old burning man's flames with their towels as Hedvig, the innkeeper's daughter, rushed across with a pail of water she scooped from a barrel and splashed it onto the old man.

In a brief glance, Ewen saw the dark mess in the corner as the smell of burnt flesh, hair, and garment followed the dark smoke, spreading across the room, choking those nearest.

"I don't care who you are or who you think you were," she mocked the burnt old man, while Ewen wondered if he was even still alive. "When you steal from a temple of Aghvr, the god of the frozen hell, there is no place you can take shelter from the cold, for the cold will come and find you."

"Aghvr?" The old man's voice croaked, to the surprise of those who'd tried to save him. His burnt head turned, cradled in his own arms. When he turned it towards Sverol, the young man backed into the wall, wide eyed and full of fear. "Aghvr? You're a priestess of Aghvr?" the burnt man asked, his voice altered by the burning ordeal.

"And I've come to retrieve the artefact you stole," she said. Her tone growing suspicious as he bitterly laughed.

A laugh that changed the old man's voice as flesh seemed to dislodge and clear from his throat. He drew his knees in to push himself up onto his shins, facing the corner of the room. Bjoric and his son stepped away, not taking their eyes off the burnt man while all Ewen could see was the remains of his hood and scalp, blackened and still smoking.

"I've been to no temple of Aghvr," the old man said condescendingly. "There's nothing for me there."

"But you spoke of the artefact," she said, confidence escaping her accusatory tone.

The old man scraped at his face with his hand and tore blackened skin from his skull, throwing it onto the floor in burnt clumps as he slowly stood. "Had you not been so petulant, interrupting my story, young woman, you would have learned that I have yet to even discover the location of the artefact that *I* seek. For it is no mere trinket of the young gods, who govern the hells or various other low realms of Etherius. Nothing fashioned by some enamoured devotee, but one of the great works taken from a shrine of the ancients, in devotion to one of the first gods. Something made when the tribes of men still dwelt in caves, shivering naked in the cold." The old man turned to face the room, tearing another piece of blackened skin from his head, revealing a skull with two small horns upon his temples pointing upward. Tiny flickering red lights danced deep in his dark empty eye sockets. His fingers were bone, partially blackened like his skull from soot and burnt skin. "That disguise was meant to see me to the north." He shook his fleshless head.

"Who *are* you?" Silana asked, as everyone else stood in stunned silence. "What are you?"

"Oh, *now* you're interested in hearing an old man's story to completion," he said, amused. "I first came to this land when I was a young man. I travelled south when I met the most important person I'd ever meet. An Ijcari necromancer."

"Ijcari?" Ewen asked, not knowing the word.

"One of the frost elves of the deep south," Silana found herself explaining as fear and regret washed across her face.

"I also took one as my wife, living in a place called Aelighold, after which I fashioned my surname, when I eventually required one. I gathered tribes from all over Froskheim and built a force of invaders, leading them to Southmarch of the Umberlands. I took the capital, Whiteburrough and slew the king, Tholmis Armont the third. I took the throne in One-Hundred-and-Ninty-Six of the New Kestrian calendar and was crowned King Garaug Aeligis," he said, through skinless teeth in a voice that did not require flesh but instead emanated from within the dark magic that sustained him. "When I died, after a near ninety-year reign, for more than the blood of men ran through my veins when I had flesh, this necromancer took me back to the place where we had first met. There, he brought me back to the world within the year. That is the debt that must be repaid, for my own skill has still not matched his."

"You're King Garaug Aeligis?" Ewen asked stunned. "From, what, four, five hundred years ago?"

"I am king no more," the skeletal figure said. "And, from what you've told me, neither are my ancestors. Damned Citadel of Light stole their birthright." Tearing burnt cloth from his body, he turned to the priestess. "I thought that's what you were, for a moment. Someone they had sent after me. For they too would desire what I seek. To add to their horded collection of holy ancient relics. But they won't stop me. You won't stop me."

"I…" Silana started but looked back at Ulfrem by the door. "Gods no. It was *him*," she said, with realisation and regret, pointing at him before being startled by the sight of her own hand, when she raised it. For the skin upon her hands had turned horribly black and red. She checked the other and found it afflicted the same. "What's this?" she asked, in a panic.

"Necrosis," the horned skeleton said, as it continued to pluck burnt cloth from a hardened leather harness now exposed about his fleshless chest. "Before you froze the skin on my hands, I killed the skin on yours."

"What?" she yelled, horrified.

"The old man who gave me his skin did so of his own free will. Now he's a soldier in my service," Garaug, the horned skeleton, said. "I'll need a new volunteer, so that I may once again pass for normal," he said, grabbing Silana by the throat before she could get to Ulfrem.

"Not me," she protested, as she grabbed his bony arm with her blackening necrotic fingers.

"No, not you. But what you just did requires recompense, you reckless lunatic," he said, lifting her off the ground. "Your service to Aghvr has come to an end, while your service to me is about to begin. If it makes you feel any better, know that my first command, when your body rises again, will be to return the trinket you came to collect."

"But he…" she choked, looking to Ulfrem.

"He was the obvious culprit, but you had to show off," he said, tilting his head. "So, instead of confronting him you thought you'd toy with your prey and make him sweat and look what happened. For it happened to you. But don't worry, he too will pay his price. For I need a donation of flesh to conceal this walking horror I call a body."

"What?" Ulfrem said, turning back to frantically try the door again.

Another shriek of ice magic crackled from Silana's black hands. "Your magic cannot harm me. Only the flesh I had borrowed," Garaug assured her. "And thanks to you, it's gone."

"I didn't know what she was going to do," Ulfrem pleaded, as he side-stepped his way past the bar, not turning his back on the skeleton, currently choking the life out of the priestess with his fingerbones. "It's not my fault."

"You could have spoken up at any time, thief," he said, watching the man look around panicked, making for the stairs. "But you didn't. Instead, watching me burn."

"So did the others," Ulfrem said, quickly making his way to the stairs and up to the loft, opening the door of every room. "There has to be another way out of here," his voice echoed from above.

"Ewen and Wenbry here, on the other hand, had no idea what was happening and are about to make more than enough coin to see them through many winters to come," he promised, as Silana let out her last breath. Her hands slipped off the bones of his arm and, when he released his grip, she fell lifelessly to the floor. "Far more than your longfrost would have paid, my fellow Southern Umbers."

"What are you asking of us?" Ewen asked nervously, as the bony figure made its way past him to the base of the stairs.

"The three of us will travel to every city, town, and village in Froskheim to find the descendants of the raiding tribe who stole an abandoned an object they called Blacktooth." Garaug said, slowly climbing the stairs.

"So, you will leave the rest of us be?" the innkeeper asked, as his family huddled around him in the corner.

"I shall," he assured him. "But unless you would have me smash your door and expose you to the cold, we're all stuck together for the night. At least until the priestess's spell upon it relents." Dragging his boots upon the wooden walkway above, he slowly closed in on the faster steps of Ulfrem. "Time to sleep," the walking skeleton said, before a whimper could be heard. The panicked steps above suddenly halted, followed by the loud thud of a collapsing body. "So," Garaug shouted from above, "keep my new companions fed and filled to their hearts' delight while this guest and I exchange appearances. I shall pay extra for the mess I'm about to make."

Ewen looked to his confused and fearful companion, Wenbry, who had understood none of what was said, once the madness unfolded. Only that the old man he'd spent the night chatting with was now some walking horror.

"Where do even I begin translating all of that?" Ewen said to his confused companion, in the Kestrian tongue. "Well, firstly… change of plans for tomorrow."

Barend Nieuwstraten III grew up and lives in Sydney, Australia, where he was born to Dutch and Indian immigrants. He has worked in film, short film, television, music, and online comics. He is now primarily working on a collection of stories set within a high fantasy world, a science fiction alternate future, as well as a steampunk storyverse, often dipping his toes in horror in the process. He is currently creating short stories and stand-alone novels while also working on an epic series. A discovery writer not knowing what will happen when he begins typing, he endeavours to drag his readers on the same unknown journey through the fog of his subconscious.

The Concealed Witness

by Alex Minns

Four sharp knocks on the door broke my reverie. Such precise movements - it must have been Helios. I took a deep breath and centred myself. I had sat in this house for two days, ensuring no enquiring eyes came too close, that no-one had followed me here. I had seen no-one since I had arrived. The neighbours all kept to themselves. The house was down a private road, trees lining the perimeter so even the nosiest of neighbours couldn't peer out their window and see anything. It was the reason I had picked this place. It was an asset I had obtained when I had assumed leadership of a gang that had been giving us some trouble; sort of a hostile takeover I suppose. The members of the outfit had been let go unless they showed potential and a new-found loyalty to me; then they were assimilated into my employee base. I was quite surprised when I saw the portfolio of real estate that came with the gang's territory, and this safehouse was perfect for what I needed. This house wasn't recorded anywhere in my paperwork; it was completely off the books so that only two people in my employ knew about it. Although that number was about to rise.

    I stood up and adjusted my clothing, pulling it straight. My cardigan had a metal clasp at the front and long flowing sleeves. It wasn't the most practical, nor were the silver chains and charms that rattled as I moved, but they fit the image. And image in my position was everything. It had taken a lot of time and effort to gain standing in the mage underworld but now very few would dare cross the Witch Queen, not a nickname I would have chosen for myself.

    I could hear grumbling from the other side of the door but no more knocks came. Helios, my most trusted lieutenant, was a patient man;

Remi was not. Three locks kept the door secure which I promptly undid before whispering a few words to lower the ward I had placed on it for safety. I opened the door with a flourish to be greeted by four incredibly suspicious-looking individuals loitering on the step. Victor started to move forward but Helios put an arm out to block her way.

"What?"

"Is it you?" I asked as I raised a hand to touch Helios' forehead gently. He did not flinch or complain. I could sense no glamours, only the energy signature I had become so familiar with. You couldn't be too careful when dealing with the Mage Council. They had tested the strength of my position early on, but as I didn't cause many direct problems, they didn't pose too much of a nuisance. Of course, all that was about to change. Their whole house was built on a pack of lies and held together with manipulation and control. I'd been searching for years for the seed to bring the whole rotten megalith down and finally Victor had brought me the way in. A long-forgotten memory held the key to everything; I should have known the answers always lie in the past. No matter how hard you run, it always moves faster.

"Shucks, you got me, I'm really the tooth fairy. Just let us in." Remi tried to jostle forward but Helios held firm. I stepped back and whispered the final word to lower the last defences; a shimmer of static flashed before disappearing. Anything that had tried to come through from that side wouldn't have been able to control their body for two days. A frown creased Remi's forehead. "That's a Selkan ward. You are expecting trouble."

"I knew you were the right man for the job." I grinned as I moved back into the living area of the house. The room was full of soothing yellows and oranges, decked out in stained pine wood. It had the kind of rustic feel you'd find in a holiday home, not exactly the décor I went for, nor expected to find in a vampire den but I suspected this was more of a halfway house for drones, especially after I saw the basement. I moved over to the glass doors at the back of the room and looked out in the vast garden. It was green and perfect, completely tranquil. I tried to siphon that kind of calm into myself but I had a vague sense of unease that had been building all morning. The fourth individual in the room was probably to thank for that.

"Right, he's here. Now what?" Remi never was one for small talk. I had known he would take the job, playing on his desire to get revenge on Castigan did not sit well with me but I needed him. It was a dangerous game I had pulled him into, and the others. I only hoped we all lived long enough to regret it.

Helios stood by the door, alert as ever, his face unreadable. Little Miss Victor was wandering around, surveying the downstairs and poking her nose into different rooms, with a permanently raised eyebrow. Such an inquisitive creature and still so ill at ease. We had our differences, ever since we trained in the same Lodge but she was not meant for this world of politics and crime. An air of nervous energy surrounded her at all times. Remi on the other hand was completely relaxed on the sofa, his arms laying across the back and his feet up on the coffee table. I knew better though. He was a cunning man. He let you believe he was kicking back and not paying attention but he already knew how many exits and entrances there were to this house, and how to respond if a threat came into the house from any of those points.

The last member of the band was sat on the armchair next to Remi. He was perched on the end, looking like a child on a seat that was five sizes too big. His eyes flitted from one thing to the next in microseconds. His hands were folded into a ball on his lap, clasping and unclasping multiple times every few seconds.

"Mr Baxendale," I greeted and went to sit on the sofa next to Remi, who reluctantly moved his feet.

"Hello." His voice was no more than a whisper.

"Tell me about yourself."

"Huh?" His face creased in childlike confusion. I found it so hard to believe what was really sitting in front of me. "Um, well, I'm a publisher. I work for a publishing company. I live, well, I thought I lived next to the beach but… well it turned out to be a box in a warehouse." I glanced at Remi who shrugged.

"They had him in a construct, loads bigger on the inside. Lovely little place by the sea it was. Might go back if this all falls through."

"You were living in an illusion." Baxendale squirmed at my words. "What about family?"

"No," he shook his head.

"Friends? Co-workers?"

"I live far from the nearest village. I see friends online and I work from home. Least I thought so. What's going on? Had I been kidnapped? Have I been kidnapped now?" His voice was starting to tremble. I got up and moved to him so I could place my hand on his head, easing his fears and helping him relax.

"I could do with a bit of that," Remi muttered beside me.

Something tugged at my subconscious and I focused back to Baxendale. My hand was still on his head and I could feel so much lying deeper within. Including something red that was screaming at me.

"They tagged him," I muttered.

Remi stood up. "No, I swept him for devices. Gave him a once over for enchantments."

"They put it deeper, right into his psyche," I cursed. "This is going to shorten our timeframe."

"For what?" Victor called out. "I'm not being funny but how can this guy help us. He doesn't even know about mages."

"Lee Baxendale doesn't, no," I shook my head. "Help me put him on the sofa." Baxendale was in a trance-like state now, almost asleep. Remi helped me manoeuvre him onto the sofa and sat him on one end, his head back.

"Then how?" Victor pressed. I turned to look at her and found three expectant faces watching me. They weren't going to like this.

"The box you found him in was just one prison. Lee Baxendale is the second cage we need to break through." Helios' eyes widened slightly as he realised what I meant. The others took a few seconds longer.

"No," Victor muttered. "You're not serious."

"What? Someone want to catch me up?" Remi took a step away from the sofa instinctively. Victor came closer, her face set in anger. I recognised that look, the one that always came before a talk on what was right and wrong.

"The rebellion. The one the Council are worried we'll find out about, must have been ages ago," she began. "I'm talking centuries, and this guy can help give us evidence. Why did I not see this coming? He was there wasn't he?" I stayed motionless.

"This guy, but," Remi stopped suddenly. "Holy crap." And there it was, now we were all caught up. Anger, fear, and something more primal flooded out of both Remi and Victor. Helios had learned a long time ago to keep his emotions much closer to himself but the other two were so easy to read. Remi stepped closer, his eyes wild with anger. "You're saying Lee was there, at the rebellion, because he's a host. There's a centuries-old demon caged in his head?"

"Yes." I nodded and smiled.

"Are you out of your tiny witchy mind?" Remi continued. I glanced over Remi's shoulder at Helios. He was still by the door, motionless but there was an undeniable tension in his body now. Even he was annoyed, brilliant. "You got me to break a demon out of a cage? A demon that has a beacon in his head which is currently drawing those lovely Enforcers ever nearer to arrest us all? I'll be off then." He turned and stepped over the small coffee table in his way as he headed for the front door. Helios didn't make a move to slow him down.

"You won't get even with Castigan if you leave now," I pointed out.

Remi spun on his heels. "If I stay, all I'm getting is a home in a very small cell in the very dark hole the Council throw us in, assuming they don't just execute us all for freeing a demon." His eyes blazed with fury. "I think I'll give Castigan a pass this time. And if I were either of you two, I'd leave now too. I can drop you off anywhere you need."

Helios didn't move. His jaw was set and his eyes fixed on a point past me. He would stay, his loyalty to me wouldn't let him leave but he would want words later, that much I could be sure of.

"No, Big Man?" Remi waved a hand in front of his face. "Fine, what about you Vic? Council might want you now, but they catch you in on this, you're done for. Leave now, give it a few years, heat will die down and they'll forget about you."

Victor turned to him and then back to me, her eyes wide, displaying her indecision. Her emotions were warring in her so much it was as if she was screaming in my face. Every one hit my psyche like a battering ram. She had no idea I could feel her every emotion; my abilities had widened with practise once I had left our lodge. Being a mage was so much more than being a one trick pony, but that's not what the Council told you.

Still, she didn't speak, she just kept looking between the two of us. Her hands were moving constantly by her sides, fingers scratching at each other, and I could tell she was biting her tongue to stop herself from getting tearful.

Eventually, she spoke, "They won't forget this one, they think I have information. I won't last a few years out there. I'm just a glorified librarian." Her voice was trembling as she fought to stay calm over every word.

"Fine. But this will not end well," Remi glared at me. If I didn't know better, I'd say he really hated me. He hauled open the front door as Helios finally looked at me, his eyes full of warning. My eyebrow raised – he wanted the mercenary to stay? I couldn't deny, if we wanted any chance of finding the truth and surviving, we needed him. Especially as I couldn't draft in many of my usual employees for this. If we were to succeed in taking on the shadowy side of the Council, we needed to do it quietly and with as few people involved as possible. I went with my instinct and lifted my arm mumbling a few words I'd picked up when travelling in Eastern Europe.

The door was ripped out of Remi's hand and slammed shut. He stepped back instinctively and when he turned to me, his expression was guarded. Victor beside me was making small noises of surprise and confusion.

"You're a psychic mage, how did you do that?" Remi asked slowly.

"You know how the Council tells us we fit in a box and that's it? You're a temporal mage, you can manipulate time in one maybe two ways. We'll teach you that and that's it?" Victor nodded at me, Remi only sneered. "Well, they lied. By omission at least. Just because you're a natural temporal mage doesn't mean you can't learn how to manipulate other forms. It just takes more incantations, more power and more will."

"Where did you...?" Victor began.

"Oh, duckie you wouldn't want to know where I've been and who taught me. Would make your hair curl," I grinned at her discomfort. "But if the Council lied about that, what else do they lie about? A secret rebellion it would appear. And that all demons are evil."

"Now you sound like a conspiracy nut." Remi still wasn't buying it but he had at least stopped trying to leave. He leant against the wall next to the door with, I noted, a direct line of sight out of the window, between the curtains.

"In South America, there's a village where some demons have taken refuge, they live amongst the locals. About one hundred and sixty people in all, and fifty of them are demons. I've been there, learned a lot from them. Demons are like humans: they can be good or evil. Yes, most seem to choose evil and yes they are incredibly powerful but it's a choice not a default setting."

"What if the one in his head decides it wants to be evil?" Victor pointed at Lee who still sat on the sofa, swaying gently side to side.

"Then we barter with him until he agrees to help. Just like a human," I shrugged.

"This is dangerous," Remi shook his head.

"Yes, so was breaking him out. So is allowing the Council to be overrun by zealous power-hungry madmen. Not doing this is dangerous. I'm doing this whether you stay or not, but I won't deny it will feel less dangerous if you stay. I need to break through his barriers and find the demon before the Enforcer squad turns up so hurry up and make your decision, Remi," I crossed my arms, my sleeves floating through the air as I moved.

He stared at me. A weaker person would have withered under the weight of his gaze. He took a deep breath before casting one last look at the others. "Right oh," he pushed off the wall and went for the door.

The three of us stared at him as he left. We kept staring at the door after it closed.

"Huh," was all I could say as I pushed the lump of unease deeper in my gut, trying to ignore it. I didn't have time to dwell. I swung Lee's legs up on top the sofa and turned him round to face the empty space which I then took. Crossing my legs, I settled myself into position.

"Emily?" Victor's voice was full of doubt.

"It will be fine." I flinched as she used my first name, the one no-one around me dared use since I left the lodge. I didn't even look at her. "There is a protective ward under the sofa so he can't leave unless I allow it and another one around the edge of this room. And for good measure another outside the house. If it goes wrong, you two just get out and go far away. But it won't."

The door suddenly burst open. Helios' hands were up in a second. Victor leapt backwards and took up residence behind the nearest chair.

"Unless the Enforcers turn up." Remi kicked the door open again and let two heavy cases drop onto the floor in front of Helios, whose hands were still raised, ready to unleash fire on an incoming enemy. "Alright sunshine, cool it yeah? I've got another case in the car we'll need; can I get it without you singeing my hair?"

My eyes closed for a second; I didn't want him to see my relief.

#

"What do we do?" Victor's voice was subdued.

"Simple really. You three make sure the Enforcers don't get in here before I've finished. I need to stop him broadcasting that signal and unlock the cage in his head." I didn't need to look to feel the unease flooding from them all. But they stayed quiet. After a few beats, Remi started moving around, issuing orders to Victor which she silently accepted. I risked a quick glance over at Helios before starting on my work. He was staring at me. It has always amazed me how the man could portray the whole gamut of expressions and emotions with just his eyebrows and set of his jaw. Right now, he was thoroughly unimpressed.

I didn't need his approval. I had been waiting a long time to find a way to strike out at the Council and Victor had brought it to me. We had to find out about this rebellion that no-one had ever heard of and preferably before the shadow elements in the Council installed their fake Kezio Constantin in charge of all Mages. Once that happened, everything was going to get a whole lot harder. Now I had a sneaking suspicion the one place I could find more information was in Lee's head and I would get it. I raised my hands and placed them on his temples. His skin was cool, pulsating slightly in time with his heartbeat. I listened, tuning into him. Once I found his frequency, my awareness of the outside world disappeared. My body felt like it was rising up off the sofa but I knew from previous experience I had actually fallen back into the seat. I pushed conscious thought away and allowed the drifting sensation to carry me, to wherever it felt I needed to go. Higher and higher I rose, everything around me was a strange lavender colour. Above me there was a dark patch. A primal part of my brain wanted to get away from it. I fought the urge to kick my legs to try and force me off course. I carried on slowly lifting, starting to rotate as I made my slow progress.

Something tugged at my feet, pulling me round faster. I craned my neck up, it was like I was sat in a rubber ring in a pool and a strong current was starting to drag me. The edge of the purple came closer. This wasn't right, I needed to go further up. That darkness was where I needed to be. I reached up and tried to propel towards it but it only dragged me away quicker. The cloud of lavender enveloped me as it deposited me somewhere else in Lee's psyche.

"Very nice," I muttered to myself. I'd ended up in a rather nice seaside flat. To my left was a window that looked directly out onto a deserted beach. Lee sat on a sofa directly ahead of me. He was staring at a television that wasn't switched on.

"Thanks." His voice was slow. His head turned towards me; his eyes narrowed. "I know you."

"We just met. My friends brought you to my house." I moved over to sit next to him.

"This is my house. I think." He cocked his head.

"Do you remember when you moved here?"

"No."

"Do you remember where you were before?"

"No."

He went back to staring at the television. I'd dived into people's subconscious before but I had never encountered someone so docile. Usually it took all my effort to keep them calm so I didn't get kicked out or worse. It had to be something the Council had done to him; the magical equivalent of a tranquiliser, it was almost like he had taken Vision. Rising from the sofa, I manoeuvred myself between him and the screen. A frown flashed across his face and was gone as quickly.

"Try and think Lee. Can you remember moving in?"

Finally, he made eye contact with me. He took a deep sigh and his shoulders sunk a little lower as he began to think. He stayed quiet for a long time, blinking more regularly as the seconds passed.

"I don't remember."

"But you had to have moved in right?"

He gave a half-hearted shrug.

"Seems like a pretty big event to me. Think back. How far back can you remember?"

He groaned. It felt like I was dealing with a petulant schoolchild who'd been asked to do their work.

"I've been here ages. I saw the World Cup on television here. That was cool. Never been on television before," he nodded slowly.

World Cup? Never been on television? "Lee, what year is it?"

"Year? It's..." His face screwed up. "It's." He rubbed at his forehead as if it were hurting him.

The light in the room flashed. It was as if the sun outside was flicked off for a split second. Lee hadn't noticed, he was still trying to think. His face was starting to flush as he let out a small whimper. The room flashed again, as if it were glitching and for a moment I could see the box that had been his prison. The real box, the one that had been rigged to hold his fake home for who knew how long. The Council had known about demons for a very long time. How long they'd known about this one and at what point they decided to keep Lee prisoner, I had no idea. A contact of mine had heard whispers but no-one seemed to know when it had happened. Which meant this person was much older than he looked, as my contacts were incredibly old indeed. I hadn't mentioned that to the others. The older a demon was, the stronger it was and if I was right, this was the oldest demon still walking.

And yet right now he was sat in front of me almost weeping, looking like a lost, little boy.

"When's my birthday?" His eyes were wide and afraid. They started to shift from side to side as the glitching of the room became more regular. He was starting to notice now. It was agitating him. If he became too afraid, it would force me out of his mind too soon.

"Lee, it's ok. We all forget from time to time." I reached out and took his hand, patting it reassuringly. "Do you remember one of your birthdays?" The room settled again as he calmed down.

"My twenty-first was important."

"Okay, do you know why?"

"No, but it was a big occasion."

"Okay, try and picture it," I urged. Something distracted him. His head cocked to the side.

"Do you hear that?"

I listened. I did hear it. Beeping.

"Do you know where it's coming from Lee?" I tried to keep my voice steady.

"Not here," he shook his head. His hand twisted under mine so he could grip round my fingers. The room started to melt away from us. Lee didn't seem worried at all; his head was still cocked as if he were still listening. Walls drifted downwards as everything shifted around me. Pine darkened until it was silvery. We were standing now. Surrounded by metal walls, a plinth took centre position in the room. The room was empty apart from this, a small square space with just the one item. On top of the plinth was a lock box.

"Oh no," I muttered as I let go of Lee's hand and got closer.

"What's wrong?" He moved beside me.

"The beeping is coming from inside here. I need to turn it off but it's going to take me a long time to get in. We don't have that long." I studied the box more closely but my initial fears were right. If I didn't do this correctly, unlock the wards in the right order with the right words, it would blow up in our faces. The beeping echoed around the metal room, taunting me.

"Let's go back to your birthday." I turned my back on the plinth. I couldn't do this now, I needed to get to the creature locked away and get us all out of danger. Assuming freeing the creature didn't make things worse.

"My parents were there." The room swirled again but the block on Lee's memories made it impossible for him to find something to hold on to. Colours swarmed around us. Wind pulled at my sleeves and tugged at Lee's hair. Every now and then an object seemed to try and break through but as soon as I focused on it, it became abstract and disappeared again.

"Try and focus Lee. Your parents were there, you said it was a big occasion, were other people there?"

"Yes. But I don't know who," he shook his head. The colours were moving faster. It was starting to make me nauseous. A cloud a green mist passed between us as a red hue rolled under my feet. There was no floor, nor a ceiling. Lee was staring to lose himself in the colours. If I weren't careful, not only would I not get the demon, but I'd lose Lee in here too and then there would be no way out.

I reached out for his hands again. When I made contact, he looked at me. The touch anchored him to me again.

"Your parents. Can you remember them? Picture their faces," I instructed.

His gaze rested on our hands as he started to think. The colours around me dimmed. I tried to keep watching him but I couldn't resist looking around. It was getting so dark. My grip on his hands tightened as panic became to lodge in my gut. It was still getting darker.

Then his head rose and he looked over my shoulder. I turned and saw a pinprick of light. A candle. Keeping hold of his hands, I stepped to the side so we could both look. That's why it was getting dark! I felt something more solid under my feet. Rock flooring helped the room solidify around us. The only light in the space was from the candles dotted around. Lee shifted next to me. I blinked as I looked back at him. Gone were the clothes he had been in, replaced with old brown cloth items. He looked like he'd been playing in a museum dressing up box.

"Holy…" Realisation dawned on me. He really was older than I had thought.

A loud crash shook the space. Lee's head whipped round to me, his face full of alarm.

"It's ok, it's something outside." My voice was soothing and calm but it was far from what I was feeling inside. That must have been the Enforcers. I had not expected them to find us anywhere near as quickly. I only hoped Helios and the others could hold them off long enough.

#

The space around us flickered, as if glitching in a game. I needed to keep him focused. I squeezed his hand a little tighter to draw his attention back to me. "Think about your parents Lee. Can you see them?"

His head moved around as he looked for them. As he did, the room seemed to open up. There were sconces along the walls the whole way round. It was a much bigger space than I'd realised. This wasn't his home; it must have been a hall or something similar. The walls were made of jagged stone and handmade wooden benches sat around the edges. We were in the middle of the floor. The benches were set around us, as if we were performing in the centre.

"They were there." He pointed towards the long, side wall roughly in the middle. Two ghost-like figures emerged before us. They looked like holograms, flickering and faded. Memories are supposed to be much clearer. The levels of shielding the Council had put in the man's head was enough to reduce most to gibbering wrecks. Lee shuffled towards the two people, nervous but driven at the same time. Thankfully, he was concentrating on them enough to not notice the room shake around us as the Enforcers continued to attack the house. I heard a voice whisper at the back of my head.

"No pressure," the female voice began. "But they are coming at us pretty hard. We think we can only hold them five minutes more." I ground my teeth. I wanted to snap back at Victor but it would do no good, she couldn't hear me from here. If I tried to hurry, I would only end up doing more harm to Lee and we would never get what we needed.

"Caleb." I looked up confused. The woman was reaching out to Lee. Of course, Lee Baxendale would never have been his real name. Having his true name might help him reach the hidden areas. His mother stroked his face as he stood before his proud parents.

His father nodded resolutely, "It is time."

"What's it time for Caleb?" I asked.

"The ceremony." His voice was dreamlike. He was starting to realise the memory more fully now. As he felt more comfortable, more figures began to appear. People were sat on the benches. It looked like the whole village had turned up to watch.

"The ceremony?" I spun slowly, studying the gathered people. There was an air of mixed trepidation and excitement drifting through them. And they were quiet. Not a word was uttered. It was as if they dare not even breathe.

"It is my birthday. It is time for my birth-right." He turned to me and smiled. He surveyed the crowd, pride swelling his grin. But I noticed him stop. It was as if his head had been trapped in a vice. His head jerked to a stop and went back to looking the other way. That was when I realised that everyone else was staring not at Caleb but the spot behind him that he had just avoided. I moved carefully towards it.

"Caleb?"

He half turned towards my questioning voice but he would not turn to me completely. Something was stopping him.

"Caleb, what is your birth-right? Where is it?"

He frowned. The room shook again and this time he noticed. The crowds on the benches disappeared.

"Caleb. Focus, what's your birth-right?" I moved out of his blind-spot and back into his view. Only then did I notice the markings scratched into the floor. They were not deep but had been done very carefully. The intricate pattern filled a large circle but a smaller circle was enclosed within. Just at the point Caleb could not look at.

"Something's missing." Caleb started turning on the spot, his hands needling at his forehead. His parents were frozen in they proud pose as Caleb warred with the contents of his mind.

"Yes, what's in the circle Caleb. Who should be there?" I pointed at the smaller carving, urging him to look. It was risky; I was probably pushing him too hard.

"I can't. There's nothing."

The room shook again. The crashing noises were getting louder. The last one definitely sounded like glass smashing. Time was not on my side. I grasped Caleb and turned him to face the spot he was avoiding. His head tucked away to the side, still refusing to look.

"Caleb. You're not going to get your birth-right if you don't look at it," I urged.

"But I must! The village is in danger if I don't." His eyes were full of alarm as he locked gazes with me.

"Then, look." He chewed his bottom lip as he began to breathe heavily. His eyes darted to one side for a split second, then again for a little longer. This happened a few more times until he plucked up the courage to finally look. When he finally settled on the space, his brow knitted in confusion.

"It should be there." He marched over to the circle that was still empty.

"What should?"

"I can't remember." He covered his face in his hands as the frustration overwhelmed him and washed over me too. I steadied myself, trying not to be carried away by his emotion.

"Yes you can. You protected your village by submitting to the ritual remember?"

He nodded, "My ancestor had been the first to make the deal. It was my turn. Every seven generations a new host was needed."

The enormity of what he was saying did not pass me by: willing hosts? Deals? I froze. On another day, this would be huge. Evidence that people willing submitted to host demons? The sheer scale of this Council cover-up probably dwarfed what I had already uncovered since I had left my Lodge. However, it was not another day and I was on a deadline.

"So, you stepped up," I carried on. "You were the new host."

"Yes." He started to pace around the circle, his hand reaching out and tracing a line absently around the edge of the circle where an invisible barrier would have been. He froze, his body starting to tremble. I stepped forward; I'd gone too hard and now he was losing himself. I was about to grab his shoulders when he put out a hand to stop me. His head snapped up. "Emethus!"

I tumbled backwards as the ground seemed to rush away from me. I reached out for Caleb but I was dragged upwards by an unknown force. Air flew past my face as I soared through the air, the room we had been in long disappeared. Colours of the rainbow swam around me as I tumbled over myself continuing my upward journey. As I upended again, I caught sight of Caleb just behind me. And then he was in front of me as our direction changed. My stomach lurched as I plunged to the left. A patch of darkness lay ahead of us. The darkness I had seen when I had first entered Caleb or Lee's subconscious. We sped towards it. There was nothing I could do but close my eyes.

#

I came to a very abrupt halt. Suddenly glad I had closed my eyes, I swallowed hard and tried to regain control over my stormy stomach. But when my brain registered the voice that began to speak, I almost lost control again.

"Caleb." The name was simple but the power that flowed from the voice would have knocked me flying had I not already been down. The tone was calm but lying underneath I could still sense the true emotions warring. "It has been a long time."

"I am sorry Emethus. I was so lost." Caleb's words were drenched in apology and sorrow. As I opened my eyes, I wasn't surprised to see the man on his knees in front of our new guest.

"It was not your fault." His voice seemed to resonate the air around me, I could feel every syllable in my chest as he spoke. It was the only constant thing about him. He was dressed in a silvery garment that shifted in the light. Even his face morphed as I watched him. It was like looking at an optical illusion, every time he shifted, he looked slightly different. One minute he seemed to be made of navy mist, the next a silvery skin covered his face with gills and lines traced across his cheeks. I lowered my eyes again as it was almost too much for my brain to conceive. Now I understood why some went mad when first encountering a demon.

"It was Mages that tore us apart," the demon spoke again. "And now another Mage has intruded." Heat washed over me as I felt the intensity of his stare.

"She helped us Emethus."

I took a deep breath and centred myself, drawing on methods I had picked up in South America for calming the mind.

"She is Mage." The hatred dripped off his tongue.

"And you are demon but I haven't started throwing insults about have I." I stood, channelling more confidence than I actually felt. The demon's face was now red, resembling the more stereotypical image and I swear he raised an eyebrow at me. I took that as a good sign. I sniffed disinterestedly and brushed my braided hair back off my shoulder. "The Mage Council locked you away and put Caleb here in a box. My friends and I broke him out and I've been helping him remember you."

"And why would a Mage do that?"

"Because Mage and Mage Council are two different things. You know something that threatened them so you were imprisoned. My friends and I are also considered threats to the Council's new plans."

"The enemy of my enemy?" He raised a hand and rolled his wrist letting the rest of the sentence hang, unspoken.

"Something like that."

"But I'm an evil demon?" He smiled. His glowing yellow eyes seemed to twinkle, contrasting against the red hue of his skin. He looked like some cartoon devil, obviously playing on the images he could pull from my mind. This one was going to be a slippery customer.

"We both know that is also creative story telling by the Council. Demon's aren't evil just self-serving. Now, Caleb has remembered you but you are still stuck in this cage." I indicated to the black mist around us. Emethus' eyes flicked around us; I could sense he had not realised that yet. "I can break you out. All I'm asking is you help my friends and I dismantle the corrupt element of the Council."

"You want me to help you get revenge on the ones who imprisoned me? You drive a hard bargain," he snorted in amusement.

"With conditions, of course. While we are working together you will be bound by my commands so you will only be able to act within the parameters I set forth." Emethus changed back to his silvery appearance and stepped closer to me. I felt him reach out with his aura to test at my mind. I let him. I let him see what I was truly capable of. True, I might not be a match for a demon when caught off guard. But on a good day, I was not the enemy he wanted.

"You, Emily, The Witch Queen," he lingered on my name, as if the conjuration of it would impress me. When I refused to react, his smile deepened. "You intrigue me." He took a deep breath his chest expanding as he drew himself to his full seven-foot height. "Once our work is done, you will release us from your binding?" I nodded once. "Then I agree to your terms. Working for a master would be preferable to an eternity in this hole. No offense Caleb." Caleb looked confused, not knowing what he meant at all. The air around us shook. "It seems that my help is needed quite urgently? "

"Yes, they put a tracker in Caleb's psyche too, warded beyond belief. It's going to take me a while to dismantle it."

"Break free my chains My Witch and you can leave that annoyance to me." The air shook again. "However, I suggest you hasten your work?"

I closed my eyes and opened my mind to see the wardings encasing Emethus inside Caleb's mind. It was like a spider's web wrapped around his limbs. Although he seemed to move freely in the space, he was bound tightly, not able to bend an inch of his subconscious. The trick with wardings such as this were that you didn't need to cut every tie, you just needed to find the key strands that were holding the tension. But I didn't even have time for that. Instead, I grasped hold of two strands that held Emethus in place. I felt the magic flowing through them as if I had grabbed hold of electric cables. I could taste charcoal and spice, the signature of the Mage who had cast this. It had a nasty barb to it too, the more Emethus struggled the tighter it became. The demon had been trapped here for hundreds of years. I had felt his pain when I first encountered him but he must have been able to hide the true extent of his agony. Once I had absorbed the rhythm of the magic, I sent out my own to merge with it, poison the strands. I spoke the words of my evocation, one no Council Mage had even learnt, and felt the fire rush beneath my fingers without burning me. Every single strand holding Emethus went up in flames instantly. I heard the demon howl as the magic was destroyed. For a moment, I was afraid I had consumed him as well. But when I opened my eyes, he was kneeling before us, his skin the colour of pearl as he stared at me in wild relief.

"Emethus, with this act of freedom, I bind thy power to my command. You may act to preserve your life and the lives of our companions but do so within my guidelines until such a time that our work is complete. Do you accept the bargain?"

"I accept Witch Queen." His voice sounded more raw this time and it clawed deep in my soul. His hands reached out in front of him and the box with the tracker materialised.

"There are fail-safes so you need…" my warning was cut off when he squeezed the box between his hands and the whole thing exploded in sparks. I held my breath, waiting for the mechanisms to unleash magical hell upon us.

"It seems My Queen, that there are some tricks you do not yet know. Perhaps I can teach you in time."

The offer was incredibly tempting. To have the knowledge of demon power alongside my own magic. That would be advantageous against the Council. However, Emethus was a demon; evil he may not be, but he would want something in return and for now, we had work to do.

"In time perhaps. But now we need to return." I moved over to Caleb and put my hands either side of his forehead as I had done on the sofa. Emethus seemed to float round behind him. His eyes were fixed on me the whole time. "Time to wake up Caleb."

#

I was brought back to reality by an almighty explosion as glass shards flew above the sofa. Some dropped on top of me but thankfully we were shielded from the high velocity pieces.

"That ward is failing," Remi yelled. "They're going to be able to get through in seconds and then we're done for." I sat up and surveyed the scene. Remi had ducked behind a window that no longer contained any glass. A gun was resting over his shoulder as he tracked people's movements outside. Helios must have been upstairs as a jet of pure fire rained down from the sky and scorched the ground just inside the ward, urging Enforcers back. I started whispering, channelling more power into the ward. Blue energy flared within it as the strength returned.

Remi glanced back at me, "You're back your Ladyship, marvellous bring anything that might help?"

Caleb was stirring on the sofa next to me. His eyes flickered open. He looked the same as he had when I had first met him as Lee.

"What's...?" The voice was Caleb's.

"Caleb?"

His eyes focused. Good he knew his true name.

"Is Emethus there? We could use his help."

Caleb nodded before whispering the demon's name. If the world around me wasn't burning I would have found it fascinating. His eyes flashed and settled. They were the same shade of brown but there was something new, a glimmer of power made them shine unnaturally.

"You called My Queen?"

"Could you perhaps...?" I indicated the chaos around us. He gazed around, calmly taking everything in.

"Are there any further instructions or codicils needed?"

"Anyone in the house is good and I'd prefer you leave the Enforcers alive. They may be working for the Council but they may be good people."

"As you wish," he inclined his head as his eyes went dark blue. As he did so the light evaporated from the room. It took me a second to realise it was actually the sky outside. The sun had been blotted out with black clouds and with the first rumble of thunder, lightning crashed down to the ground right outside the house.

"What the bloo…" Remi leapt backwards in surprise. The thunder roared again and more lightning crashed to the ground. "They're falling back."

"Time mage," Emethus called out.

Remi glared back at us, he oozed suspicion.

"Can you get the vehicle started?" Remi didn't bother to reply he simply disappeared in the blink of an eye.

Emethus stood up and grabbed my arm to follow.

"Helios, Victor! We're moving!" Heavy footfall rang out on the stairs as the pair joined us at the front door. They both stared warily at the demon beside me but stayed quiet. Noticeably, Victor stayed behind Helios. The light dimmed even further and I couldn't see a thing, it was as if the light was being sucked out of the room.

"Follow me," Emethus instructed as we heard the car start outside. Helios' hand reached out and grasped my shoulder to follow my lead. It was impossible to even see your own feet, let alone where to go. The darkness was claustrophobic to say the least. Lightning hit the ground a foot to my left lighting the area up for a split second, letting us see the car. We didn't waste the opportunity to reach for the door and pile inside. The vehicle shook as a roll of thunder made the very Earth beneath our feet reverberate.

"Follow the light time mage. Once we are far enough, I shall restore the sun." Emethus had managed to get the front seat next to Remi. I leaned over the person next to me, who I realised was Victor when she squawked at me. Peering out the windscreen, I saw a ball of white light hovering in front of the car, incredibly close. Everything was still pitch-black outside when there was no lightning. Without arguing, Remi let the car roll forward and followed the light. He drove faster than I would have dared down the stone drive, trusting that there weren't any other cars coming towards him but then I felt the barest shimmer of magic and realised he was manipulating time, giving himself extra seconds to read the situation. Hopefully, he wouldn't have to do it for long as he would tire quickly.

The darkness started to lift as if responding to my concerns. It was just enough to give Remi enough vision to join the main road. Anyone else caught in it would put it down to a freak storm and slow down to a crawl.

"Anyone care to tell me where we're heading?" Remi's voice was strained. Helios and Victor had been uncharacteristically quiet too, well Victor had been.

"I hear South of France is lovely these days," Emethus settled into the seat and draped his arm along the edge of his window.

"You did it then," Victor muttered. "He's not Lee anymore."

"He never was Lee," the demon turned to face us. "His name was Caleb, but don't you worry he's still here and can come out to play when needed. Now, how exactly do you intend on besting the Council?"

"What do you know about a rebellion during the inauguration of a new Council head?"

Emethus fixed me with a long stare, "Well then. Scrap the South of France driver, it seems we're going to York."

Alex Minns is based in England and has worked in forensics, teaching, PR and been paid to wield custard flamethrowers. She writes sci-fi, fantasy and steampunk and can be currently found forcing her mother to listen as she tries to untangle the timelines of her time-travel steampunk novel. You can find her obsessively creating blog stories and micro-fiction on https://lexikon.home.blog/ and on Twitter under @Lexikonical

Demon Dave: Dinner Time

by Andrew P. McGregor

"Hello, Dave," a slippery voice slid into my ears. I opened my eyes but soon shut them against the harsh midday sun. The sun took centre stage in the clear blue sky, so I figured it must've been the middle of summer, but I felt as cold as if someone had thawed me from a block of ice. I wrapped my arms around my chest to ward off the unnatural chill.

A moment later, the pain started.

Spreading like an earthquake from the epicentre of my stomach, the pain spread to every extremity of my body. My hands curled into shaking fists, and my pointed nails pierced the thick skin of my palms. My mouth clamped shut, knife-like teeth narrowly avoiding a spasming tongue. My back arched and the crown of small white horns on my head dug into the red dirt where someone had dumped me on the ground. Seconds later the pain abated and my muscles relaxed, but only for a moment. "Embrace the pain, my dear traitor."

"Who. Are. You?" I screamed between bouts of pulsing agony that continued shooting through my body. I smelt smoke and opened my eyes again, creating twin slits through which I searched my surroundings. My vision blurry from pain-induced tears, I found what looked like a horse standing over me, its long tail swishing back and forth. Except, it wasn't a horse, its skin formed scales like a crocodile's, and the head...

The head looked like the black bones of a goat's skull, contorting and twisting as it spoke.

"Oh, Dave," the creature standing over him replied, "do you really not recognise me?"

The pain wracked me for a moment, and once I recovered I wiped the tears from my eyes. My eyes found the monster that stood over me, and I recoiled in horror.

"Tell me, Dave, do you know who you are? Or what you did?"

I tried to think. Pincers of pain sliced through my brain, and as hard as I tried, I did not know who I was. Flashes of a former life bubbled to the surface, quickly swallowed by waves of pain. I might've been a soldier, fighting in trenches somewhere. I ran away, killed people. I was on a ship somewhere. Perhaps I was a sailor?

Children, yes, I had two sweet daughters; they missed me so much.

I had to get the bread, but I forgot to look both ways. Someone bumped me onto the road.

The front of a fast tram greeted my brittle body.

I'm dead, I realised, *and I deserve to be*. The pain eased a little as I recalled running from the Western Front, leaving my soldiers to their fate.

"You remember, don't you?"

I peered at the grotesque face of the creature that stood above me, its feminine, snake-like voice giving me shivers. I knew that voice from somewhere. I *hated* that voice. "I'm dead," I told the monster, my voice delivering animalistic words despite me talking as normally as I could.

"Good, now get up, Dave."

That's not something I wanted to do. What I wanted to do was tear the head off of the creature standing over me, but I did not know why. I could do it, too, I thought, using the corded muscles in my bestial arms and claw-like fingernails at the ends of my hands to carve that monster's face into multiple strips. I stopped thinking for a moment and looked at my hands and arms. Brown fur covered my arms, hiding taut muscles.

When I looked up again, I stared at dark shapes beyond the monster, seeing demons in place of men.

"Get up," the monster demanded. Pain radiated from my stomach each time she spoke. "Get up." I shook as I stood, not used to the alien body I now inhabited. "There, that's better." The creature wasn't as large as when I'd been lying on the ground. It wasn't as large as a horse, but it was still as tall as a man and as long as a crocodile. I feared the creature as much as I hated it.

"What do you want?" I grated with my unnaturally guttural voice. I looked down at my body, and saw that they had dressed me in an ebony cuirass, with black greaves covering my shins. A demon standing nearby approached, its features becoming more defined as my eyes adjusted to the harsh light of the midday sun. The demon carried a large, circular

Demon Dave: Dinner Time — Andrew P. McGregor

shield and a long, ash-coloured spear. The pain in my stomach returned for a moment, and I shivered as a hot breeze brushed over my body, cooling me down.

"I want you to fight, Dave."

"Why would I fight for you?" I asked the creature, despite the rising stomach cramps and searing coldness.

"Because you hunger, Dave." The creature's face contorted and twisted, morphing into a mockery of an elderly woman's features. She was smiling. "Because your guilt compels you."

The accusation of guilt hit harder than the pain or the memory of the tram flinging me onto the pavement. I closed my eyes for a moment, trying to erase the image of the distorted woman from my mind. When I reopened my eyes, the creature had reformed its face into the black sheep's skull. "What are you?" I asked it.

"I am your master." The creature's tail cracked like a whip. "Fight, kill, and the pain will lesson. Now, take your gear and join the others. You will attack the farm full of enemies. I need you, Dave. I need your leadership to win this battle. Take your place at the front of the formation and win."

The demon that held the equipment looked identical to me. He handed me the ash-coloured spear and obsidian black shield. The moment I held both spear and shield, I recalled a decade of experience with them, as if their presence implanted memories in my mind. I even knew what the spear and shield were called, a dory and a hoplon, the equipment of ancient Greek hoplites. The demon who gave the equipment to me led me over the top of a small, dusty hill, and a small army of demons greeted me.

The coldness I felt dissipated when I approached the army, and my desire to fight increased, as if I could feel the collective bloodlust emanating from the hundred or so other demonic hoplites. While I joined the ranks of the demons, the four-legged, black-scaled, sheep-skulled monster followed, but stayed at the top of the hill to oversee the preparations for the attack.

Below the hill were several farmhouses and a small, empty riverbed, where water used to run. Eucalyptus trees shaded patches of dusty landscape, and barbed wire fences cordoned off areas where a herd of starved cattle roamed. A man ran from a large shed into the main house, carrying a rifle of some sort.

"Dave, join front rank," one demon, the strategos of the small army, told me. I knew this demon from memories, either implanted or real. He was a favourite of the monster, a general from ancient Athens brought back to life as a demon. His rule was absolute, and his cruelty legendary, even amongst the denizens of the volcanic underworlds from where all had spawned. I obeyed the strategos without question and pushed my way through to the front of the army to join the wall of shields and spears there. The other demons kept a close watch on the building below, or stared at me as I pushed through. Whether they were angry with me or surprised that I'd come to take command of the front rank, I couldn't say, but their faces were gargoyle carvings, ugly stone visages animated by evil purpose. Many amongst those watching me with yellow eyes regarded me with wariness, as if I were about to gut them with the tip of my spear.

The attention made me uncomfortable. "Eyes forward," I barked at my otherworldly underlings. "Lock shields and obey commands." Perhaps feeling the pain in their bodies as much as I, or fearing the whip-like tail of the sheep-skull master, the demons fell into line without a word of complaint.

One other soldier stood in the middle of the formation, at least twice the height of any other, and roared, signalling the attack to begin.

I did not know who we were attacking or why. I only knew that the humans sheltering in the houses below us had to die. I held my shield in the correct fashion, the left of it covering the body of the demon to my left, and the demon's shield to my right shielding the right side of my body, so that we were all interlocked, each protecting the other in a line of demons fifty wide. Two more lines of demons pressed in behind us, forming a unit a hundred and fifty strong.

I felt warm amongst my peers, our combined body heat scorching the red dirt wherever we trod, but the pain remained, spurring me onwards. The desire to kill, to quench the pain and slake my hunger, rose with each passing step. The pace picked up as we reached the bottom of the red hill.

One section of the phalanx slowed, having to cut through barbed wire, but it didn't take long before the ash-coloured spears had sliced through.

A buzzing sound zipped over my head. *A bullet!* My long-dead memories informed me, fired from one of the buildings. Moments later bullets whizzed over our heads or buried in the dirt near our feet.

"Fire!" a shout echoed from the house where the first shot came from. The human's voice seemed distorted and twisted to my ears, as if the speaker were an alien speaking some strange language. I could tell the man was speaking English, and I had to resist the temptation to drop to my knees and cover my body from the expected incoming fire.

Demon Dave: Dinner Time — Andrew P. McGregor

A torrent of metal zipped towards us. The ground seemed to come to life; the dirt bubbling where the bullets hit. Lightning lit up the windows of the houses, and thunder struck our indestructible shields and greaves. One demon fell as a bullet zipped over his shield and into his forehead, and another demon from the rank behind him took his place.

"*Backchos, attack,*" the strategos ordered the army's giant. Backchos, crouching behind the formation until that moment, picked up a large rock in his fiery hand, and rose to his full height to tower over the smaller hoplites. Several bullets pinged off his black armour, and he threw the rock with great accuracy at the main house, roaring like a tank engine as he did so.

The rock smoked as it flew, leaving a thin trail of black and grey wisps before it struck the house, smashing several wooden weatherboards inwards. The firing from the house stopped for a moment, but increased in urgency as those inside realised how much trouble they were in.

A grenade flew from the roof of the main house, landing short and exploding in a hail of fragments that drew blood from the hoplites but didn't kill anyone. Pained grunts and frustrated screams rose from the throats of the wounded hoplites.

The combined body heat of the packed ranks of demons ignited nearby shrubs lucky enough to have survived what appeared to be a long hot drought, and insects and rodents scattered before them. Upon hearing the gunfire, the cattle in the yards fled further into the desolate paddocks, abandoning their precious shade and picking up the pace when they heard Backchos roar again.

"Reloading," a human yelled.

"More grenades, throw 'em Ava!" another shouted.

Backchos took aim and flung another rock at the roof, where the grenade-wielder was hiding. The right-side top storey window shattered, and I saw someone inside the window fall down. A few seconds later, the woman named 'Ava' and the entire room she was occupying exploded outwards as the grenade she must've been about to throw ignited.

Screams and curses rang from within the house, and gunfire pattered against my shield, making me flinch, but I didn't stop marching forwards. The gunfire became more sporadic, the shouts of those in the buildings higher pitched, panicking. I imagined it must've been a horrible sight, being confronted by a wall of black shields wielded by brown-furred demons marching in step at them, impervious to modern weaponry.

One man ran out the back of the left-most house, and Backchos hurled a fist-sized rock in the man's direction. The man fell dead, his chequered shirt ablaze and the blood on his back bubbling where the rock had embedded within his body.

A loud crack and boom ripped through part of the phalanx to my left and a hundred heads turned to see what had happened, while those that were injured by the blast gurgled inhuman screams or ducked behind their shields. A handful of hoplites had fallen to the ground, spraying red dust over black shields. Blood joined the mix, and one of the fallen hoplites lay still, while another's legs spasmed, lashing at those around him with clawed, leathery feet. Several demons from the front rank moved forwards to protect the downed troops from the distant gunfire.

"Formation, halt," the strategos, his voice a grotesque, beastly groan, yelled over the sounds of rifle fire and echoes of the explosion. Bullets continued raining against our shields while our strategos assessed the situation. The main building was burning where the hot rocks had landed and the grenade exploded, but those inside kept up their frenetic rate of fire. The strategos turned his burning gaze on me, and I felt the cold all over again. "Explain."

The strategos and the rest of the soldiers had died well before me, hundreds and thousands of years ago, so knew little of modern warfare. I squinted at the ground where the explosion had killed the hoplites and then peered over the top of my shield to scan the area surrounding the houses. There were several places on the ground that were a little darker than the rest, or where the ground was a little higher.

"Minefield," I explained. "Weapons buried beneath the ground attack us when we step on them." The only mines I'd seen on the western front were anti-tank or anti-ship explosives, but the other officers in my division often talked about how useful smaller versions could be throughout the Great War.

I frowned, thinking the mine that had incapacitated two demons and knocked three others to the ground should've killed a dozen, even with their shields. But then I saw the burning grass and tufts of smaller plants wilting from the combined heat of our massed bodies. The mine must've detonated early, triggered by our combined heat.

Two more demons fell from rifle fire, one clutching his neck and the other at his foot.

Demon Dave: Dinner Time Andrew P. McGregor

The strategos snarled, running out of patience. A shot of pain drilled its way from my chest to my left leg and I looked down, expecting to find a bullet hole, but there was none. Finally, the strategos gave me a command. "Dave, take your rank, *attack*."

Relieved that I would soon be out from underneath his gaze, I nodded at the strategos and nominated a dozen demons surrounding me to follow. The rest of the front rank I commanded to surround the other houses while I led my squad into the main house.

"Forward," I told my chosen squad, "spears out, shields over top." The orders came as naturally to me as if I'd practiced all my life, but the closest I'd ever come to hand-to-hand combat in my former life was hiding in trenches and fixing a bayonet to my trusty rifle to prepare to run across an open field.

The front rank split into three smaller phalanxes, while the second two ranks kept their position and Backchos hurled more rocks at the houses, suppressing the constant gunfire and allowing me to get closer. There was what seemed like a narrow path through the suspected mines, so I led my troops through it. Bullets hit my shield more and more as I moved towards the house's white picket fence. Flaking paint and wood chips went flying as bullets tore through the fence and deflected off our shields.

The front door opened, and a man stepped onto the house's verandah, bearing a grenade. "Die you devils!" he shouted, while pulling his arm back to take aim at us.

"Loose spears," I shouted to those around me. Those of us in the front kneeled so that those behind could throw their spears. They were too late. The spears flew while the grenade torpedoed towards us in the other direction. "Down!" I yelled. A split second later, the grenade hit my shield and bounced onto the ground in front of me. All the hoplites kneeled together and locked shields. The grenade exploded, knocking against my shield as if Backchos himself had punched it, but we held firm and the grenade did little more than feed hot smoke into our already burning lungs.

The gunfire ceased for a moment, and as my hearing returned, I heard the screams of men and women from the house. A couple of the spears had struck their targets.

Sensing our moment, burning saliva dripping from my mouth and excitement coursing through my arms and legs, I roared, "*Charge!*"

We sprung upwards, smashing through the flimsy fence and gate, holding a loose formation while running at the grey-white house. Without the interlocking shields, several demons fell to renewed rifle fire, reducing our numbers. I no longer cared, but leapt onto the low-lying verandah, took two steps towards one of the large windows, and smashed through it, leading with my spear and shield. The spear slashed through flesh while the shield took care of the glass, and I almost stumbled over the debris.

I withdrew the spear from the man's body and kicked him away. I felt the man's life leaving his body like a drug that soothed my pain. The feeling of relief was intoxicating, and the feeling gave rise to instant pleasure. The fire in my body cooled, and I no longer felt the coldness of the blistering sun. The pain in my stomach dissipated, and a sliver of clarity crawled into my mind. The clarity brought with it a sickly sweet aftertaste as I realised it was the man's death that had lessened my pain.

More, my body screamed at me, urging me to reduce the pain further, *kill more*. With hunger clouding my judgement, I wholeheartedly agreed and searched for my next victim.

Elsewhere the slaughter built to a crescendo of shouts and screams as my hoplites crashed through more windows and smashed through the front door, which had been shut by the grenade-wielding man. The grenade-wielder, a bearded, wide-bellied man of great height, toppled under the might of the demon that had crashed through the door. The walls of a kitchen were on fire, and a woman in a flowery dress fired a rifle at another hoplite, hitting its shield, while an older white-haired woman in leather attire sporting tattooed arms flung a kitchen knife, hitting the same hoplite in the side of the head. Another hoplite braved the knives and rifle fire and jumped onto the kitchen bench before slashing his spear across both women.

A man dressed in a blue uniform yelled something alien at me and pointed his pistol, expertly flinging bullets at my shield. One bullet grazed my right cheek. I snarled, and then tossed my spear when the uniformed man ran out of ammo, lancing him in the chest. As the man lay dying, a feeling of euphoria spread from my stomach, soothing my aching muscles. It was as if a cup of cool water had just been poured into my burning mouth. Then the tap stopped, and I searched the house for more.

I heard a loud thud above my head and smiled. *Victim found*. After picking up my spear from the blue-uniformed man's bubbling chest, I ran through the warm fire in the kitchen and found a narrow flight of stairs near the house's back door. The shield didn't fit across the staircase, so I held it sideways as I ascended, desperately seeking my next hit of pain-reducing murder.

Demon Dave: Dinner Time — Andrew P. McGregor

Two doors greeted me at the top of the stairs, one in front and one to the left. The one to the left was open and on fire, as was the room beyond where the grenade had exploded, so I used the hot, obsidian-sharp point of my spear and thrust it into the handle of the door in front of me. The spear point easily sliced into it, turning the handle and lock to molten slag, and the door popped open.

On the other side of the door was a child, no more than sixteen years of age and probably younger, pointing a small rifle at my face. Her hands shook, and she dropped the gun.

I paused, lowering the shield.

Just a child.

I couldn't kill a child.

The pain flared up, beating upon my back as if it were forcing me onwards. "No," I grated, shaking my head. The pain increased, and my stomach rebelled. I was so hungry...

"No," I repeated. I squeezed my eyes shut and warred against the pain and hunger. "Go," I growled at the girl. I opened my eyes and fixed her with them. "Go," I repeated, trying to sound as human as I could.

"W-what?" she asked in a voice that sounded alien to me. She didn't move, scared stiff.

"Go!" I snarled at her. "Leave. The. Gun. And... *go*." I struggled with the words and hoped she understood. "Hide," I hissed, as much with pain as urgency.

"I can't," she cried. "The house is on fire. You demons will kill me if I run." She picked up the rifle, waving it in my direction, but too frightened to put her finger on the trigger.

She was right. I gritted my teeth, trying to think how the girl might escape the carnage downstairs. Too late. Someone came up the stairs behind me and hissed when looked over my shoulders and saw the girl waving her rifle.

"No," I commanded the soldier, turning around to face him.

"Need. Kill," he replied, in more pain than I was.

"No," I repeated, turning around to stare into the other demon's eyes. He glanced at me, then stared at the girl and pointed his spear in her direction. I stood in his way, gambling that he wouldn't try to skewer me. With all thoughts of taking the girl's life banished from my mind, the pain lessened, allowing me to think clearly again. I took a deep breath. "This one's mine. Tell the strategos she remains under my protection and is not to be harmed."

The demon's panting, blood-thirsty breath seized up, and he looked into my eyes, trying to understand my desire to keep her alive. He hissed again, baring sharp teeth at me. He looked like he wanted to kill me to get to her, but backed away when I levelled my spear at him. He grimaced, not wanting to let the girl go. "Strategos won't like," he said in Ancient Greek, frustration filling his voice.

"She is of use to us," I insisted, speaking his language as if I'd been born to it.

"So be it," the soldier snapped. He gave the girl one last look and turned around to head back down the stairs.

By the sounds of it, the slaughter downstairs had ended, and sporadic gunfire from the other houses had ceased.

"Come," I told the dark-haired girl, "come, or die." Still shaking, she nodded. "Leave the gun." She put the rifle down and we descended the staircase together, with her staying close. This, I decided, was stupid of me, but I had to show her trust. Even if she had a hidden knife that she wanted to plunge into my exposed neck, I didn't think I would have minded.

We made it down the stairs and crossed through the smoke-filled kitchen, heading out the front door with the girl by my side. She cast her gaze downwards to avoid seeing any other demons or the murders of her friends and family. The demons under my command were dragging bodies out of the houses and piling them together, watching me and the girl as if we were ghosts.

Dozens of yellow eyes tracked our movements while we moved to the wrecked fence, and four demons approached us from the ranked soldiers that had watched the battle from afar. One demon was the one I'd told to inform the strategos of my decision. Two others held no spears or shields, but carried black iron chains to wrap my prisoner with. The fourth was the strategos, his fiery gaze bathing me in hatred.

"Take the girl," the strategos ordered. The two demons with chains wrapped the girl's hands and led her back to the rest of the army. "Dave," he addressed me, spitting fire from his mouth, "you commanded this one to keep her alive?"

"Yes, strategos," I replied, expecting retribution.

"And this one disobeyed?" he asked, pointing to the demon I'd commanded.

I frowned, my mouth falling open. *I'm not the one he's angry with*, I thought, and nodded at the strategos. The strategos nodded back, turned to the demon that had disobeyed, and slashed clawed hands across the demon's throat. The demon's eyes widened, and he dropped his spear to hold his neck. The cuts were deep, and the demon fell to his knees, his death assured.

Demon Dave: Dinner Time   Andrew P. McGregor

"Come with me, Dave," the strategos demanded, heading towards the house. I followed, wary of his deadly claws. Hoplites moved out of our way and we headed to the burning kitchen, where the four-legged monster greeted us.

"Well done, Dave," she said, her sheep-skull face twisting with each word and her tail slashing across the kitchen walls. "You are wounded." She pointed at my left leg, where a trickle of blood escaped from a shrapnel wound I hadn't noticed before. "Now, eat. You've earned it."

A man's body, dressed in a blue uniform, lay across the kitchen bench, and the hunger in my stomach grew to overwhelm my senses. The girl was one thing, but the body of a dead man was something else. I dug in, ignoring the knives to use my claws, tearing meat from bone. The pleasure I derived wiped away any sense of disgust and hatred I had for myself, but only for the few minutes it took to finish.

When I'd swallowed several mouthfuls, I wiped blood from my mouth and looked upon the world with cooler eyes.

As the flesh of the man rested in my stomach, my wound started knitting back together. The human flesh soothed my pain, I could think clearly again.

My thoughts were not kind.

We just slaughtered people. I'm dead. Why am I killing people? I just ate part of a man. Why did I do that? But then I looked at my hands, those furry, hot, clawed hands, and remembered what had become of me. I furrowed my brows, remembering other battles in my demonic form, fighting for the demonic invaders and against them. I looked into the sheep-skull monster's alien eyes and remembered what had happened to those eyes the last time it had brought me back to life.

Finally, I remembered the monster's name. "Lucy," I snarled the name and snatched for my spear. A second later, her whip-like tail had lashed around my neck and she yanked me downwards, slamming my back into the floor before pinning my chest and arms with her forelimbs.

"That's right, my rebellious demon Dave. You remember killing me now, don't you? Helping your great grandson shatter my eye and destroy my brain with your dory. That wasn't a pleasant experience."

The intense pain returned, and if the monster who liked to call herself Lucifer wasn't pinning me down, I would've curled into a ball and screamed.

As soon as the pain had arrived, it stopped, as if Lucy had turned off the tap that fed fire into my body.

"You set my plans back years. That's right, Dave, you killed me *years* ago. It's taken me that long to reconstitute myself and rebuild my army, all because one traitor wanted to help his descendants survive."

"Why bring me back?" I croaked, barely able to breathe with her tail around my neck and her clawed forelegs on my chest.

"To punish you. Here's a little secret, Dave. Inflicting pain and death on humans brings relief to my soldiers, but *creating* pain, especially psychological pain in my soldiers, brings *me* pleasure. And trust me, you're going to suffer. You're going to kill for me, *willingly*, and you're going to hate yourself for it."

"No," I yelled, trying to rip her tail from my neck and roll from under her forelegs.

She laughed at my feeble attempts. "No? But look around you. You willingly led the attack on this little farm and gained *pleasure* from the slaughter. You didn't hesitate to eat the flesh of one of your great grandchildren a few moments ago."

My eyes popped open, and I looked at the blue-uniformed body on the kitchen table. *My great grandson? No!*

"I'm afraid he isn't the descendant of yours that helped kill me, but that man's time will come, and when it does, you'll be the one to thrust the spear."

"Never," I whispered.

"*Inevitably*," Lucy corrected me. "Strategos, time to go. We must reach the mountain by sunrise if we are to awaken our reinforcements."

The pain washed over me again, and Lucy let me go. Too weak and in pain to fight, I allowed two hoplites to grab me under the shoulders and carry me outside, where several white delivery trucks full of demons were already waiting. They'd driven over the small hill where the army had traversed and gone around the small minefield to park between the houses and sheds of the farm.

The demons of the phalanx were born millennia ago, and the heat in their hands could melt plastic, so teenage humans were forced to drive, and my captive was being inducted into the role by one of the other human teenagers. My captive looked out of the window at me, pleading for me to help her, but I could do nothing. The hoplites threw me inside, and as they closed the truck's rear doors, I heard Lucy's horrible laugh, and that half roaring, half hissing laugh echoed over the red sands.

I clenched my teeth and screwed my eyes shut. I knew, somehow I knew, that when our small army reached the mountain that hid the reinforcements, millions of demons would be loosed upon the world. I

Demon Dave: Dinner Time   Andrew P. McGregor

thought of all I had done, of all the guilt and blood spilt in the name of an alien demon, and let out an anguished roar.

To my surprise, the hoplites that rode in the back with me, those I'd led in the battle, responded by roaring their anguish as well. I opened my eyes again and stared with hope at the surrounding soldiers.

"Master," the closest demon said, nodding in my direction.

"Master Traitor!" another shouted in triumph. Others took up the title, chanting it over the rattling and bumping of the truck on the rough dirt road.

Despite the aching pain that pulsed from my stomach, a thin grin disfigured my leathery face. *Perhaps Lucy could die again,* I thought with a vengeance. *Perhaps the world won't burn.*

Andrew P. McGregor lives in the rural town of Inverell near the East coast of Australia. He writes science fiction and dark fantasy short stories, most of which are collected in 'Tales of Starships & Apocalypse.'

Astounding Performances

by Joanne Blondin

Welcome to Cirque de Oiseaux, or Circus of the Birds to you non-Frenchie's. Step right in folks! Come see astounding performances by men, women, beasts, and clowns.

You'll see trapeze artists flying, tight rope walkers running, dwarves dancing on horseback, and lion tamers controlling ferocious lions, tigers, and bears in the same cage. If that ain't enough, there's an elephant parade too!

We got outstanding food cooking up, cotton candy, fire roasted peanuts and popcorn, and flame grilled hot dogs. Remember the last time you smelled those aromas? You gotta have one of each. Dontcha? Your kids sure do.

Listen! The horns and trumpets are warming up with today's popular songs "Earth Angel" and "Moon River" setting up the dreamy romantic rhythm for the aerial artists. We got a drummer practicing to introduce death-defying acts.

Here come some clowns dancing in their big clunky shoes. They are so fun.

We got a side show and carnie games. Test your strength with the strongman's game, hit the bell, knock over the bottles, pop the balloons, and win a prize for your mother or girl.

Got your ticket? Better hurry. You don't wanna miss a thing.

There's Princess True Blue, our youngest bird, only thirteen-years old, dressed in her shiny blue costume, smoothing her feathers just like a seasoned performer. Autry, her partner, is doing the same thing with his bright green suit. Both are chalking up their hands and stretching. They're ready.

Step right in. Look up! It's show time!

With the smiles of experienced performers, Princess True Blue and Autry flew smoothly through their flying trapeze routine, easily soaring back and forth, catching each other or the catch bar. Until—

unbelievably, Autry was late. Their fingers touched lightly and slipped apart. Princess True Blue fell down and down. Her smile became a frown for only an instant. Flapping the feathered arms of her costume didn't slow her fall. The crowd gasped and then applauded as she scrambled out of the net and took her bow smiling with relief. The rubes were sure her fall was part of the act. The horns and trumpets played their theme song "Earth Angel."

Autry leapt down into the net, jumped over the side, and was applauded too. Grinning and waving, Autry and Princess True Blue ran hand-in-hand out of the ring and out of the tent.

Away from the crowd, Princess Blue turned to Autry and screamed, "Why the hell didn't you catch me? We practiced the triple somersault a hundred times. Where was your mind at?"

"Blue, are you okay? I lost count. I lost my focus," Autry blurted and contorted his face so he wouldn't cry.

"You could have killed me! What if I landed on the edge of the net instead of the middle? We're four stories up. Thank God I know how to fall!" Blue shouted.

"Maybe I should take care of the animals or be an extra. Blue, I couldn't put Mom out of my mind. One side of her face doesn't move. She's slurring her words and you know she never drinks. She won't get on a horse and says she's taking the summer off. She wants a vacation, but Mr. Jeffries refuses," Autry said. "The worst part is Dad, is oblivious."

"You're the one who's oblivious! You missed *me*! This was my—*our* performance, not some practice." Princess True Blue took a deep breath and continued, "Sounds like Rita has something real serious. What did Doc Matthews say?"

"We haven't gone to see Doc Matthews. Mom won't go. She doesn't want any bad news."

"You or Cecil better go with her, maybe both of you. I gotta go chill out. I'll see you tonight," said Blue, trembling as she turned to go to her parents' tent. I'll never fly with Autry again. Blue thought. Touching fingertips doesn't count.

Blue lay down on her cot and was up in a minute, her heart pounding. She paced back and forth. I'll never relax. How am I going to fly tonight? I gotta speak to Bobby, my elephant friend. He'll listen and understand. They had been friends from the moment he first put his trunk around her as she skipped past. Somehow Blue learned his language. She made the same deep rumbling and growling sounds that he did.

Astounding Performances — Joanne Blondin

Blue meandered through lanes of straw and wood shavings over to the animal area. She patted and spoke to each animal in its language even though she was still shaken. The bear, camels, horses, and big cats responded with soft growls, purrs or whinnies. The boa constrictor was silent, but he wrapped himself around her and squeezed gently.

She took a quick look around to see if the elephant trainer was nearby. The last thing she needed was Alvin's negativity. To her dismay, he walked out of a nearby tent.

"Hey, Blue, how ya doing?" Alvin asked with a cigarette dangling from his lips, "You're lucky you can practice falling. I can't practice being trampled by an elephant. I'll never forget how Nicky's body looked after his elephant got spooked and trampled him. That could happen to me. Us elephant trainers never get the recognition that aerialists do."

"That was sure terrible. Falling really hurts. I hate it. I gotta talk to Bobby. I'm way shook up," said Blue. She had heard about Nicky's elephant a hundred times.

"Oh. Sure. Sure. No problem. Come over to the elephant enclosure. I'm sure he'll be glad to see you."

"Aren't the big cats more dangerous?" asked Blue, blowing her hair out of her face.

"Big cats? Dangerous? Give me a break." Alvin scoffed. "The lion tamer got you and the rubes fooled. He keeps the cats doped up with sleeping and allergy pills."

"Really?"

"Look at the pill bottles in the trash around his trailer. No one needs that many pills to sleep. He don't got allergies either. I'm sure he feeds the pills to his lions and tigers."

"I didn't know," said Blue. Tears started to come to her eyes. "Please, I gotta speak to Bobby right now."

Alvin flipped his cigarette butt onto the wood shavings. The glowing end hissed "Lemme burn. Gimme my air." Alvin crushed the butt and walked with Blue to the elephant enclosure. As usual, Bobby had one foot chained and was eating a trunk full of hay. When Bobby smelled Blue, he dropped the hay and trumpeted a soft low hello. Blue rumbled a greeting of love to him and patted him with swift strong motions. Bobby growled with pleasure. Dipping his trunk into his water trough, he turned and sprayed her gently with a trunk full of water.

"That feels so good. It's so hot today," she gushed, as Bobby patted her with the tip of his trunk. Blue was sure Bobby could feel she was big time upset. Next Bobby curled up the end of his trunk to make a place for Blue to stand and swung her back and forth, just like her parents used to when she was younger. She loved it.

"You are so good to me, Bobby. What would I do without you?" said Blue holding on to a tusk and his trunk. Bobby growled pleasantly. Tears rolled down Blue's face. She was starting to feel better. She wanted to fly but for sure not with Autry.

#

While Blue talked to Bobby, Autry and other performers gathered in the circus' backyard away from the crowd. They stretched, drank as much water or soft drinks as they could, and reconnected with each other. They were glad to be away from the spectators until the evening show.

Blue's father, mother and a couple of other performers sauntered into the gathering. The minute he saw Autry, Blue's father yelled, "Autry! What the hell happened out there?"

Autry hung his head. He explained that he got distracted and was worried sick about Rita, his mother.

"You gotta know whether it's okay to perform or not. You're the catcher for Chrissake! Thank god we taught her good. She coulda missed the net and broke her neck like that tightrope walker did. Only twenty-five years old and totally paralyzed. He's a friggin' exhibit in the Circuit Circus sideshow. Every rube that comes by pays a dime to poke him," Blue's father said.

"I know. I know," Autry said.

Rita, dragging one foot, limped over to the crowd of performers around Autry.

The shouting and accusations stopped.

"Hey Rita, how's it going?" someone asked.

She gave a thumb up with her left hand. Her right arm hung limply, and only half her face held a smile.

"Leave Autry alone," Rita shouted, shaking her fist at the other performers. Turning to Autry, she stood on tiptoe and hugged him around his waist. "Don't let them give you a hard time, Sweetie. Everybody has an off day. Blue knew how to fall. That's what's important."

"I'm worried about you, Mom," Autry choked out.

"I'm fine kiddo. Not to worry."

"Your mom will be fine tonight. She had a bad case of nerves," his dad interrupted, "I ought to know. We've shared a tent for 25 years and got married too." The other performers started shouting back and forth.

Astounding Performances — Joanne Blondin

"Rita says she's fine," one performer said.

"She looks like she's hurting," said another performer.

"She's always complaining," a third performer said.

All at once, the back and forth arguing stopped. Mr. Douglas Jeffries, the circus head honcho and owner, wearing his dark blue suit, white shirt, and red tie, while smoking his fat stogie, strode over.

"What the hell's going on, Autry? Why the hell didn't you catch Blue? She's our star performer. She keeps these bumpkins coming in and keeps us afloat. I didn't name her Princess True Blue for nothing. I'm docking your pay for that performance. Reggie's going to catch until you get your act together. Blue's flown with him before. He don't look like you, but the rubes won't know the difference, if you loan him your costume."

Autry didn't say a word. No one argued with Mr. Jeffries.

Mr. Jeffries went on to his next problem performer.

"What the hell's wrong with you, Rita? Why the hell are you limping? What does Doc Matthews say? Have you talked to him?"

"Not exactly."

"Well sweetheart, go see him. If he says you're okay, you're getting on your horse for tomorrow night's show. I treat you good even if you are a stunty; sorry, I mean shorty. Didn't I get special hay and vitamins for your nag, too? I pay you and Cecil good. Got it? If you don't get it, you and Cecil can pack up and get the hell out."

"Okay. Okay, Mr. Jeffries. I'll see Doc Matthews first thing tomorrow." Rita said loudly and under her breath she said, "I wish I felt better, but I gotta perform whether I like it or not."

"Like I don't have enough worries with performers getting dropped, animals eating us out of house and home, clowns looking glum when they are supposed to look funny and happy," Mr. Jeffries muttered. He ranted some more about not making enough money to make ends meet. Finally, he walked away, puffing on his cigar as he relit it. The burning end shouted "Great. Gimme more air. I wanna burn big like my dad. He burned down a whole house with people inside." Then Mr. Jefferies flipped the flaming wooden match onto the shavings covering the ground. The flame hollered, "No! Don't step on me," as Mr. Jeffries crushed it out.

"Autry, I'll pound you if you have another off day," Blue's father called as the performers dispersed.

Autry cringed and walked hurriedly back to his tent, grabbing a couple of cotton candy cones from a cart on the way. He sat in his tent unconvinced by his mother's assurance. He stuffed himself with the cotton candy. What was wrong with him? He had never dropped anyone during a performance. Blue was so brave to tumble through the air with nothing to hang on to. He could always feel the reassurance of the trapeze bar. He bowed his head in his arms and cried.

He heard people walking past his tent. The concession man's voice came through the canvas interrupting his thoughts.

"No more cotton candy for you, fat boy. I'm making it for tonight's crowd now. Get off your ass. Move around. Do some pushups. That'll make you feel better."

"Okay. Okay," Autry yelled, "Jeez, can't a guy take a break? You're starting to sound like old man Jeffries." Crying is girly stuff, he thought. He wasn't a wuss – he could pull himself together. He always felt better when he pounded the strongman's game and heard the *Bing* of the puck hitting the bell. He ambled over to play.

#

At the evening show, Mr. Jeffries stood as unobtrusively as possible near the side entrance of the main tent. He anxiously puffed his cigar. "Keep that air coming. I love it," The burning end of the cigar muttered.

High above Blue performed with Reggie. There's the double somersault. Drum roll. There's the triple. She's gorgeous. Right into Reggie's hands. Thank god. The crowd whistled and applauded.

Blue and Reggie took their bows and ran out of the ring hand-in-hand.

"Thanks for catching, Reggie," Blue said.

"My pleasure, Blue. Any time," Reggie said putting his arm around Blue's waist, pulling her close, and passionately kissing her on the lips.

Blue pushed him away.

"What's the matter, sweetheart? You don't like that?"

"Sorry, Reggie, I'm still a little shaky from the matinee performance," said Blue thinking how good-looking Reggie was in Autry's costume even if his kiss felt wonderful and even if all the girls said he was a wolf.

#

The next day, Rita, subdued by Mr. Jeffries threats, found Doc Matthews pouring a shot of whisky into his coffee. He was having a late breakfast at two p.m. She apologized for interrupting.

Astounding Performances — Joanne Blondin

"Two shots used to get me right on track. Now I better have three. How's it going, Rita? What brings you over?" Doc Matthews asked.

"I'm fine, maybe a little tired. I could maybe use a break, Mr. Jeffries wants me to get back on my horse. He says I need your okay."

"I can okay you no problem. I'll do a couple of tests to make sure. Sit up on this here table."

Doc Matthews tapped each of Rita's knees with his reflex hammer. Each leg jerked out. Pulling his stethoscope out of his jacket's pocket, he listened to Rita's heartbeat and breathing.

"Your reflexes are fine. Your heart and lungs sound good. You're good to go. Gimme a minute and I'll write a note to Mr. Jeffries."

"Thanks, Doc Matthews," said Rita taking the note. "Come see Cecil and me tonight."

"You betcha," Doc Matthews said.

Rita hurried back to their tent, eager to tell Cecil about her visit with Doc Matthews. Seeing him she said, "Hey, Cecil, I got okayed. I'm gonna go talk to my nag. I've been neglecting her. Then I'll get into my costume for tonight's performance."

"That's great sweetie. I knew you'd be all right. We can perform tonight and start getting paid again," said Cecil as he hugged Rita and kissed her on the nose. "What do you say we do some practice?"

"Nah! I'm fine. Balancing is in my blood. I had a good break. Coulda used a vacation, but I'll never get that off old man Jeffries."

"You sure you're okay?"

"My nag will know what to do. I been stretching and exercising. I'm good to go," Rita replied.

#

The trumpeters announced the start of the evening show. Blue and Reggie flying on the trapeze was the first act. Their second aerial performance was near perfect. The crowd applauded, whistled, and stamped their feet.

After they took their bows, Reggie kissed Blue again.

"Hey, Reggie, leave me alone," Blue said, gently pushing him away.

"What's the matter, Babe? It was just a friendly kiss. Still got Autry on your mind? Let's you and me get away from this dump and get an ice cream soda."

He took Blue's hand firmly, pulled her to him, and said, "I can show you a real good time."

"No thanks, Reggie," said Blue as she tried to walk away. How can a wolf be so attractive? She wondered. Can I keep saying "no" like Mom and Dad tell me to?

"Gimme a chance to get to know you, Princess. We're working together now. I wanna be your Prince Charming," Reggie continued. "Go out with me, just one time."

"Okay, I guess." Blue said as she thought, he sure seems really nice. The other girls must be wrong. "Lemme get changed."

"Great! Meet you at the popcorn stand in twenty minutes." The two of them rushed off in opposite directions.

Back at the stand in less than twenty minutes, Blue smiled at Reggie. He winked, pulled her close, and kissed her gently.

Does he really like me? Am I pretty enough? Does my powder blue skirt and blouse look okay? Worried thoughts flitted through Blue's mind. Thank god I wasn't named Red, White, and Blue like Mom and Dad wanted to. Thank god they listened to the other performers.

"Let's go to that soda shop over the hill. They stay open late to catch the crowd coming from the circus. Their sodas and shakes are out of sight. Lemme hold your hand to be sure we don't get separated in the dark. Catching always ramps up my appetite. I'm ready for something sweet."

"Me too. I'm starved," Blue said. She wanted another kiss too. His arms around her felt so good. Mom and Dad told her not to let a boy kiss her, but Reggie wasn't a boy, he was nineteen.

The two walked quickly through the grassy field away from the circus toward the lights of the town.

#

Back at the circus, it was time for Rita and Cecil's horseback balancing act. Special ramps had been built so that each of them could jump onto their horses as they galloped past. They looked perfect together standing easily on the backs of their mounts. The audience had no idea that Rita had been unwell.

"Lookin' good, Sweetie!" Cecil said with a big grin.

Rita, happy to be back at work in spite of her protests, started to dance on the back of her horse. Suddenly her leg crumpled, causing her to lose her balance. She grabbed the reins as she fell onto one of the bales of hay surrounding the ring. Her horse, disoriented by mixed messages and lack of practice, bolted into the audience. Screams erupted from the crowd. Frightened spectators tossed whatever was in their

Astounding Performances — Joanne Blondin

hands, popcorn, candy, lighted cigarettes, and cigars, onto the straw and shavings-strewn floor, igniting it. "Finally! It's *my* turn. I'm no rinky-dink sideshow cooking fire roasting peanuts and hot dogs!" the fire screamed. Clowns ran over and quickly stomped on the flames with their oversized shoes putting them out—almost. They helped Rita up, grabbed her horse, and led them both out of the ring. The audience relaxed, certain that everything was part of the act. Then a sudden wind revived the flames. The flames got higher and licked the sleeve of a clown's costume, setting it on fire. The clown shrieked and shook his arm to try to put it out, which made the fire burn more fiercely.

The circus extras rushed under the seats and grabbed buckets of water stored there for emergencies. They tossed one of them onto the burning clown. The water ran down the over-sized smile painted on his face.

"Get that water off me! I'm the star," the fire crackled. "I'm my own spotlight. I'm hungry. Lemme catch that kid holding onto her daddy with her sticky hand. Yum, I've caught her short pink party dress. She's screaming too, 'Daddy, put me out!'"

An extra doused the little girl with a bucket of water.

The fire hissed "You can't put me out. My grandpa was a forest fire. Lemme grill up some animals like he did. I'm hungry for roast tiger and elephant steak. Gimme more wind. I'm ready to be an inferno. What else can I burn up? Who else?"

The wind is the rain's harbinger.

"No drizzle is going to extinguish me," the fire spluttered. "I gotta burn. Gimme one more person."

The horns and trumpets began to play "Stars and Stripes Forever" to calm the crowd. The song was a signal to the performers and extras that the fire was an emergency. One extra rushed to get the circus truck to drive around to find volunteer firemen in the nearby town. He sped off down a country road honking the horn.

The smell of smoke and burning canvas filled the air. The crowd stampeded out of the tent, until someone tripped and fell. Others tripped over him again and again. The pile of bodies grew blocking the exits. Performers ran around frenetically trying to wrench people out of the big tent to safety.

In the animal enclosure, Bobby coughed and coughed and trumpeted "Help me!" as he yanked and yanked on the heavy chain around his foot. Lions and tigers locked in their cages bellowed and roared.

Blue heard Bobby and saw the fire far in the distance. She pulled away from Reggie and ran as fast as she could back toward the flaming circus, stumbling over rocks and roots in the field. Reggie ran after her.

Blue ran to Bobby stamping on small burning clumps of straw and sawdust on the way.

"Lemme catch that girl in blue," the fire shouted, "I can grab her skirt, no problem."

"Get away from my friend!" Blue yelled as the flames licked her skirt.

"Stop crushing me!" the fire yowled.

Blue stamped some more, flicking the fire off her skirt.

Bobby had fallen over with the chain clamped to his foot. She put her head, first at his mouth and then at the end of his trunk. Only the faintest breath came from his mouth. She pounded and pumped on his chest to try to get him to breathe. She screamed for help, but everyone was running around intent on saving people. When no one came, she rushed around to find help. Running past the animal cages, she roared and growled at them. No animal answered. Devastated, she returned to Bobby, who was now wheezing. She collapsed sobbing, with her arms wrapped around him.

Reggie ran his comb through his greasy hair. He slid it into his back pocket and sauntered over to Blue. He tried to pull her away from Bobby.

"Come on, Babe. Leave that scuzzy old elephant alone," said Reggie, wiping soot from his face, "He's a goner."

"No! He's my friend," said Blue hanging fiercely onto Bobby.

"This rain will put the fire out. Let's you and me go find a dry place to get to know each other better."

"I'm staying with Bobby. He's my best friend," said Blue her tears mixing with the rain, "I love him."

"And give me up? You're missing a swell time, kid," said Reggie as he turned and ambled away, "There's plenty more girls who want a good time."

The drizzle became a rainstorm. "No! I gotta burn," the fire gave a last gasp and fizzled out.

#

When the fire trucks and ambulances arrived, the tents had completely burned, and the survivors sat in groups holding each other or staring vacantly. The horns and trumpets played the sad, lonely song "Heart

Astounding Performances — Joanne Blondin

Break Hotel" to match the feelings of the crowd. The smell of smoke and burning fur permeated the air.

As the ambulances' sirens faded, the crowd and ringmaster heard cars rumbling up the road. As they approached, the crowd read the giant letters painted on their sides. NEWS! JOURNAL! UP TO THE MINUTE!

The ringmaster, standing to the side of the crowd, dusted himself off, wiped his sooty face with the wet sleeve of his grimy suit. He looked around at the newspaper reporters and photographers, checking to be sure their cameras had flash attachments. Then he addressed them and the crowd.

Adieux, Cirque de Oiseaux. That's goodbye circus of the birds to you non-Frenchie's. We got no more circus.

Goodbye spectators. No more performances today—or ever. No more blue and green trapeze birds flying or horseback riders dancing or ferocious animals performing. No more cotton candy spinning, popcorn popping, peanuts roasting, or hot dogs grilling.

*How come this fire happened is a mystery. We did everything for the circus right. We treated every performer good even the shorty's. We provided on-site competent medical care for our performers. There were certified trainers for all our animals. We were well prepared for a fire. We didn't con the rubes that much. That's what circuses do for Chris*sa*ke. We gave the rubes a splendid show.*

Cirque de Oiseaux is extinguished.

Joanne Blondin lives and writes in Cambridge, Massachusetts. When not writing, she is paddling a canoe or kayak.

Theo Klaaggorn, Private Eye

by James Pyles

I left the werewolf in my car, and with a fairy in my jacket pocket, shuffled short, stubby legs across the street. It was a rundown North Las Vegas neighborhood and I was at the front door of one of the trashier shacks. Just half an hour past sundown, and I was hoping I could get to the Lillian before the vampires did. If we were too late, Angie would probably be sent up for life and I'd have let down a five-year-old kid who deserved to have her Mom back.

"Theo, I can hardly breathe in here."

Maddy was all of five inches tall and me being only four feet taller, she made a big lump in my sports coat.

"Shut up."

My chunky fingers reached for the doorknob and turned. I pushed it open slowly and peeked inside. Not a creature was stirring, which I hoped was a good thing. Then I saw her.

Lillian was lying at the far end of the tiny living room by the entrance to the kitchen, scarlet oozing from the wounds on her throat.

I'd only walked in a few feet when the lights went out and the door slammed shut behind me. One must have been waiting outside and he threw me forward like a basketball. The other two lurched in from the kitchen. They had me pinned to the floor just like that. I couldn't tell if Maddy was still with me, but one of the attackers put a bony knee on my chest. There was enough light filtering in from outside for me to see his face. It might have belonged to an angel, except when he opened his mouth, twin fangs turned him into a monster.

"You escaped us once before, Klaaggorn. There's no getting away this time."

Then he leaned down, ready to deliver my death sentence. Oh, my name's Theograven Klaaggorn and I'm a dwarf and a Private Detective. You're probably wondering how I got into this mess.

#

"Theo! Theograven Klaaggorn! Stop snoring you son of a coal miner!"

At the far end of a dark and boozy tunnel, I could have sworn Lekisha was yelling at me. Then three jabs of her elbow to my ribs convinced me that it really was her in my bed and I was regrettably awake.

"Huh…what?" My mouth tasted like the bottom of a truck stop toilet as my words slurred out. I rolled onto my tummy, its bloated bulk trying to sink into the mattress.

"I said get up!"

Her voice was coming in clearer which meant it was too damn shrill. Then ten fingers with inch long nails filed to penetrating perfection shoved under me. My sometimes girlfriend reminded me that half-elves are stronger than they look.

I squawked as I fell and then hit the thin, beige carpet on the right side of the bed. Peeling my crusted eyelids open, I was rewarded with the blurred and blinding light of day.

"What the hell time is it?" I reached up on the night stand, thick, hairy fingers rummaging for the digital clock. I slapped at it, and in revenge the thing cracked me on the top of the head before dangling in my beard by its cord. I managed to focus on the dull red digits enough to read 10:32 a.m.

I sat up letting a wave of nausea pass. Rubbing my furry noggin, I grouched, "Why did you wake me up so early, Lekisha? I've only been asleep for…" I tried doing the math in my head, but my hung-over brain wouldn't cooperate.

"In bed? Six hours." Her "your-snoring-makes-me-want-to-smother-you-with-your-own-skivvies" tone softened. "Asleep finally, about three."

I tried putting the clock back on the nightstand but it skidded across and then fell behind, nearly knocking over the lamp.

Leaning against the box springs, I could feel her hot, moist lips kissing the bump that had just started swelling. You'd think having a mat of curly hair thicker than Howard Hughes' bank account would have cushioned the blow.

Theo Klaaggorn, Private Eye — James Pyles

"Sorry, Sugar, but I've got that gig at the Hilton…I know I'm only a backup singer, but…"

The misty haze cleared enough for me to finish. "…but it's Elvis. I get it. You don't want to go into rehearsal feeling like death on a shingle."

"So, lover boy, would you please get up and get out?"

She was leaning down further and nibbling on my ear. Suddenly I wasn't so tired anymore.

"Yeah, sure. I guess so. Hey. This is my place, shouldn't you…?"

Her expert teeth and tongue did a terrific job of convincing me that I'd probably should start my day, even though I hadn't planned to get up before noon.

I hoisted myself to my feet, rocking back and forth for a minute before my balance resurrected.

Lekisha's brown eyes looked up, well not too far up, I am a dwarf after all, into my green ones and then down at the pleasure producing member. As I saw interest put a sly smile on her face, the member started to respond with a will of its own.

She shook her head. "Nope, you brute. We get started again and I can forget about getting more sleep."

One of the nice things about being a dwarf, is we can only reproduce with lady dwarves, so Lekisha didn't worry about the pill. Poor elves on the other hand, every time they hook up with a human, well…that's where half-elves come from. Humans are responsible for a bunch of half-everythings, although what they see in Orcs baffles me.

I was about to tell her what she was missing, but singing backup for Elvis wasn't trivial. The kid had some tough breaks before escaping the Old Country and taking refuge in Vegas. I couldn't mess up her dreams.

I struggled into my boxers. "Might as well check messages, get some breakfast. If a case doesn't come along, I'll have to hit up Percy again for a temp bouncer job."

That's how I turn a buck. Theo Klaaggorn, Private Detective to the fantasy creatures in Las Vegas and occasional bouncer at "The Bum's Rush." It's one of those dive bars where you can get a lot more than drunk, and for the right price no one will ever go away lonely.

"Night, sweetie. Sorry about yelling at you."

She was already under the covers and starting to doze. I finished getting dressed in the cheap, gray suit I had on last night (well, it looks cheap, but being only four foot six inches tall and almost as wide, its custom made).

As dwarves go, I might look like a pug ugly mutt with the sensitivity of hobgoblin, but that's just for show. Inside, I'm as gooey as a marshmallow. So, I stood staring at sleeping Lekisha like a lovesick sap. Her hair made a large halo around her black face like she was an angel. Yeah, I said black. Not all elves are pale with blond hair. Regardless of our species, we don't all look alike.

I took a leak, staggered into the kitchen, and used the wall phone to call my service.

"I'm sorry Mr. Klaaggorn. No messages since the last time you called."

"Thanks, Sylvia." I hung up softly. "Thanks for nothing." She had some Orc in her bloodline and I knew better than to piss her off. I almost lost a really juicy divorce job because I'd growled at her. She withheld my messages for a week. Good thing I'm one of the few other world gumshoes in town. Everyone from banshees to brownies calls me when they get in a jam.

Checked the fridge but I hadn't gotten around to doing the shopping this week. All that was lurking inside was half a loaf of stale bread and the last of a gallon of milk that had gone bad.

Half an hour later, I was choking down my third cup of coffee and gobbling the eggs and ham special at the counter of a diner a few blocks from Fremont Street. It gets a mix of humans and those of us who can pass. That's why when I heard Big Clancy, the gentle giant (he really is…tops out at near eight feet) try to sneak up behind me, I didn't think a thing of it.

Being a dwarf, I'm short, but wide. Massive bushy hair and beard down to my nipples hides most of my face, but hands, feet, and most other parts are all supersized. However, when Clancy plopped his catcher's mitt on my shoulder, I thought I'd break.

"Pull up a stool, Luca," I greeted him without looking up. I call him Luca to tease him because he reminds me of that big dope enforcer in the movie "The Godfather."

"Buy some coffee. If you're lucky, I'll let you pay my tab."

Being a Private Eye means I'm never rolling in dough, and Clancy has a sweet gig over at the Citadel Casino working for the human owner. He could afford $4.99 plus tax no problem.

"Got no time and neither do you. Boss is waiting. You got your car?"

"No, I only live a few blocks from here and I walked. Stop. Your boss is waiting? For what?"

"He's got a job and you want to take it."

Theo Klaaggorn, Private Eye   James Pyles

The look on Clancy's sad sack mug meant business and even if he wasn't armed, he's big enough to use my ribcage for an accordion. I grabbed his jacket lapel and pulled him down until his ear was close enough for me to whisper, "Are you nuts? I don't work for humans ever."

"You will today, Theo. Look, I'm calling in a solid you owe me. As a personal favor I want you to take this one."

I did owe him a solid. We refugees have to stick together, but even after escaping the Dragon Wars, going through the underground pipeline (inter-dimensional portal that manifests between worlds about once a month), and ending up on Earth, there's nothing that says we have to back each other up. If it wasn't for Clancy though, several particularly unpleasant demons and their vampire cohorts would have beaten me into chunky salsa, turned me into the undead, or dragged me back to the Old Country. That's where they're in bed with the Shade Dragon clans, and because of some "stuff" I did before escaping, I ended up with a death mark on my head. I'm not the only one.

The Shade Dragons and Hellspawn had taken over most of the Dragon Lands, banished or "disappeared" the Golden Serpent families, and enslaved the dwarves, elves, gnomes, halflings, and all of the other kinsfolk who had lived and worked in peace for thousands of years. A few members of High Elfish royalty were rumored to have made it through the pipeline, but who they were and where they'd gone was real hush-hush.

Saw Clancy staring at me and realized I'd been woolgathering again. "Okay, but then we're even, and this better not blow up in my face." We'd been using certain places like Las Vegas, Los Angeles, and New York as apolitical refugee zones for decades, places where it's easy for us to disappear or blend in. We almost never reveal ourselves to humans. That's because some of them, probably most, are worse than what we ran away from.

"It won't if you mind your manners, Theo."

"What's the gig?" I'd been kidding before, but Clance pulled out his wallet and dropped an Alexander Hamilton on the counter next to my bill.

"Boss'll tell you. Let's go."

He was already on his feet and walking to the door. Given he's built like a skyscraper and me like a fire hydrant, I had to rush to keep up.

One quick trip down the Strip in his tricked out pink Cadillac Eldorado convertible (he needs a big car, obviously), and we were pulling in behind the Citadel Casino. It's next to the Circus Circus which employs just a ton of the kinsfolk. A lot of us work in entertainment because we like the funky hours and the customers don't notice our differences.

Riding up the elevator to the penthouse, I finally broke down and asked. "Clancy, with the gas shortage and all, how can you afford to fuel up that beast of yours?"

"Boss has connections."

Decades later, the world would remember the oil crisis of the 1970s and it made me glad that I only drove an old, beige VW Bug. It's cheap and no one pays any attention to it, so following a mark is easy. Even if it's small, I still need a booster seat and pedal extenders to drive the thing. You should have seen what I had to go through to get a license.

#

"Clancy tells me you're a pretty good PI. How come I've never heard of you before?"

Anthony "Peanuts" Brambilla was sitting behind a humungous oak desk bigger than my bedroom. This office could have swallowed my little 1920s bungalow whole as an appetizer. The carpet was so thick, I could almost sink into it up to my armpits. I don't have much of an eye for art, but the paintings on the wall behind him looked pricy. Just about as pricy as the gold chains dangling around his neck down to his gray-haired chest. Shirt was unbuttoned below oblivion. The suit was rose-colored and silk, and he had a pompadour big enough to make Wayne Newton jealous. Peanuts was the shimmering model of 1974 Vegas Mafioso chic.

"I have a specialized clientele. Immigrants from the Old Country." I was mentally crossing my fingers that he wouldn't get too nosy. I wouldn't tell him squat, but if the job was legit, I could make some real green.

"Clancy here tells me you're good, especially at the weird cases and this one's weird. It's also personal so I need you to be, how shall they say, discreet."

He reached in a bowl for another handful of peanuts, loudly cracking the shells and dropping them in a waste basket. He came by his gangster nickname honestly.

I could hear Clancy shifting his weight, standing a few feet behind me as my butt was parked in an opulently cushioned chair in front of Brambilla's desk. Turns out Clance is one of Peanuts' personal bodyguards, but given I'd never worked for a human before, he made me feel safer than his boss.

"What's the job?"

"What do you get?"

He was all business. I told him double my hourly fee plus expenses just to see what he'd do and he didn't bat an eye. Before I left his office, I had a check in my hand with a number and more zeros behind it than even I expected.

"The case." Peanuts started to deflate, so I guess he wasn't all business. "My son Tommy..." He looked like he was going to tear up for a second. "He's dead. Coroner's not sure of the cause. Some sort of toxin. Still won't release his body so I can give him a decent burial. They arrested his wife, Angela. I know she didn't do it. I want you to find out who did and clear Angie of the charges."

"How do you know she's innocent, Mr. Brambilla?" I didn't see this one coming. He's one of the most powerful men in Sin City and if someone murdered his son, I figured he'd be all for catching the killer, daughter-in-law or not.

"Trust me, Mr. Klaaggorn. They'd only been married six years but they were good for each other. I know she loved my Tommy as much as he did her. I tell you; she was framed. Over a month ago, someone killed my boy and put the mother of my grandchild in jail. Here's a check for your first week's expenses. You need more time than that and I'll pay whatever you want, but I want results. This is family. I take family very seriously."

Peanuts probably meant that as a threat as in if I screwed this up, he'd bury me right beside Tommy. Instead, it came out soft and sentimental. He turned a framed photo on his desk toward me. They really did look like a loving couple, but Tommy must have gotten his looks and his height from Mom. I'd seen Peanuts around town a few times. Guy's maybe five foot eight at best and Tommy was at least six three, plus pale skinned and platinum blond, everything Peanuts wasn't. Even the jailbird Missus was taller than her father-in-law.

After putting the picture back, he scrawled on the check. Clancy walked over, took it from him and handed it to me. I put on my best poker face, but that wasn't the last surprise.

"Grandpa."

A side door I guessed lead to his private rooms shot open and then a tiny blur of long, dark hair and a powder blue dress zipped across the room and climbed into Peanuts' lap. She was four-and-a-half or five tops.

"Olivia, honey, I told you I'm doing business. Go back to your room. Nanny will take care of you and I'll come see you as soon as I'm done." He was whispering, but loud enough for me to hear. So, this was why. As far as humans go, I'd never seen someone so in love with his grandchild.

Peanuts looked at me. "My pride and joy, Mr. Klaaggorn."

"Are you the man who's going to help Mommy get out of jail? You're funny looking."

The innocence of kids can still be insulting, but she was so cute I really didn't care. Then she was off Grandpa's lap in a flash, around the desk, and into mine. I saw Peanuts tense up, but Clancy, standing beside me, nodded. That's right, Peanuts. I'm an okay guy. I'm not going to hurt the only person you've got left to love.

"I'm going to try, Olivia." I ran my fingers through her hair, and touching one of her ears shrouded beneath, I found yet something else unexpected. No wonder Clancy got me this job. The police would be no good at it and neither were any of the usual private investigators.

"Your Grandpa is right. You'd better go back to your Nanny. I'm just finishing up here anyway."

"Okay." She raced off back to Grandpa, planted a big, wet one on his cheek, and the returned whence she came, stopping to take her Nanny's hand at the doorway.

"I miss my Mommy and Daddy. Daddy's in Heaven with God. Please bring my Mommy back home."

Then she was gone, and she took my broken heart with her.

#

Before I left Peanuts' office, I told him what I'd need in terms of access to witnesses, records, and stuff, especially the Coroner's report. Pretty odd them still not releasing the body. After all this time what did they need it for? Also, pretty odd they could say no to a member of the Brambilla family without getting their legs broken.

Clancy walked me across the Casino floor and I saw one of my favorite people, uh…creatures, Leon Chaney. He ran one of the Craps tables on the day shift. We nodded to each other as I strolled past while wondering if I had time for a little hair of the dog before getting to work. That "dog" reference and Leon's name are both gags. You see, he's a werewolf. He works mostly days because a few nights every month the full moon comes out and he's impossible to be around. The name is a small twist on actor Lon Chaney Jr. who played Lawrence "the

Wolfman" Talbot in the 1941 movie. Most of us don't keep our real names when we become refugees. I'm an exception. So Lekisha and Clancy were called a very unpronounceable something else when they were in the Old Country.

Leon retains a lot of his fuzzy "wolfishness" when he's human, but when he isn't working or being a monster, he spends most of his time at the MGM Grand in their movie theater watching old films. He's nuts for them.

"So, when were you going to tell me that Angela Brambilla is a half-elf?" We were taking a shortcut through the maintenance hallways toward the loading dock. That's where a couple of other friends are, but I'm getting ahead of myself.

"Olivia's ears gave it away."

"Answer the question."

"Long about now."

"Why not before? I mean, I get why you suggested to Peanuts that I'd be the right guy for the job. If Tommy got knocked off by some exotic poison the cops can't ID, and he was married to one of the folk, that narrows the field of suspects to witches, alchemists, and maybe the odd druid." I'd already ruled out the druids since most live in Berkeley and are constantly high on weed.

"Figured I'd let the Boss tell his story and then I'd fill in the blanks, not that I know much. I do know that Angie keeps who and what she is under wraps. Tommy knew, I knew, but not the Boss. Most of the kinsfolk didn't even know. She was real private, not part of the action like you and me."

"But you think it was an underground job. Otherwise, you'd never have called me in."

"Call it a hunch, Theo. The whole thing doesn't feel like a mob hit and it doesn't feel like Angie did Tommy in. Sure, some half-elves have a temper, but the Boss is right. She loved Tommy to the moon and she'd have never hurt him."

I thought back to Lekisha's tantrum this morning and had to agree.

"Fine. You heard me ask Peanuts to call Angie's lawyer and get me a list of people who saw her and Tommy the night he died. That's where I'll start. But I plan to see a few of the kinsfolk too and put the word out."

Clancy opened the double doors to the Citadel's loading docks. Most people don't get that a big hotel casino is a lot like a convention center. You've got to have tons of food, booze, equipment, all kinds of crap, shipped in all the time. You also had to hire a lot of strong union backs to move it all, but I didn't see Mickey on first glance.

Clancy kept walking but I stopped and looked up. Fairies were pretty rare in Vegas because they're like five to six inches tall, tend to glow, and fly around on gossamer wings. Most of the ones I know hang out in the country with fireflies. Yeah, they're bigger than insects, but I guess in the dark at a distance, people don't notice.

In spite of that, Madeline lived here and was one of Mickey's best friends, which was a pretty odd match him being a troll.

There she was near the ceiling. Easy to spot, especially if you know what to look for. She was an oddball for another reason. People knew about her, well sort of, and she didn't mind. Some places have their resident ghosts (I know my fair share). The Citadel loading docks had Maddy. To the Teamsters, she was part legend, part good luck charm.

She caught me gazing up at her, scoped out my surroundings to see if it was safe, then zipped down to me like a hornet with an attitude.

"You're here about Tommy and Angela, right?"

"You bet, Tinkerbell." I loved to mess with her.

"That's Madeline to you, Theo, and I'm not in the mood."

Like I said, inside, I'm all mush, but I kid around a lot to keep that part of me quiet, even when on a job like this. All joking aside though, if she was a little taller or I was a little shorter, I'd seriously think about putting the make on her. Snowy hair, short, short mini-skirt, and curves to die for.

"You in the mood to tell me if you know anything about…?"

"Hey Theo! What's going on?"

That loudmouth was Mickey. If Maddy was Tinkerbell, Mickey might pass for the Hunchback of Norte Dame, except he didn't have a hump and wasn't bad looking for a troll.

"Got to blow, Theo. Say hi to Lekisha for me."

She was gone in a blink. I double-checked but there wasn't a human within thirty feet of us in any direction. So why did she take off like a bat out of Texas just because Clance and Mick were coming over?

#

Clancy filled me in on the drive back to my place. Mickey was in love and believe it or not, with a human, one of the cocktail waitresses named Lillian. It wasn't like Mickey and Maddy had a serious relationship, mainly because of the size difference, but I guess she could still get jealous. I hope Mick doesn't get burned. Trolls and humans almost never mix.

#

Lekisha was gone when I got back to my place which was just as well. I called my service and actually had a message. It was from Angie's lawyer, a Mr. Smithers. Human, of course, but he said he'd meet me at the County Jail at one. He could get me into see Angie on the private saying I was working for him. He also had the list of people who saw Angie and Tommy the night the kid died. Good thing on both accounts. Unlike all of those PIs on TV, I don't have a "friend on the force." They're all human, well most of them anyway. But Smithers could probably get me anything they had on Angie.

I had to hustle since that gave me only half an hour to make tracks. Glad I had a full tank of gas. Lines at the filling stations sometimes went around the block and I didn't have time for that sort of nonsense.

I met Corrington Smithers of Smithers, Smithers, and Armani in the lobby of the jail and he did two things, well three. He handed me a sealed manila envelope with the dope I needed, he got me in to see Angie privately, like in no cops present or even listening in, and he looked at me like I was something he just scraped off of the bottom of his Guccis. This is why I don't like most humans.

So, I'm sitting across a metal table from Angela Brambilla in her matronly prison duds in an interrogation room. I would have bet any amount of money in her father-in-law's casino that she was a hundred percent home grown human. I guess that's how people didn't know. I mean the points on her little girl's ears were almost unnoticeable, and with Angie it was the same.

"I suppose you know who I am and why I'm here, Mrs. Brambilla."

She wasn't crying, and her eyes weren't even red, but she looked like she wanted to stop breathing and die. I'm the suspicious type, but I just didn't see the percentage in her having anything to do with her killing her husband.

"I've heard of you, Mr. Klaaggorn."

"Call me Theo."

"Theo, like the detective on the TV show?"

I ignored her. I get that sometimes. "You keep a low profile in the world I live in." I wanted to ask her why, but that wasn't the topic of the hour. "I know the police have asked you this, but do you have any idea who would want to kill your husband, especially someone from the Old Country?"

"I'm going to share with you something that no one else knows. Well, I thought no one knew, but if they got to Tommy…"

She lowered her lovely face, chin hitting her chest, trying to hold back the tears. Then Angie looked back up. Her eyes were piercing, like looking into ice and fire at the same time.

"I have to trust you. No one in the community, no one knows, and I want you to promise me it will stay that way."

"Knows what?"

"You'll never solve his murder if I don't tell you. Not if they are the ones behind it."

Her face twisted into anger with a hint of vengeance. She knew who killed Tommy.

"My husband, Theo, was a half-elf, and the heir apparent to the Genydark Royal dynasty."

"What the…?" You could have knocked me over with the proverbial feather, and I'm no lightweight.

"Somehow there must have been a leak. The demon houses found out and…well, the reward for the confirmed death of any Genydark…"

"I know about being on a wanted notice. But Peanuts, Mr. Brambilla, Tommy's his son, and…"

"Tommy was spirited away to this world as an infant. His elfish features were almost completely suppressed and he easily passed as human, almost as easily as I. It was arranged that he be adopted by a human family. If he weren't in the community, he'd be much harder to track. Anthony's wife Helen couldn't have children. The adoption was arranged privately. The agents who brought him here were killed shortly afterward. No one knew. We thought no one would ever know."

"So how did you meet him?"

"Is that really relevant?"

"It might be, but I'll skip that for now. He had a price on his head as a Prince. So, who got the contract and how did they find him?"

"I don't know."

"Mrs. Brambilla, I'm trying to help you."

"I'm not lying, Theo. I really don't."

"You have any ideas? Who did you see the night he died?" I had the list in the envelope in my hand, but I wanted to hear her version.

"It was our sixth wedding anniversary. Of course, Anthony pulled out all the stops."

She was smiling, remembering that last night Tommy was alive, and probably how much Peanuts loved the both of them and little Olivia.

"Dinner, a show, Anthony knows I love Don Rickles, a private party, it must have cost a fortune. Tommy grew up in wealth and I just the opposite, but the family knew I didn't care about the money. Money is how they show love, Theo."

"Where was Olivia?"

"We have a nanny, Cynthia Gilbert. Olivia was spending the night with her at Anthony's home."

"What happened?"

"Nothing out of the ordinary. We exchanged gifts. Tommy got me a diamond necklace and I got him a bottle of Black Bowmore."

She must have seen the question mark on my face.

"It's a rare whiskey. Tommy enjoyed expensive liquor. You can imagine why being raised by the Brambillas. The restaurant buyer in Anthony's casino suggested it and arranged to have it shipped in for the party."

She smiled again, but only a little.

"According to what I know, the Coroner said that a unique toxin, a poison killed your husband."

"The police said I put poison into his drink, but I swear to you, I didn't."

"When did he drink it? At the party?"

"No. He waited until we got home. It was supposed to be very romantic. We shared a toast, but I'd had more than enough to drink by then. I swallowed a little and then choked, spilling most of my glass next to the sofa. Tommy drank all his. We were both suddenly exhausted and went to sleep. Only the next morning, Tommy didn't wake up. I'm so thankful Olivia wasn't there. She misses her Daddy."

"Who else had access to that bottle?"

"Once it arrived at the casino? Al DeGeorgio, he's the head of purchasing."

"He gave it to you personally?"

"No. I wanted it wrapped up so I suppose someone at the hotel did that. A waitress came out and presented it to him."

"Do you know specifically who was involved?"

"No, Al arranged all that for me."

She paused and I could see her shoulders sag under a weight of guilt.

"If I hadn't…he'd be alive. It's all my fault."

"No, no, not at all. Someone went through a lot of trouble to murder your husband. I don't know if they wanted you to be framed or if the cops just blew the investigation. My job's to see that we make this right and you get to tuck little Olivia in bed again."

"If you can do this…"

"You don't have to make me any promises, Mrs. Brambilla. I'm already being paid well. Besides, I met your little girl. Putting a smile on her face is reward enough."

#

Back in the parking lot, I was in my car thumbing through the papers the shyster gave me, looking at basically a suspect's list, though the cops thought they had Tommy's murder all sewn up. Bunch of friends and family at the celebration plus a lot of the casino workers. Tommy liked Craps, so he spent plenty of time at the table. Then a couple of names jumped out at me. One was Leon's. He didn't normally work nights, but a quick check of a calendar would later tell me it wasn't anywhere near a full moon. Lillian Ziganri, a cocktail waitress. Wait. Clancy told me that Mickey had fallen for a cocktail waitress named Lillian. I guess it could be a coincidence except I don't believe in them.

I also found the Coroner's report that had to be pried out of the cold hands of the Clark County Sheriff's Department with a court order, and that was only this morning. Peanuts must have gotten a copy of this about the same time I did.

Although elfish anatomy is different enough from human that it wouldn't go unnoticed, Tommy must have had so much human in his bloodline that he passed even when being turned inside out by an autopsy. Two big question marks turned up. The first was an attempted chemical analysis of the toxin that was supposed to have done Tommy in. I'm no scientist so I couldn't make anything of it, but I knew how I could find out. The other was some strange blood factor that the Coroner's report said has only occasionally been noted. That I did recognize and it made my blood temperature go sub-arctic. It also didn't make sense. Why would a vampire put the bite on Tommy after he was poisoned and killed unless…? Now I knew why the Coroner didn't release Tommy's body. It wasn't in the morgue anymore. Some members of the undead who weren't suppose to be on this side of the pipeline were waging a cover up. Mashed my feet on the clutch and gas pedals, turned the key, and gunned my VWs wheezy little engine. I had a bunch of work to do.

I was starving by then, so I swung into a drive-through to pick up a burger and soda. Even though I can metabolize human food, this stuff was barely editable. Next, I stopped by a phone booth and left a message for Peanuts at the Citadel. He gave me a private number to call in case I needed anything. Then I was off to the casino again.

Leon was waiting on the loading dock when I pulled up. I knew his shift ended about now. Wasn't much activity so I climbed some convenient stairs to where he was standing beside a forklift.

"You got it?"

He reached into his pants pocket and produced a key. "Yeah, Clancy gave it to me." I have no idea where he picked up an East Texas accent, but I liked it.

"Great. Let's get going. Should be dark in a few hours which is a good bad thing."

"You sure you want me to come along? This really isn't a good time."

I knew what he meant, but if I was right, it also could be a great time. "Trust me, Leon. I need you on this one and I'll make it worth your while."

"Okay, brother, but I'm afraid of what'll happen if I don't get home tonight. Just hope you know what you're doing."

"So do I, Pal."

Leon trotted down the steps first and I took a quick scan of the area. Some teamsters at the far end of the dock but no sign of Mickey or Maddy. I don't know why that bothered me.

#

Beating rush hour traffic, forty minutes later we were at the plush, ranch-style home of Mr. and Mrs. Brambilla in fashionable Paradise Estates. Their neighbors included Jan Murray and Totie Fields if that sort of thing is important.

It wasn't an official crime scene anymore so we opened up the front door and walked in. Nothing was out of place, but there was a horrifying, empty loneliness. A family had once lived here and now there was nothing.

"Here in the living room, you say?"

Yes. She said she spilled her glass around here somewhere." I pointed to the couch. "Time to turn your nose all the way up to eleven."

"I'm always a damn bloodhound for you, Theo. By the way, you should have showered this morning, and what you had for lunch reeks."

"Just do your job, please. We're running out of time."

"You're telling me."

He moved the coffee table back and got on all fours. It would have been comical, except I've seen the other side of him, and those horror movies don't do lycanthropes justice.

"Oh crap."

"Got something?"

"Yeah, and you're not going to believe it."

"Try me."

He stood up and faced me.

"I recognize the smell and you're right. Wasn't supposed to kill anyone and it's doctored to hit only elves."

"Knock out juice. Simulated paralysis. I knew it. Angela just had a little while Tommy took the full glass. She was only sedated but in Tommy's case, it induced a coma."

"If vampires are behind it, why do it this way?"

"I think they had to get him to the morgue."

"Vampires running a morgue. Well, that makes as much sense as anything."

Right then, I'd have sworn the lights flickered a little bit.

"You can come on out now, Maddy. I can smell pixie dust from a mile away."

I turned to see Leon staring up at the chandelier. Madeline came fluttering down like a leaf in autumn and sat on the coffee table.

"Maddy, what are you doing here?"

Leon and I sat on the floor next to the table so we could see her at eye level.

"I figured you knew I hitched a ride, Leon. Thanks for not tipping off Theo before we got here."

"You had your reasons, I know that."

"Fine. Will one of you clue me in to what's going on?"

"I didn't know it was the bottle of booze that did Tommy in, otherwise I'd have told you earlier, Theo."

"Told me what?"

"It's about Mickey and that tramp Lillian. I don't know if you know, but I've been pretty jealous of them lately. I mean there could never be anything physical between me and him, but it doesn't mean I wasn't in love."

"Mickey can be a real blockhead sometimes." Leon was nodding his head sadly, commiserating with Maddy.

"Anyway, I got to following Mickey around a little. I know what it sounds like and it's bad, but I couldn't help myself. A few hours before the party for Tommy and Angie, a package was delivered to the loading dock, a small one. Delivery driver gave it to Mickey personally. He rushed into the hotel and I tailed him. He handed it to that hussy Lillian. I figured it was some present he bought her. She gave that lug a big kiss and sent him back to work. He was so lovesick; he didn't even notice it was a brush off."

"You got curious about what it was."

"Theo, I know it was her. There was some sort of vial and injector."

"Did you see her do something with the bottle, Angie's present to Tommy?"

"No, I had to leave. She went into the girl's locker room and it was filing up with waitresses getting ready for the shift change. Too many eyes around."

"Theo, Lillian was the waitress who gave the bottle to Tommy. I was at the celebration and saw it myself. Didn't think nothing of it at the time, but with what Maddy said…"

"That's it, Leon. Lillian's the key to this." Lights were on and so was the air conditioning, which probably meant the phones still worked. "I've got to make a call."

#

When I phoned the Citadel, I found out two important things. The first was that Lillian had called and quit right before her shift today. The second was her address in North Las Vegas. I also put out a "Hey Rube" to Clancy because I had a feeling this was all going to go south.

The sun had been down for over half an hour by the time we got to her little hovel nestled among a bunch of other little hovels. Her lights were on.

"Leon, you wait in the car. Maddy and I will check this out and if something goes wrong, I'll send her to get you."

"We don't have the time for this, Theo."

Leon had been getting increasingly nervous, checking his watch every ten seconds. I knew what he was afraid of, but frankly, I was banking on what was about to happen.

"Just stay here."

"Whatever you say, Theo but I'll tell you right now, all of this is on you."

"Yeah, tell me about it."

Maddy climbed into my jacket's biggest pocket and I could hear her muffled voice.

"Damn it, Theo. Take a bath once in a while and save a girl the stench."

"Hush."

I got out of the car and walked across the street. Figured I'd use the direct approach and try the front door. It wasn't locked.

#

Now you know how I ended up as an early evening snack for three of the undead. But that isn't the half of it. Everything was either going to get a lot better or a lot worse, and fast.

Then someone let off a bomb and the front door exploded. Either that, or the full moon rose a minute or two ago and Leon's hirsute self made his appearance right on time.

I'd like to say that the sight of a werewolf startled the big guy on my chest enough to where I could throw him off, but when Leon barreled in, he kept going, colliding with all three of them. Then the melee began.

I don't carry a gun and it wouldn't have done any good anyway. So, I did the only thing I could think of, which was to jump into fray myself and try to help Leon out.

I could hear him whining as they clawed at him and bit. They can't turn him while he's in wolf form but I'm not so lucky. One good bite and a suck and I'll do whatever they want me to do.

One of them slammed me against the wall and made for my neck, mouth wide like a lamprey. I managed to fend him off. Strength-wise, we were about evenly matched. I heard Leon yelp again and figured the other two were giving him a hard time. I was glad the lights were out, because with a werewolf fighting two vampires, there was probably blood everywhere. Lillian, if she wasn't dead before, was going to be trampled.

Didn't know how Leon was doing, but I was losing my battle. I could feel his hot breath on my face and smell the stench of blood. He'd gotten to Lillian and I was next.

The vamp and I were holding onto each other so tight that when something grabbed him and sent him sailing, I went along for the ride. I landed on and broke a tattered recliner. When my head cleared a second later, I saw Clancy pummeling the undead person with ham-sized fists. He couldn't kill him, but pain is pain.

The Hey Rube worked. When the lights came on again, there were a dozen kinsfolk, giants, elves, trolls, banshees, ogres and even a small dragon (where has she been hiding?) in the room.

Maddy was at the light switch. She'd gotten out in time and brought in the troops.

Vampires are strong, but so are we. Plus, some of us do double duty as what I call, "Van Helsings." That is, because vampires are such pests, a few of us folk train to fight and well…end them as the case might be. I mean they had crosses, holy water, stakes and mallets, the works.

I looked at the end of the room. Leon was hovering over Lillian. He wasn't threatening her. It was more like he was guarding her. Mickey, bless his soul, sat down next to them, stroked her hair and started to sob. The poor kid wasn't breathing. None of this was her fault. The vampires had used her and the worst part was, she wasn't going to stay dead.

Clancy had the one that had almost nailed me on the floor. He was squirming like a trapped bug.

"Start talking. You don't want to be here when the cops come anymore than the rest of us do. Where's Tommy?"

He rudely told me to perform a sexual act that is probably impossible. Clancy leaned on him harder.

Theo, Theo, Theo!" Maddy was zooming in from the back of the house. She landed on my shoulder and panted in my ear. "There's a basement. Coffins. Tommy's there. You've got to hurry."

It was Tommy alright and he was alive. They'd sliced and diced him some and chained him to a wall. The vampires were probably going to wait until they got him back to the Old Country before making a public spectacle of his execution. He was alive, but it wasn't over yet.

#

The Van Helsings did their thing including on Lillian and we all blew before the police showed. For once, I was glad that they have such a lousy response time in poor neighborhoods. It's bad for the people who live there, but it gave us all a chance to get away.

The papers chalked it up to Lillian and her three pals being part of some weird gang or death cult. Out-of-town rivals came in, did a really gruesome hit, and then split again. Lillian drugged Tommy to fake his death and they were going to secretly reveal he was alive to Peanuts, supposedly for some big ransom. That was the story the law was selling, at least officially. Funny how three out of the four were also morgue employees.

Tommy spent a few days in the hospital but was out by the time Angie was sprung from jail. Peanuts invited me to his place to watch the reunion and I cried like a baby. That doesn't mean I didn't accept the generous bonus he gave me. I don't earn this much in six months. Not only that, but Peanuts personally said that whatever I needed whenever I needed it, he'd provide. He's a real standup guy.

There's still a problem. Someone in the Old Country knows an elfish Prince is here, and their hit squad failed to return as scheduled. I don't know how they found him or who else knows. For that matter, why is Angie so undercover, too? I'll have to tackle that one another day.

I did call in one of those favors. Tonight's the first night Lekisha sings back up for Elvis and I've got a front and center seat. After the show, we're going to celebrate.

James Pyles is a published SF/F writer and professional Information Technology author. Since 2019, his short stories have been featured in anthologies and periodicals. He won the 2021 Helicon Short Story Award for his SciFi tale "The Three Billion Year Love" which appears in the Tuscany Bay Press Planetary Anthology "Mars."

Beneath the Roots

by Anstice Brown

The blazing arrow illuminated the sky with silvery flashes before hitting the boulder with a resounding crack. Through the smoke rising from the rubble, Perun spotted a brown bear lumbering toward the forest.

"Aha! I see you, Veles!"

He rode his chariot through the clouds and onto Yav, blasting a pine tree into smithereens with another fiery missile. A flurry of shrieking crows whirled into the air.

"Where are you? I'll set this whole forest alight if I have to!"

His enemy's snickers provoked Perun to demolish another tree.

"Craven snake! Stop cowering behind the trees and face me!"

"This is much more fun, don't you think?"

It had been, once. But he found their annual battle exhausting rather than exhilarating these days.

Perun followed the trickster's taunts to a clearing in the centre of the forest. Scrawny deer nibbled on the brown grass by a dried-up stream. A gigantic oak towered above them, its branches stretching high into the heavens and its roots descending into the murky underworld.

A shepherd with a scruffy, red beard leaned against the trunk.

"I'm tired of fighting too," Veles grinned, scratching his curly horns. "How about we call a truce?"

"How about I cleave you in two?" Perun slashed his axe through the air, but the shapeshifter leapt away, guffawing.

"As slow as a blundering ox and twice as ugly. It's time a worthier god sat upon the golden throne."

"You are...nothing!" Perun swung the axe at him again, but Veles dodged it. "You will return the divine cows to their rightful place in Prav!"

"Your cows? I'm the god of cattle! Those cows belong to me."

"They belong to the mortals, selfish maggot!"

"Why such animosity toward your brother, Perun? What harm have I done to you?"

"You stole my first wife!"

"She chose me. She belongs to no one."

"You kidnapped my son!"

"I raised him as my own. Didn't I return him to you, virtually unharmed?"

"That's not the point!"

Veles shrank into a horned viper, dodging the path of Perun's axe as it flew past him and embedded in the trunk of the World Tree.

"Look what you made me do!" Perun wrenched out the blade, sticky with the sap of life.

The viper slithered toward the tree roots which led to Nav. Perun pulled a golden apple from his quiver with a shaking hand and hurled it straight at his serpentine foe. An electric crackle, a burst of brilliant light and the snake disintegrated into ash. Perun ground the charred remains into the dirt.

"Come back from that, demon!"

Perun ascended to the holy citadel of Prav in the crown of the World Tree to bask in his victory. He lay back on his throne smiling as the divine cattle bellowed and brayed. The goddess Dodola milked them and soon the heavens opened, showering Yav with a glorious rainstorm. Mortals danced in the downpour, filling clay pots with the life-giving liquid. The dry season was over. Tonight, they would sacrifice a bull to the god of thunder.

\#

Perun loathed the so-called 'Great Night'. Veles's rebirth meant another six moons of torment. He couldn't stand to watch the foolish mortals parading through the villages in their grotesque masks and jingling costumes, eager to meet the spirits of their ancestors. When they lit lanterns carved in Veles's image and chanted his name, Perun surprised them with a freak lightning storm which sent them skittering back to their huts.

"Perun!"

Zorya descended from the sky, her silver skin shimmering in the dawn light.

"How are you, my love?"

"Didn't you hear? Veles hasn't returned. I can't sense him anywhere on Yav."

"Well, what is it to me? Let him languish below where he belongs."

"You may despise him, but we need him."

"Preposterous! That snake is a curse upon the Word Tree. If he never returns, then all the better. There shall be no more dry seasons, no more blight and famine."

Zorya narrowed her eyes. "What did you do?"

Perun glanced at the golden apples hanging from the branches above them.

"Tell me you didn't? We're not supposed to touch Rod's fruit."

"He shouldn't have left them lying around if he didn't want us to use them."

"It's a test, you fool! You could have destroyed the whole World Tree!"

"Enough!" Perun balled his hands into fists and thunder rumbled around them. "You shall not question my authority again, Zorya, or by Rod's name I will strike you down!"

The goddess stuck out her chin and stared at her husband.

"Don't ever speak to me that way again, Perun. In fact, don't ever speak to me again."

Perun seized the hem of her cloak, but she vanished, leaving him with a handful of stardust. He let the sparkling powder slip through his fingers and sprinkle to Yav. He didn't need her. He didn't need anyone.

#

Perun slumped in his golden throne, tossing scraps to his imperial eagle and watching her catch them in mid-air. What a dismal Perun's Day. Where were all the mortals? Where was the lavish feast in his honour?

Zorya emerged through the clouds in a gust of wind, her face flushed.

"So, it took you a whole twenty-three moons to come crawling back to me," Perun drawled. "I'm impressed."

The goddess shot him a withering look.

"I'm not here for you. I have no other choice. The three realms are in grave danger."

"Always so dramatic. You can't stand the idea that I can run Prav perfectly well without you, can you?"

"Perun, this is serious. I've just been to the hall of the Little Bear." Zorya pursed her lips together.

"Well? What of it?"

"It's Simargl. I fear his bindings will not last another moon."

"Impossible. Those chains were forged in Svarog's fire!"

How the savage dog had howled when Perun bound his wings to Polaris.

"As the mortals' faith in us weakens, so do Simargl's chains. They're even neglecting our idols."

"Fear not. I'll create a spectacle grander than any—"

"Stunts aren't enough. They want miracles that matter. But what hardship can we save them from? What cosmic victory can they praise us for without Veles to challenge us?"

"I'm not bringing him back. Not a chance."

"You have to, Perun! If Simargl breaks his chains, he'll devour the whole World Tree."

"You're the hound's guardian. Why don't you bring Veles back?"

"Because all this is your fault! If you don't put this right, everyone will suffer."

#

Zorya's words haunted Perun all night. The mortals were ignorant and unsophisticated creatures, but they didn't deserve to perish. And what would become of the gods if the World Tree fell? He didn't want to find out.

When Dazhbog arose in the East, Perun swallowed his pride and rode his silver chariot to Yav. He knelt before his brother, shielding his eyes from the bright rays. Though he appeared an infant, Dazhbog had nurtured the World Tree when it was a sapling.

"Great sun god, I seek your counsel. I must retrieve Veles from the underworld, but I am too large to slip beneath the roots."

"Then you must visit Morana in her Mirror Palace, as mortals do."

"Wait, you mean…?" Perun shuddered. Though death was only temporary, regenerating his material form was a painful and tiresome process.

"If you defeat Zmey Gorynych in combat, he will let you cross the Smorodina in your corporeal body."

Ah, yes. That minor detail. Thank Rod he was armed.

"Follow my path across the sky, and I will deliver you to Kalinov Bridge."

Dazhbog mounted his flaming chariot, and his four white foals stretched their luminous wings and rose into the sky. Perun thundered after him.

When they reached the highest point above the World Tree, Dazhbog had grown into a handsome sandy-haired man and his foals into powerful stallions. Hours later, his hair was as white as swan feathers. They descended toward the blazing Smorodina river which separated Yav from the afterlife.

Perun grimaced as they parked their chariots on the riverbank beside the stone bridge. The stench of thousands of burnt corpses rose from the bubbling lava.

Dazhbog drew deep, ragged breaths as he climbed from his chariot. His rays were no longer blinding but soft as candlelight, and his sagging face resembled melted wax.

Perun ran his hands through his hair. What does one say to a dying god?

"Do not mourn me, brother. Here my path ends, and Jutrobog's begins. Our eternal cycle brings balance and order to the mortal world. You must strive for the same."

Dazhbog dived into the molten river, his chariot vanishing.

Perun did not wait to welcome the moon god. He loaded his bow and mounted Kalinov Bridge. The noxious smell from the river made Perun thankful that he lacked a digestive system.

When he was half-way across, the rock beneath his feet cracked and crumbled, throwing Perun out of his chariot. Scrambling to his feet, he drew back his bow and glanced around. Silence save for the ominous gurgle of the Smorodina.

"I know you're there, zmey. It is I, Perun, god of war and thunder. I command you to—"

A sharp pain seared across Perun's back and a huge, clawed foot slammed him face-down into the bridge.

"Arrgh!"

Perun kicked hard and the beast recoiled. He rolled onto his back and the zmey's bulbous, glowing body loomed above him. Three twisting necks writhed like serpents, each topped with a monstrous head.

"None command me!" The giant lizard hissed.

"But I am a child of fire."

"I do not care who you are. You are not mortal, nor dead...yet. You do not belong here, son of Svarog."

"I seek the Goddess of Winter."

Zmey Gorynych's amber eyes narrowed. "You have two options. If you defeat me in battle, you will be granted passage."

"I do not wish to harm you, great zmey. What is the other option?"

"You must look deep within yourself to perceive the ultimate Truth of your existence. You must sacrifice your pride and glory, becoming humble as—"

"I choose to fight."

"Very well. If I vanquish you, your soul shall be lost to the Smorodina." Zmey Gorynych licked his gleaming fangs.

Perun's arrows were useless at close range, so he drew his axe and silver shield. Better not go for its heads as they would regenerate if decapitated. He hacked at the beast's sturdy legs, but the powerful blade barely scratched his thick scales.

Three hideous jaws snatched at Perun, and he bellowed as the creature ripped into his shoulder, sending his axe clattering to the ground. He tried to wrench the sharp fangs from him, but the zmey held fast. Indigo blood soaked his white cape. He strained to reach his quiver, grasped an arrow and pierced the zmey's amber eyeball. The monster screeched and convulsed as lightning coursed through him.

The electrified head flopped to one side while the remaining two snarled and snapped at Perun in a vengeful rage. The zmey's scales smouldered like molten rock. Perun rolled away before a burst of orange fire hit the spot where he lay. Flames licked at his cape and he shrugged it off, wincing as he patted his raw forearm.

He stumbled back across the bridge and Zmey Gorynych stomped after him, blasting fire and billowing smoke.

"Gods, help me!" Rain lashed down, drenching Perun to his skin. "Really? That's the best you can do?"

Perun dashed away again but slipped on the wet stone, falling to his knees. He shielded his head, expecting to feel the white-hot kiss of death. But Zmey Gorynych coughed and spluttered, raindrops sizzling off his scales. Perun dived forwards, sliding on a puddle and slipping under the creature's forelegs. He swung back his axe, preparing to drive it into the zmey's fleshy underbelly.

"Stop!"

A hunched figure shrouded in a gray cloak stepped toward him, leaving a frosty trail in her wake.

"Throw down your axe, Perun!"

"Are you insane? Call him off first!"

"One cannot give orders to an angry zmey."

Morana raised her arms to Prav and summoned a blizzard. As snowflakes swirled around them, the great zmey gave a tired moan and grew still. Perun shivered. His fingertips brushed cold stone. He crawled out from underneath Zmey Gorynych and marvelled at the magnificent statue he had become.

"Don't worry, he merely sleeps."

"Your pet almost killed me."

"He is trained to protect me. He is a good boy." Morana's wrinkled face twisted to reveal a mouth of misshapen, yellow teeth.

"I require your assistance, crone. I must return Veles to Yav, if it can be done."

"Follow me."

Perun followed the old woman across the bridge to her wintery kingdom. Skeletal trees clawed at the dark sky and snow-capped mountains stood like sentinels on either side of a sparkling palace. A pulsing tangle of black serpents covered the frozen ground.

"You didn't think the three-headed zmey would do?" Perun mumbled as he picked his way through the slimy web.

"I do not care for visitors."

"I can see that."

Morana led him up the crystal steps to the Mirror Palace. The oak door swung open to reveal a dark hallway. It led to a large, circular room filled with ornate mirrors of all shapes and sizes. The view of the starry sky through the glass ceiling was breath-taking.

Perun admired himself in the nearest mirror, holding his axe aloft and his shield in a blocking position. Despite the soot covering his face, he was intimidatingly handsome.

"This is how you perceive yourself."

Perun glanced at the next mirror and frowned. "This one is the same."

Morana shook her head, dusty hair flying about her pale face. "Look closer."

Perun scrutinized his reflection. His face was etched with thin lines like a withered leaf. His arms looked thinner and less rugged.

"This is my true self?"

Morana nodded and Perun made a mental note to build in more bicep curls.

Perun found his many different aspects in the other mirrors. The five-faced god Poverit with his shield and lance. Erisvorsh, god of storm and winds and Perkunas, the northern god of thunder and lightning.

But then he came face-to-face with a three-headed god he did not recognise, riding a black horse. One face was his own, another belonged to his father, Svarog. When Perun leaned closer to observe the third face, he recoiled with a start. Veles.

"How can this be? Veles is my archenemy."

"Tell me—if the trunk of a tree is felled and the roots hacked away, do the branches remain in the clouds?"

Perun furrowed his brow.

"Harmony is born from conflict, not compatibility. Triglav represents the union of our three worlds. The realm of men balances between opposing forces. Without either extreme, it is thrown askew." Morana passed Perun a vial. "You must capture Veles's spirit and return him to me. My deadwater lake will restore him. But be warned. Veles has been connecting with one of his aspects."

"What does that mean?"

"I am sure you can handle it. You would not have fought Zmey Gorynych only to return empty-handed."

They wove through the glass labyrinth to an oval mirror lying in the center. Morana shattered it with her staff and Perun peered through the jagged edges at the unwelcoming abyss below.

Before he could muster the courage to jump, an ice-cold hand gave him a push and he plummeted into darkness.

#

The silence and gloom went on even longer than Zorya's lectures. Just when Perun feared he would never feel the ground under his feet again, he splashed into a deep, foul-smelling pool. Blind and spluttering, he groped along the rocky tunnel until he found an opening and pushed through into a vast underground cavern.

He dragged himself from the swamp and squelched across the mossy ground. Flocks of screeching nawie hung from enormous tree roots above, occasionally swooping into the dense mist.

The nawie fell silent as a dark shadow passed over the cavern. Perun spun around, drawing his axe and shield. The shadow crept across the rock, stretching until it eclipsed the whole cavern. A muscular torso solidified from the darkness, followed by a thick neck. Two sword-like horns protruded from an angular head and huge, leathery bat wings unfurled across the creature's back.

"The supreme ruler of Prav! To what do we owe this great honour?" The demon's deep chuckle shook the cavern.

"I seek to return Veles to the mortal realm."

"Nav has a new ruler now. Chernobog, devourer of souls." The demon seized a claw full of trembling nawie from above.

"Stop! Those souls must be reborn!"

"Why prolong their suffering?" The demon flung them into his gaping mouth. "The World Tree shall fall before Dazhbog's rebirth. Do you not hear Simargl howl and gnash his teeth? Tonight, he breaks his chains."

"No! I won't let that happen."

"Your power is waning, Perun. The mortals have forgotten you, as they have forgotten me."

Chernobog raked his sharp claws across the ground, forcing Perun to jump out of the way. He hurtled at the demon, driving his axe into its huge forearm, but Chernobog swatted him away like an annoying bug. Perun's axe slipped from his fingers and sank into the murky depths of the swamp and his shield slid toward the demon.

He pulled out his bow and fired a lightning arrow at him, but Chernobog grabbed Perun's shield and deflected the beam back at him, hitting him square in the chest. The bolt of pure energy blasted him across the cavern, and he collapsed in a sizzling, blistered heap.

Chernobog plucked him from the floor, snaring him in his gnarled talons. He dangled Perun's limp form over his terrible mouth, his yellow crescent-moon eyes boring into Perun's own.

"Veles? Is it you?"

"I no longer answer to that name."

"What happened to you?"

"You named me evil, so that is how I shaped myself. I fed upon your hatred and grew stronger."

"I was wrong. Your powers are the roots that anchor the World Tree. Without you, I'm nothing. Come back with me and put things right."

"Only now your destruction is imminent, do you regret murdering me."

The demon formerly known as Veles released his grip and Perun tumbled into his vast jaws. Refusing to be swallowed, he grabbed onto Chernobog's tongue and held on tight as it thrashed about. The demon gurgled and snapped his overgrown fangs furiously. Perun kicked against the demon's swollen tonsils. Chernobog's choking cough sent him flying out of the hideous mouth and he fell to the ground in a puddle of mucous.

"Don't you just hate those tickly coughs?"

"I'll end you!"

"You can try. But I'm not giving up. I know you care for the mortals. You protected their hunters and shepherds, blessed them with the harvest, wealth and music. In truth, my hatred sprang from envy. The mortals love you more than they will ever love me."

"They have forsaken me."

The demon thumped his fist upon the ground in frustration and Perun was knocked off balance. An avalanche of rocks fell upon him, pinning him to the ground. He heaved the rubble from his chest and crawled toward the demon, panting heavily.

"They will worship you again if you help me."

The demon raised a huge boulder over Perun's helpless figure. The god of thunder reached for his shield and his fingers closed around the handle just as Chernobog brought the boulder crashing downwards. Perun thrust his shield forward to block the blow, but it never came. He looked up at Chernobog's wide, glassy eyes as they stared into his silver shield. The demon slowly lowered the boulder, letting it drop to the ground.

"You see? This isn't you," Perun wheezed, clambering to his feet. "Return to your true form and together we can bring balance to the World Tree."

Chernobog let out a great sigh and closed his enormous eyes. His hulking form dispersed into smoke and Perun stumbled forward to coax the dark tendrils into the vial.

#

When Perun emerged through the broken mirror, burnt and bedraggled, a beautiful raven-haired maiden greeted him.

"Morana? What happened to you? You look—"

"You no longer fear what you do not understand. You have done well."

"That thing nearly swallowed me! And my axe is lost. You could have helped!"

The corners of Morana's mouth twitched. "I knew you could talk him down."

Perun limped out of the palace after her. She smashed the frozen lake with her staff and bathed his wounds with the healing deadwater. Perun released Veles's nebulous essence beneath the surface, and they waited.

Perun coughed. "Did we do something wrong?"

"Ssh!"

The surface of the lake cracked, and a fist broke through the ice. Veles clambered out of the freezing water, his fur coat dripping, and weeds tangled in his beard.

Perun looked at his feet. "Welcome back."

"You can kiss and make up later. Make yourself known to the mortals again before it's too late!"

Perun nodded. "Farewell, goddess."

"See you don't disturb my solitude again, or you shall suffer an eternal winter."

"A pleasure to see you too, fair lady."

The god of thunder and his adversary bolted across Kalinov Bridge, pausing only to recover Perun's chariot from the shadow of the colossal three-headed zmey statue.

By the time they reached Yav, Simargl's growls echoed all around them. Veles took the reins and drove the chariot skyward, whilst Perun aimed his flaming arrows at the earth, shattering rocks and reducing trees to ash.

Confused mortals gathered on hilltops, wide-eyed and open-mouthed as they took in the spectacular cosmic display.

"Perun speaks to us!"

When a dazzling lightning bolt set Perun's neglected effigy alight, the blazing beacon on the hilltop could be seen for forty verstas. Golden seas of wheat sprang from the barren earth, and the mortals were even more delighted.

"Veles has returned! He has not deserted us!" They set about preparing sacrifices.

Perun and Veles travelled to the four corners of Yav, gifting the mortals in every settlement with weapons, crops and cattle. As the sky lightened to soft pink, they rode high above the World Tree into the hall of the Little Bear. The doomsday hound curled his lips and licked his fangs as they approached, straining against his chains. Drool dripped from his chin and he whimpered in frustration.

Zorya greeted them with a relieved smile.

"The chain has been fortified! You have saved us all."

They returned to Prav as the first shafts of sunlight peeped through the clouds. Veles looked around the grand palace in awe, his gaze hovering on Perun's golden throne.

"Er—if you like it, I can have one made for you. Engraved with snakes instead of eagles, of course."

"It would add a touch of glamour to the swamp." Veles cleared his throat. "I suppose I should thank you for bringing me back, even though you caused all this in the first place."

"I suppose I should apologise for killing you, turning you into a demon and almost bringing about the apocalypse, even though you goaded me into it."

Veles raised his bushy eyebrows. He drew Zorya into a tight embrace, his lips grazing her cheek and lingering a fraction too long. He smirked at Perun before transforming into an adder and slinking down the trunk of the World Tree.

Anstice Brown works as a Literacy Learning Lead in England, where she lives with her wonderful husband, daughter and two mischievous cats. She adores speculative fiction and all things retro. Previous publishing credits include Fairytale Dragons (Dragon Soul Press, 2020) and Masquerade: Oddly Suited (Dancing Lemur Press, 2019).

Three Drops in the Snow

by J.C. Pillard

My father loved to tell me how my mother had wished me into being. He would take me on his knee as he told the tale, his breath heavy with the scent of cardamom and cloves from our dinner. "She wished for you my dear," he'd say as he ran a hand over my coal-black curls.

"One day, when she was sewing in her garden, she pricked her finger. Three drops of blood fell on the snow and seemed to her to form a face. She sighed and wished for a child just like you: lips red as blood and hair black as a raven's wing." He always smiled at me then, the embodiment of his wife's wishes alive before him.

My father seemed to think the story a beautiful one. I was not so certain. What kind of woman saw blood and thought of a child? I longed to know more of her—what were her favorite songs and stories, her pastimes and interests? But when I begged my father to tell me more, he would trot out the same tired tale: that she was kind, that she was beautiful. That she knew her duty well. She was the barest outline of a woman.

After a time, I realized he couldn't answer my questions because he did not know the answers. He wanted me to remember her fondly, but not deeply. "Be grateful," was his constant refrain. I wished I felt gratitude. For many years, I tried to mourn a woman I'd never known. I'd stare at her portrait in the great hall of the palace and will tears into my eyes, but they always refused to come.

When I was nine, my father left for a month and returned with a woman who he told me was my new mother. The next day, he took me to meet her in what would become the terrace of her rooms.

Her name was Velda. The first time I ever set eyes on her, she was seated at a small breakfast table. She stood when we entered, straight and taller even than my father. Her dark hair was pulled into a severe bun. And her gown. An austere, dark-red dress that trailed along the floor like a river.

"My dear," he said proudly. "This is my daughter, Blanche."

Her deep brown eyes met mine, and I squirmed beneath her gaze. A slight smile curved her lips.

"Blanche," she said, tasting my name like a fine wine. "Your father has told me so much about you."

I wondered what he'd said, but I knew better than to ask. Instead, I dipped a curtsey. "Your Majesty." I didn't think this was a woman who would like to be called "mother."

"Please sit." She motioned to one of the tall wooden chairs at the table.

At that moment, a messenger came breathlessly into the hall. Velda frowned as he bent to the King's ear. My father cleared his throat.

"Please forgive me, my love. Urgent business. The Sassalian ambassador," he explained to his new wife with a regretful look.

"Ah, of course," Velda assented, watching him go with affection before she turned back to me. I felt her gaze like a physical force.

"You're pale as a ghost."

I swallowed my nerves. "My father doesn't allow me to play outside."

She arched an eyebrow. "And why is that?"

"He says the sun would damage my skin," I replied slowly.

"Do you agree with him?"

"He says it's what my mother would have wanted."

She leaned towards me. "And what do you want, Blanche?"

I glanced out over the gardens that ran away from the palace. The little rivers that you could jump over, the trees to climb, the bushes to ramble through.

"I'd like to play outside," I said, almost too softly for her to hear.

She smiled. "Then you shall play."

#

It took only a day for Velda to convince my father to let me out in the garden, and another for her to arrange for her Seven to guard me, at my father's request.

Three Drops in the Snow — J.C. Pillard

The Seven made up Velda's retinue, and Owain the Scourge was their leader. I was terrified of him initially. A jagged scar ran the length of his face, turning his right eye milky and his smile into a grimace. The first day he came to escort me to the gardens, I shook so badly I could barely stand. But then he knelt, and we were eye to eye. He wasn't quite so terrible then.

"You must be Princess Blanche," he said. I nodded timidly.

"Have you ever met a knight before?"

I shook my head. My father had kept me away from the training grounds and barracks.

My father had kept me away from pretty much everything.

He chuckled. "Well, you're about to meet seven of us." Standing again, he offered me his arm. "I've never escorted a princess before, so you must tell me if I do it wrong."

The Seven all looked as frightening as Owain but were just as gentle, at least with me. Eloisa was short, nearly my height, but much more muscular. Her brother, Wyat, was taller and carried a bow. Rainier was lanky and black-cloaked, and wickedly good with knives. Like the others, he always had a kind smile for me. Then there was The Hobb, a man with a fiery red beard and a powerful laugh. He was matched in his gregariousness only by Inaret, who had a wit as sharp as her blade. And last was Albree. She was older and quieter than the others, but in time she became one of my most valued confidantes.

All of them were knights, but all of them put aside that knightly training with me. They taught me Hide and Seek, Grapes in a Barrel, and Free the Flag. I think they had almost as much fun as I did, darting along the garden paths and laughing at my shrieks of joy.

I asked Albree about it once, about a year after Velda's arrival.

"You're knights," I said. "Shouldn't you be training with my father's companies?"

"My Lady Velda requested this of us, and so we do as she asks." Albree spoke with a lilting accent, drawing out the vowels as though savoring them.

"How did you come to work for her?" I asked, staring idly over the brimming blooms of the summer gardens.

Albree leaned back, her greying hair glinting in the sunlight. "Because she saved all of us."

I glanced at Albree. "Saved you?"

"It's not something you will understand now. But when you are older, there may come a time when you will wish to be saved." She pointed to Wyat and Eloisa, who wrestled in the courtyard.

"Those two used to be thieves."

I gasped. "Really?" Thieves and highwaymen were suited for stories, I thought, not courtyards. I could hardly imagine Wyat and Eloisa as such.

Albree nodded. "One night, they tried to rob Lady Velda's carriage. Her guards subdued them. But rather than have them killed, Velda offered them work. She promised that if they changed their ways, they could live the kind of life they had always dreamed of and make something of themselves, too. They agreed."

She closed her eyes. "Lady Velda is like that. She believes in being able to change a life, to chart a new fate."

I couldn't help but glance towards the tower where my stepmother's study was. I wondered if she might be watching, and what fate she imagined for me.

#

Six months later, in the dead of winter, I began to understand what Albree meant when she said I might wish to be saved.

It was a clear, cold day. We were playing Hide and Seek, and I'd found a perfect hiding spot at the edge of the gardens, wedging myself between a bench and a high hedge. Sitting there, trying not to laugh lest I give myself away, I heard the crunch of footsteps. At first, I thought it was one of the Seven. But then a man I didn't recognize entered my grove.

He wore a white cloak over gray clothing, and the cold steel of daggers gleamed in his hands. A scarf hid all but his eyes, which glittered in the dim light. His gaze darted around the clearing before landing on me. I scooted backwards, the bare branches of the hedges digging into my shoulders through the heavy wool of my cloak.

He approached, flipping a dagger in his right hand. I scrambled away, trying to burrow through the bushes, but he caught my arm.

"Where are you off to?" he growled.

"Let go!" I shrieked. I tried to twist away, but his grip was ferociously strong, and I was only ten. He raised his dagger, and I screamed, squeezing my eyes shut.

The blow never came. A high whistle pierced the air, and a gurgle followed. I glanced up at the arrow now embedded in the man's throat. Blood spurted from his neck, hissing as it met the snow, and he toppled away from me. I couldn't tear my eyes from his body, staining that white snow red. I should have been horrified to watch him die, but all I could think of was my father's story, my mother's bleeding finger.

Owain knelt in front of me. The other Seven came into the clearing behind him, Wyat with a second arrow nocked.

"Are you all right?" Owain asked.

I didn't know what to say. I wasn't all right. I was scared. I didn't know who that man was, or why he'd wanted to hurt me. I stared blankly at Owain, unable to form words.

"I'll take her to Lady Velda," Inaret said.

"Take this, too," The Hobb said, handing her a piece of paper. "We found it on 'im."

Inaret carried me to Velda's study. I was too shocked to say much of anything, but I couldn't help wondering why she brought me there. I hadn't seen much of my stepmother in the past year that she'd been here. I didn't know why Inaret would take me to her now, instead of my nursemaid.

Velda sat in her study overlooking the gardens, her black-green gown pooled around her feet.

"Lady Velda," Inaret said, her voice low. "Blanche has had quite a scare." Quickly, she told the whole of it to my stepmother, handing her the paper the Seven had found on the man's body. I stared at the floor the entire time, feeling distant from myself. It was beginning to sink in that the man in the gardens was truly dead, that his corpse lay in that hidden grove. I felt the ghostly pressure of his hand on my arm.

I started shaking, my hand trembling violently in Inaret's. Suddenly, Velda's face was before me as she knelt.

"Go fetch the others," she commanded.

"Milady, are you sure?"

"Go," Velda repeated. "We'll be fine."

Inaret left, the door clicking quietly behind me, and Velda pressed her warm, solid hands against my freezing cheeks.

"You are safe," she said, holding my eyes with her own deep brown ones. I felt as though I was falling into those depths, as though they were carrying me to a safe shore, away from murderers in my father's gardens.

A warmth emanated from her hands, sweeping through my body. The shaking subsided, and I found I was able to breathe again. I blinked, staring at my stepmother.

"How did you do that?" I whispered.

She paused. "You noticed," she said with a frown. "If I tell you, it must be our little secret. You cannot tell even your father. He wouldn't understand."

"I promise," I said, because I knew she would never tell me otherwise.

Velda sat me on her blue settee, wrapping a blanket around my shoulders. "Long ago," she said, sitting beside me, "before your father's kingdom even existed, there were people who could shape the world to their will. You've heard of them in your stories. They were called sorcerers."

Sorcery. The word sent a shock through me. Velda had brought more than highwaymen out of storybooks and into the castle. I examined her, thinking of the way the warmth had flowed from her hands. "You're a sorceress?"

"I am, though nowhere near as powerful as those ancient magi."

"Did you use a love potion on Father?"

She raised an eyebrow. "Do you think I'd need one?"

I looked at her unearthly beauty. Even without magic, I had no doubt she could hold all the kings in the world spellbound. "No."

"No," she repeated. "No, I didn't enchant your father. And all I did to you was a simple enchantment to calm you. Now, we're going to have to do something a little more complicated."

Standing, she strode to the wall of her chamber where a swath of green silk hung down as though covering a painting. Pulling the silk aside, she revealed a gilt oval mirror, tarnished a little at the edges.

Turning back to me, she gestured to the mirror. "I'm going to look for whomever tried to harm you."

I shuddered. "He's in the garden."

"Yes, he is. But he was not acting alone. Someone sent him. This," she said, holding up the paper from Inaret, "includes commands to kidnap or kill you." I flinched at the words, but she didn't pause. It was not in her nature to shrink from truths, no matter how frightening.

"We're going to find out who sent him."

She turned back to the mirror. The air in the room seemed to still, the world growing quieter. "Mirror, mirror hanging there, who's the killer? Who would dare?"

The mirror flickered, as though it contained a light within. Slowly, the image of the room where we sat faded to reveal the very man who had accosted me in the garden, breathing and standing in a doorway. I gave a little squeak and spun towards the door. Velda turned me back around.

Three Drops in the Snow — J.C. Pillard

"This is the past, Blanche," she said. "It can't harm you. But that is him, isn't it?"

I nodded, barely.

She returned to the mirror. "From where did he come?"

The image changed again, soaring across plains and through forests to a village on a river. Velda hummed to herself.

"Who sent him?"

A new image: a palace covered in snow, a man with a black beard standing before a window while a younger man poured over books in a dimly lit room. The two were speaking, their words too low for me to hear, but Velda listened intently.

After a time, she turned away from the mirror with a sigh. The glass darkened, then returned to normal. Velda gestured towards the door, and it opened on its own to reveal the Seven, standing outside as though they'd been waiting. Owain entered, his mouth in a hard line.

"Milady, what would you have us do?"

Velda pulled the note from her sleeve and handed it to Owain. "You are to return this and the assassin's body to the Sassalian royal family in Casmeir. Let them know that we don't appreciate underhanded dealings here. And if any more northerners are found within these walls, I will not tolerate them to live."

Owain nodded, and the Seven turned to leave. The Hobb came and ruffled my hair.

"No hide and seek for a bit," he said gruffly. "But we'll see you soon."

"More games?" I asked hopefully.

The Hobb glanced at Velda, whose face was carefully neutral. "More games," he said after a moment. "But 'haps some different ones."

The Seven departed, and Velda rang for tea. She pressed a warm cup into my hands before taking a sip of her own.

"Well, I'm done for the rest of the day," she said with a weary sigh. "It's not easy to look all those leagues into another country."

I kept my eyes on my cup. The wonder of my stepmother's magic was quickly fading, replaced by a cold numbness. "Why...why would someone want to kill me?" I asked. There was a fleck of red on my right wrist, I realized. I couldn't tear my eyes from the spot.

Velda set her cup down with a sigh. "You have been too sheltered," she said. "Your father believes he can raise you to be a princess, but he forgot that princesses become queens."

She pulled a handkerchief from her sleeve and gently brushed away that bright speck of blood. "You are a royal. Your life is not your own: it belongs to your country. If someone wants to hurt the country, they can do that through you."

"But I'm <u>not</u> the country!" I insisted. "I'm...I'm just..." I stopped. She was right, of course. I was not an ordinary girl. I was the princess of a nation, my father's only daughter. "Why would they want to hurt me?"

"To destabilize our kingdom," Velda said. "Sassal is our closest neighbor, but they have long had their eyes on Prathia. We have access to the sea, which they do not." She lifted my chin, forcing my eyes to meet hers. "Do you understand?"

I nodded. "What can I do?" My gaze strayed to her mirror, its gilt edges glinting in the dim light. "Can you teach me to do what you did? Perform magic?"

She smiled sadly. "Would that I could. But magic is carried in the blood and you have none of mine. But," she said, standing, "we can do the next best thing."

#

My father swiftly forbade my play in the gardens after he learned what happened. I don't know that he would have let me leave the castle again, were it not for Velda's intervention. My hours of play were moved inside and slowly replaced with something quite different: lessons. In the morning, Velda tutored me in the politics of our continent. I learned to speak multiple languages, how to read and write trade agreements, and the distances between my kingdom and all our neighbors. She taught me to conceal my feelings beneath a veneer of civility, to calm the storms that sometimes raged in me when I couldn't understand something.

"You are not the hurricane," she would often say. "You are its eye."

In the afternoons, Owain took me to the private training field of the Seven. There, under the watchful eyes of the Queen's guard, I learned to fight. Archery, knives, even axe-throwing were included in my daily routine. Inaret taught me swordsmanship while Owain taught me hand-to-hand combat. And Albree taught me poisons.

"Because sometimes," she would say with a smile, "you needn't fight your opponent directly."

Four years passed this way. There were no more assassins in the garden, though Velda kept me informed about Sassal and their intentions towards us. I grew beneath the weight of my position. I was not happy with it: can anyone be happy in a life that is not their own? But I came to accept it and even embrace the mantel I might one day wear.

My father, however, was unaware of my transformation. He still thought me a little girl, pliable to his will. Perhaps that is why he reacted how he did, when he finally realized who I'd become.

#

The morning of my fifteenth birthday, my father summoned me to his chambers. I slipped on my best gown, nervous but excited. I could not recall the last time we'd shared a private moment together. He was always attending matters of state, traveling between the duchies and outlying provinces. I hurried to answer his summons, wondering if he'd called me because he'd remembered today was my birthday.

As I pushed open the thick oak doors, I realized that there were two other people in the room with my father. One was a tall man, thin and bald with pale blue eyes. The other I recognized from the mirror vision all those years ago; the man with the black pointed beard. I had learned that he was chief advisor to the Sassalian royal family.

"Ah, Blanche," my father said, giving me a strained smile. "Come in."

I approached, keeping my chin firmly up. A princess does not bow to strangers.

"Blanche, this is Lord Remzi of Miotus and Chancellor Soeren. They are here bearing an offer of good faith from Sassal."

"Princess." The bald man, Lord Remzi, bowed. "It is an honor to meet you."

I stared at him the way I'd seen my stepmother do, keeping my eyes distant. "A pleasure," I said, inclining my head enough for civility. What was my father doing? He knew very well that this was the country that had tried to murder me only a few years ago.

Chancellor Soeren stepped forward. He moved like a snake, oily and insinuating. He removed a scroll from his robe and unfurled it.

"Prince Ulrik von Verstein of Sassal most graciously requests the hand of Princess Blanche of Prathia in marriage. Let us unite our two glorious kingdoms, too long at odds, under one flag," he read magnanimously.

I stared at the three men. Marriage? What on earth could any of them be thinking of? I was barely fifteen and not finished with my studies. I had no interest in being sold off to another kingdom, let alone one that wished to kill me.

"My lords," I said carefully. "I am sensible of the generous nature of your offer. I am sure Prince Ulrik is a good young man. But as I have no formal acquaintance with him, I must gratefully decline."

They laughed, then. As though it was a joke.

I did not.

My father must have read my face, for he leaned forward. "Blanche, this would be a most advantageous alliance."

"I would be very happy to draw up a treaty that would align us without a marriage."

My father frowned. "You cannot decline."

The two Sassalian representatives glanced at each other uneasily. "You Majesty," Chancellor Soeren said, "we will leave you to discuss the matter with your daughter."

They left. My father rose from behind his desk.

"You cannot decline this offer, my dear child."

"I just did."

"Blanche." His voice hardened. "You do not know what you are risking. If you refuse, it will ruin years of planning. You must do as I say."

I could feel my temper rising. "There is nothing I _must_ do."

"You will marry the Sassalian prince."

"I will not."

"What has gotten into you?" he demanded. "I raised you better than this."

"You didn't raise me," I shot back. "You know very well they tried to have me killed!"

"And they did not succeed."

"This is just another way—"

My father brought his hand down on his desk, the thud startling me. "You will do as I say. I am your father—"

"And _I_ am a princess," I snapped, drawing myself up. "Not some sheep. Can you not see what they are trying to do, what they have been trying to do for years? They want to ruin us!"

"They will ruin us if you do not!" my father thundered. His words seem to echo, leaving silence in their wake. He sat abruptly, looking tired and old.

"You don't understand. If you do not marry him…" He sighed deeply. "We are greatly in debt to Sassal. They began demanding payment years ago. This was all I could do."

Three Drops in the Snow — J.C. Pillard

I stared at him, bewildered. My own father would sell me to settle debts he alone had incurred. I understood now why he wanted me to be grateful to my mother. He had hoped I would grow obedient under a yoke of guilt for her death.

I turned and left, silent as my mother's grave.

#

I went straight to my room. I took the lovely vases lined up along my bookshelves and hurled them at the wall. I wanted to scream, to tear the brocade curtains from my bed. Rage boiled beneath my skin like lava from the volcanoes I'd read existed in the Southern Reaches. My father saw me as a mere child, a pawn to be moved at will. Even should the prince be kind, I would have to spend the rest of my life looking over my shoulder. Sassal wanted Prathia, and they would have it through me. My father had crippled us with debt: if I married the son of our enemy, it would be the death of our kingdom.

I turned to my shelves. They were crammed with books and notes from hours of study and preparation. Preparation, I realized, for a role into which I would never step. I felt suddenly foolish for believing that the throne might ever be mine.

Was that why he'd married Velda? To produce a new heir, one that would take my place once I'd been sold off? Had they been planning this together, all along?

I imagined my stepmother's eyes, the careful façade she always wore. She had treated me kindly these years, but what did I really know of her? Nothing.

I wanted to scream, to throw the books to the floor. But I didn't. I remembered instead my lessons with Albree, her neat little vials lined up in the sunny courtyard where we discussed poisons.

"There are poisons for everything," she'd said, swirling a deep purple liquid in a vial. "This is *Atropa belladonna*. Slip this into someone's tea, and they will experience muscle paralysis. A little more will stop the heart completely. While this one," she continued, picking up a second vial, "will cause complete paralysis and stop the breathing. However, a small dose will merely make the individual *appear* to be dead. Dosage is essential."

I went to my bookshelf and began pulling out my notes. The Sassalian prince wouldn't want to marry a corpse, after all.

"Most women wait until after the wedding to kill their husbands."

I whirled to my door. Velda stood there, tall and unyielding. I felt rage rise in me.

"If he's sent you to talk sense into me, you can go."

"No, he didn't send me," Velda said, easing into the room and closing the door. "Eloisa heard that Sassalian representatives arrived yesterday." She nodded at the books in my hands. "Are you planning on murdering the prince?"

"What if I am?" I said recklessly.

Velda sat in a chair beside my hearth. "You wouldn't be the first unhappy wife to do so, you know. Your grief is not unique."

"It is my life," I spat. "I'm not letting him sell it to the highest bidder."

"Your life—"

"Is not my own," I finished bitterly. It was well-trod territory, an oft-repeated adage whenever I bridled against my position. "But it is no one else's either. Not the prince's, not my father's, and not yours."

Velda stared at me. "What makes you think I would want it?"

"Because you married him!" I screamed. "Because you married the man who would sell me away. Why? So you could take my place? So you could rule without a rival to your power?"

Velda looked taken aback. "Is that what you think of me? That I am some power-hungry monster, here to steal your seat from under you?"

"What other reason could you possibly have?" I was crying, I realized. Hot, angry tears that coursed down my face.

"Blanche," Velda stood, setting cool hands on either side of my face. I swatted her away, turning towards my window. Below, the gardens stretched away to the high wall that encircled the palace. I stared at the rolling hills beyond, the green that disappeared into the forests, blending into the sky.

"Blanche, when I was very young, I was not a princess like you." Velda's voice was soft behind me. "I was a maid in the kitchens of this very palace."

Her words went through me like a shock. I couldn't imagine it: her cold, austere beauty in a servant's frock.

"Your father became my friend when he was a prince here. I fell in love with him. He was charming and kind. But he was a prince, and I was nothing.

"When I was fourteen, I went to live with a wise woman. My mother had seen that I would have a gift, you see. One greater than her own small magics. I went away, and I learned how to see things far off. The past, the present. Sometimes, I could even see the future. I sold my

Three Drops in the Snow   J.C. Pillard

talents and rose in society. I became a noblewoman in my own right. When your father came to me five years ago, it was for you. He thought you needed a mother. I said yes because I loved him. I still do."

I heard her sit, and I turned to face her. She smiled faintly from my bed. "I came here because I love him. But I have come to love you dearly. I would not have you sent away any more than you would."

"Then talk to him," I begged, falling to my knees before her. "Tell him what a fool he's being."

"I've already tried," she said. "But there is no other way. Sassal is going to call in our debts unless we agree to unite the kingdoms. Prathia has been borrowing from them for too long, and if they withdrew their support..." She trailed off, her mouth a grim line. "You cannot imagine the harm it would do. You're the only leverage we have."

I glanced towards my notes, the poisons Albree had so clearly outlined for me. "What...what if there was another way?" I asked slowly.

My stepmother pursed her lips. "What did you have in mind?"

#

The night before my wedding arrived. After my outburst in his office, my father didn't trust me not to do something foolish. He moved me from my rooms to the East Tower, which boasted a single door. I was a prisoner, but no word of complaint crossed my lips. I didn't want him suspecting my plan.

It was late when the knock came. I cautiously opened my door to find Velda upon the threshold, wearing a long black cloak. The guards behind her were slumped at their posts, asleep.

"May I come in?"

I opened the door wider, and she crossed inside. She took the seat beside my bed, lifting the cloak from her hair. I returned to my bed, twisting the nightgown in my hands.

Velda examined me, her face serious. "Are you sure you wish to go through with this?"

"Yes," I said. I had never been more certain of anything.

She did me the courtesy of not objecting, and simply nodded. From the sleeve of her robe she withdrew an apple. Its skin was so red that it almost looked like a plum.

"This contains a small dosage of the poison you suggested. It will make you appear dead to all who behold you. In three days' time, you will awaken, and your life will be your own."

I reached for it, but she drew back. "Don't be hasty. I have not finished. When you begin to wake, it may take some time for your senses to fully return." She grimaced. "It can be unsettling."

"I understand," I replied. "I am ready."

Velda nodded once and handed me the apple. I held it between my palms. There would be no return from this.

I brought the apple to my lips and bit into it. The flesh inside was white, whiter than any apple had a right to be, white as the snow. The taste was fresh and cold.

The world around me dimmed, and the apple slipped from my grasp.

#

I remember nothing after that bite. I learned later that the kingdom was thrown into disarray when I was found dead the morning of my wedding, and even greater disarray when the poison that had apparently taken my life was found in Chancellor Soeren's chambers, courtesy of the Seven. My father was overcome with grief, but my clever stepmother used it to our advantage. Sassal agreed to forgive much of Prathia's debt in exchange for averting all-out war. Their coffers were fuller than ours, but when it appeared they were looking to murder royal families, our other neighboring countries rallied to our aid. Sassal's small army was no threat after that.

My body was moved to a special mausoleum which Velda had prepared for me. A glass coffin, lined in silk, had been fashioned for my body, though I didn't get to appreciate it while I slumbered there.

The world came back to me slowly and dimly. First, I became aware that I had a body. Then, I began to hear again: the sound of blood rushing in my ears, my own breathing. And then, gradually, I regained my ability to see.

Velda was there when I finished coming back to myself, a small smile on the edges of her lips. Behind her, the Seven were dressed in traveling clothes.

"Welcome," Velda said, offering me a hand. Slowly, I sat up. My head ached—an after-effect of the poison. Albree came forward, handing me a bundle of clothes, and I realized that I was in my death shroud. I brushed it from my shoulders.

"I've instructed the Seven to take you far from here. My sister, Orella, lives in Arilon. She will help you find your way in the world." She leaned forward, kissing my forehead. "I will miss you."

Gratitude filled me, so overwhelming that I couldn't stop the tears that came to my eyes. Swiping at them, I threw my arms around her. I had never thought to hear words so sweet from anyone. I could feel the shackles I'd worn all my life falling away. I would leave them behind in my coffin.

"Thank you," I whispered. "Thank you, Mother."

J.C. Pillard lives at the foot of the Colorado mountains. She has a master's degree in English literature and her recent publications include stories in *Broadswords and Blasters* and *In the Wake of the Kraken*. When not writing, J.C. can be found prowling through her local bookstore. Find her at www.jcpillard.com and on Twitter @JCPillard.

Flight of the Fae

by Linda M. Crate

Isegal was fine with being labeled the villain. She knew that Leflar was going to play the victim no matter what. She knew that since he was the king, since he was so charismatic and charming, and because she was already seen as weird and an outcast for being one of the only female knights that he had...that few people were going to believe her side of the story even though it was the truth.

Sometimes it was exhausting to be a woman, but this was nothing new.

People always tried to suppress the power and magic of women since the beginning of the ages or so she had been told. The fae liked to pretend that they were better than the humans in this regard, but they were not. Nor were the elves. In fact, the only ones she had ever met that treated their women with equality were the dwarves and surprisingly the orcs; both of these peoples considered barbaric by her fae counterparts.

Clearly, however, they knew how to treat the women of their kingdoms. Something the fae could certainly stand to learn.

Brushing coifs of long black hair from her dark face, her honey brown eyes glanced over her shoulder.

She wondered when they would begin looking for her. She knew by now that Leflar would have told his wife that she seduced him and not that he had cornered Isegal and demanded that she give him what he wanted or else he would kill her little sister. He ended up killing her sister before her very eyes anyway. Clenching her fists, she bit down hard on her lip to prevent herself from keening. Now wasn't the time nor the place. There would be time to mourn her sister later.

The scene danced vividly in her mind, though, as if it had just happened in this moment and not two days before. Her sister, her beautiful sister, with her lovely green wings was wearing a matching green dress that day. She had laughed seeing Isegal, asking her why couldn't she be more feminine sometimes. She didn't see her impending doom. Before Isegal could open her mouth, her sister Essie was taken from her in one fell swoop.

The king was smirking, brushing a loc from his dark black eyes, he stepped before her. "You are nothing, no one will ever believe you. You will regret the day you were born unless you give yourself to me always. You have nothing now. Your parents are dead, your brothers have died in war, and you no longer have a sister. You are mine. I am your god."

"You are delusional," Isegal had snapped, snatching one of the braiding beads from his hair she used the golden hair accessory to slash at his face like a dagger, impressed to see that he actually bled. "Gods don't bleed," she retorted, before she leapt from the window of the room; using her shifting abilities to turn into a raven. Not every faerie could shapeshift, but it was a talent that she had always possessed.

She flew and flew and flew until her wings had grown tired in raven form and then she switched to a swan to see if that were any easier, but the wings still ached and throbbed. So she eventually resumed her natural form, and had flown until she had reached a different faerie kingdom.

Isegal had only been here for a few hours. She didn't know how she was going to manage it, but she knew that she would have to start over. Begin again somehow.

First, she would have to disguise herself because she knew that Leflar would likely try to drag her back to the kingdom. Isegal knew he would never anticipate her to wear something overtly feminine and so she went to see what dresses the merchants were selling.

Isegal had always been fierce and powerful and whilst her dresses had always been more simple she thought that women should be able to both be strong and feminine even if they weren't all too excited about frills and corsets.

She remembered Essie had once told her that she looked good in pinks and purples.

"Hello there, traveler, what have ye come for?" one of the merchants asked. She was a lovely and tall black woman with her hair held back in bantu knots.

"Something very feminine, I guess I'm trying to deviate from this as much as I can," she said, gesturing to her armored dress. "It's time for a change in pace."

"Ah, so you're a woman with a past. I can respect that," the woman chuckled. "What's your name?"

"Essie," Isegal answered without thinking it through. She felt bad for lying, but she also knew that her real name would get her caught more quickly by Leflar.

"A beautiful name for a beautiful woman. Do you know what colors you're looking for?"

"My sister always told me that I looked good in purples and pinks," Isegal said.

The woman nodded. "Come, we have many different pieces like that to choose from."

Isegal followed the tall woman into her merchant tent, and almost immediately her eyes caught a beautiful and elaborate purple gown unlike anything she had ever wore before. It reminded her of Essie. It had poofy sheer purple sleeves, it had a corset that didn't actually look as if it would be the most physically painful thing in the world adorned with tiny moons and stars; but it was the bottom of the dress that had caught her eye. It was layered fabrics in hues of purples and pinks she had never even imagined could exist that had large crescent moons, stars, and flowers of many different varieties on it. "How much for this one?"

"Ah, you have good taste. That just came today." She looked at Isegal before nodding. "Ten gold pieces."

"Ten?" scoffed a blonde haired woman with green eyes. "You told me a thousand gold pieces."

"For you, that's what I'd charge. You can feel free to leave if you'd like," the woman snapped, folding her arms.

"But you're the best merchant in of all Everdalia."

"So I suppose you'll just have to deal with my attitude then. So what say you, would you like the dress or not?"

"I would," Isegal nodded, procuring ten golden pieces from her bag. "Why would you charge her so much?"

"She's a snot that thinks that she's above everyone else just because she has a rich daddy. You know the type. I would rather see anyone but her in this dress," the woman admitted.

"Can I change into it here?"

"You're in a lot of trouble aren't you?"

Isegal hesitated before nodding.

"Very well, I don't usually allow it, but..." She threw up her arms before instructing Isegal to follow her with a hand gesture. She led Isegal to a room. "Be quick, won't you?"

Isegal nodded. She stood before an ornate mirror with many charms and jewels glittering on the outside edge. She pulled off her armor as silently as she could manage before she pulled on this purple dress. It fit like a glove upon her form and even pulled hints of purple and gold from her wings, making her smile. She knew that Essie would be proud.

She sighed, as she looked at herself in the mirror, though. She would need shoes and not the armored boots she was wearing. Dressed she left the room as quickly as possible, keeping her dagger holster attached she had removed her boots, and now searched the woman's vast array of items before settling on a pair of leather flats that the woman only charged her five coins for.

She was aware that the blonde was absolutely fuming at her, by this point, but Isegal wasn't concerned. She could defend herself if need be, but she hoped that it wouldn't come to that.

Fortunately, she noticed that the white woman quickly paid for her items before leaving.

Isegal also decided that it would be safer to adorn her face with some make-up so she bought some of that. The merchant led her to a room where she could ready herself different from the one she had just changed in.

As she secured her purchases in the bag she had just bought of silk linen, the woman stopped her.

"What about your armor?"

"You can sell it if you'd like, I have no use for it anymore."

The woman nodded.

Isegal smiled her thanks, and then left the merchant's tent. She managed to slip into the crowd and searched for someone selling food. She found massive gyros with cucumber sauce and lettuce at one merchant's tent. Her stomach growled, and though it was pricey, as she bit into the gyro, she knew that it was worth it. Her mouth watered in anticipation of the next bite, much to her embarrassment. For it was, at this moment, she noticed a man was staring her down.

"Can I help you with something?" she asked, giving him a dark look.

"I don't mean you any harm, it's just that you're so lovely...you seem familiar. Do I know you?"

"No," Isegal answered.

"I'd like to know you."

"No, thank you," Isegal growled.

"Come on, why not?"

"Well, for one, I prefer women," Isegal retorted. "For two, I don't owe you my time or my consideration just because you find me attractive."

"Oi, leave her alone, Rufus," came a familiar voice. It was the woman from the merchant's tent in which she had bought the dress.

"Come on, Izzy, I didn't mean any harm."

"She clearly doesn't feel comfortable around you. Let the woman eat in peace," Izzy insisted, folding her arms. "So you can leave now unless you want to be banned again, this time permanently."

The man grumbled beneath his breath before stomping off.

"Sorry that he noticed you," Izzy sighed. "He seems to creep out all the young women," she muttered. "He doesn't seem to realize no one is going to be attracted to some weirdo that makes them uncomfortable. He was good for a minute, but you are very beautiful. I suppose he just couldn't help himself this time," Izzy grumbled, sounding disgusted.

"What did he do the first time he was banned?"

"Tried to touch the king's daughter. Of course, the princess was in disguise so no one knew it was her. Because of that, the king spared his life, but he was banned from this premises for six months. Honestly, I think it should've been permeant," Izzy answered.

Isegal nodded.

"So do you have anywhere to stay?"

Isegal shook her head, frowning.

"I thought you might say that. You can stay with me, as long as you earn your keep," Izzy responded. "I have a business to run, after all. I gave you quite a discount on everything you bought from me, after all."

"Why did you do that?" Isegal asked.

"A lapse of judgment, I guess. You remind me of my little sister. Unfortunately, she was a knight for our king and lost her life in war or so they say. I don't think that's the real story as her body was never found, but I have given up hope thinking she's alive...it's been over twenty years."

"I'm so sorry," Isegal frowned.

"Don't be, had nothing to do with you," Izzy shrugged.

"I know, but that's still sad," Isegal remarked.

Izzy nodded. "It is sad, but what can you do? I wasn't there when it happened, and I wouldn't even begin to know to look for her if she were alive. I just hope that if she is alive, she is happy and well wherever she is."

Isegal nodded.

"So what happened to your sister?"

"What do you mean?" Isegal asked.

"I knew something happened to her by the way you spoke about her. I guess it was just a sixth sense," she laughed.

"She was killed right in front of me, after I did something that was supposed to spare her life from being lost," Isegal gulped. "It only happened a couple of nights ago but...I feel like it happened yesterday."

"I knew Leflar was a liar," the woman responded, tutting. "He always makes everyone out to be the villain, but he forgets that our people know how vile and repulsive he could be. He forcibly stole one of his wives from our kingdom. We have never forgiven him. Don't worry, your secret is safe with me. But that means that your name isn't Essie, doesn't it?"

Isegal sighed, nodding. "That was my sister's name, but I don't feel safe uttering my own name."

"Very well," Izzy nodded. "Come, Essie, if we're lucky we might sell more before night falls."

Isegal nodded, not knowing just how difficult this job would prove to be. Isegal had worked hard as a knight defending her own kingdom, but this was a different type of hard work. Dealing with people wasn't the easiest thing in the planet yet Izzy seemed to have a silver tongue that could soothe any serpent. "I don't know how you do it, Izzy!"

Izzy laughed. "Just takes some practice, I guess."

Isegal's feet were aching by the end of the night, but Izzy was generous and let her take a seat, and as she looked out of the tent she noticed the carnelian and amethyst of the sunset sparkling. Just how many hours had she been working? She couldn't even quite remember when she had arrived. So much had happened since that moment. She was grateful that Izzy had taken her under her wing, so to speak.

Isegal glanced over at Izzy as she began slowly rearranging the tent. "Come on, let's close shop for the night. We'll have more sales to attend to in the morrow."

Isegal nodded and helped Izzy rearrange the tent so that it was closed to the outside elements and the public. She followed after Izzy, and found comfort when Izzy gave her a private place to sleep.

"Also here are some night clothes that once belonged to my sister. You don't need to sleep in a fancy dress and shoes. Unless, of course, you wish to."

Isegal shook her head.

"I thought not," Izzy grinned. "Good night, I'll see you in the morning."

"Good night," Isegal responded.

When Isegal laid down, she found that she couldn't fall asleep right away. Her thoughts were racing. She thought of Leflar finding her, of Izzy getting hurt, or that weird old man coming after her when she tried

Flight of the Fae Linda M. Crate

to sleep. She thought of Essie's laughing face when they were children or the way her sister used to smell always of lilacs. She felt a tear slip from her eyes before she could stop it, and she just let it slide silently down her cheek.

Then, all at once, her lids felt heavy and the world fell away with all of its troubles.

Isegal woke up to find a freshly washed robe that resembled Izzy's laying on the ground. She slipped on the robes, finding that Izzy had placed a more practical pair of shoes her size right by the leather flats she had purchased the night previous. She placed her feet in the shoes and admired how smooth and nice they felt.

"Good, you're awake," Izzy said, popping her head in. "You got ready pretty quickly," she remarked. "It takes me a while to wake up," Izzy laughed. "You're a lot like my sister in more way than one. Come on, we've got to open up shop."

Isegal nodded wordlessly, following after Izzy with a yawn.

"Oh, don't start that. That's contagious," Izzy muttered, shaking her head. "After this, I've got some breakfast for us before the shop opens up completely."

Suddenly a breeze swept past and Isegal smelled bacon. "Is that bacon?"

"It is. Bacon, sausage, eggs, and some freshly baked warm rolls."

"That all sounds delicious," Isegal responded.

The two women finished setting up for the day before walking back to where the food was. Izzy snorted at the speed of which Isegal was eating her food.

"Are you sure you're even tasting that?"

"Sorry, I guess I'm a bit hungry."

"Here's some water before your throat goes dry," Izzy chuckled, handing Isegal a silver goblet.

Isegal held the silver goblet to her face for a moment before drinking any.

Izzy nodded. "It is a hot day already. Can only imagine how warm this day will be. At least the tent will protect us from most of the heat," she remarked.

"Thank you for all of your help, Izzy. I don't know why you took it upon yourself to help a stranger, but I am grateful that you did," Isegal said.

"Don't get all emotional on me," Izzy snorted. "It wasn't entirely altruistic. After all, it's easier to open the shop with two people rather than one."

Isegal nodded. "I surmise it would be."

Izzy's face was devoid of emotion as suddenly someone broke into the room. "I beg your pardon, but these are private quarters."

"We were told there was a fugitive here."

"Well, that's news to me," Izzy remarked. "Just me and my worker here."

"Are you sure there's no one else?" one of the guards snapped.

"I'll have you know that we hate your country even still," Izzy spat in return. She folded her arms, rising to her full height. "There's no one else here."

"Do you know where the person came from whose armor you sold?"

"No idea," Izzy shrugged.

"You don't keep tabs on things of that nature?" the guard snapped.

"Why would I? Money is money no matter where it comes from," Izzy shrugged. "So why don't you tell your king that he's going to have to look a little harder than bothering a merchant if he wants to find whomever he is searching for."

The guards all looked angry and disgusted, but they all left. None of them seemed to recognize Isegal much to Isegal's amazement.

"Do you really have a silver tongue? I know some faeries have that ability."

"I do, and I can cast illusions with it. They only see what I want them to see," Izzy smirked. "They could look you dead in the eye and not recognize you, and tomorrow we'll be on a ship taking us somewhere else so they won't find you unless you want them to."

"Certainly not," Isegal scoffed.

"I rather thought not," Izzy winked.

"I'm still keeping my dagger, though," Isegal shrugged.

"I would expect and accept nothing less of one of Leflar's knights. So when are you going to tell me your name?" Izzy asked.

"It is Isegal."

Izzy nodded. "Unusual. My sister said if she had a daughter that's what she would name her."

"Izekeniah?"

Izzy looked at Isegal in both terror and surprise. "No... you...you're Delilah's daughter?"

Isegal nodded.

Tears spilled from Izzy's eyes. "She was so close this entire time. Tell me, how is she? How is my sister?"

"She's gone. I'm sorry," Isegal remarked.

Izzy nodded slowly. "It's okay. I found you, and that's enough," she responded, a smile spreading across her face. "I'm so happy that you happened upon me. Merlin only knows what could've happened if anyone else found you."

Isegal hadn't known she had any family that was still alive, but she was so thankful that she had found the aunt she had never known she had.

"My mother said her sister was reckless as the day was long."

Izzy nodded. "That's a valid criticism, but it's just my truth. She was always too boring, never had enough sense of adventure," Izzy tutted.

Isegal laughed. "I told her always that she needed to get more of a sense of adventure. She didn't like that I became a knight, she didn't think a woman should be that bold. But I always thought that women shouldn't owe the world beauty as our rent. We can be both strong and effeminate. Nothing about a woman says we have to be weak. We have magic and power all our own, and I'm finally okay with being the villain in someone's story because people only see what they want to see. My truth is true, and I know what I lived. I don't need anyone to tell me who I am because I define myself," Isegal stated.

Izzy smiled. "A woman after my own heart, perhaps that's why we get along so well. I am so glad that I found you and that you found me."

Isegal smiled. "Me, too. I never knew when I would start anew that I would find you, but I'm glad that I am not all alone in this world."

Izzy nodded. "Well, come on, niece, we've got a long day of sales ahead of us."

Isegal turned as Leflar stormed into the tent.

"Is there no such thing as privacy any longer? No one's supposed to be here except for me and my coworker," Izzy snapped, eyes flashing.

"Where is she?" Leflar demanded.

"I'm afraid I don't know whom you speak of," Izzy answered.

"The woman who sold you her armor!" Leflar roared.

"I'm afraid we didn't ask her who she was or where she was going," Isegal snorted.

"Purple eyed tart, no one was asking you!"

Purple eyes? Well, Izzy's illusion was working wonderfully then because Isegal knew her eyes weren't purple.

"Well, you did ask and she did answer. Even if your question was directed at me. You can leave, however, unless you want me to inform the king you're here. I'm sure he'll take kindly to that."

Leflar let out a long string of profanity, turning away. It was then that he decided to turn around and he shoved a sword straight through

Izzy's heart. As she fell to the ground, the illusion she had cast upon Isegal had fallen away. "I knew it! You're coming with me."

Isegal ran from the tent. "Leflar has stabbed Izzy!" she shouted, hoping that this was enough to garner attention.

Suddenly a mob of people surrounded Leflar, and in the chaos she took to flight as a raven once more. She hoped that Izzy would be okay and get the help she needed. If fate were kind then she knew she'd see her aunt again.

Linda M. Crate's (she/her) works have been published in numerous magazines and anthologies both online and in print. She is the author of eight poetry chapbooks, the latest of which is: *follow the black raven* (Alien Buddha Press, July 2021).

The Each-Uisge

by Matthew McKiernan

The carriage collapsed, jolting Achaius awake. He bounced in the carriage and hollered. "What's going on, Mr. Woodsworth? Did we hit a rock?"

For a few moments there was no response, then the sound of Mr. Woodsworth's cockney accent filled the carriage. "Just stay inside, Lord Sutherland. I…I…need a moment to figure things out."

Achaius thought for a moment that his father was in the carriage with him. Then he remembered that he was now Lord Sutherland. The year was 1837 and Achaius's father had died from the pox two weeks ago. It gave Achaius comfort to know that his father had lived long enough to see Victoria become queen. Afterwards, Achaius's mother sent him from Edinburgh to the Scottish Highlands to spend the summer with some distant relatives. She said it would be good for his health. Although Achaius was only twelve, he was smart enough to know that there were already suitors courting his mother, and it would be much easier for her to find a new husband without a hemophiliac son around.

Hemophilia, that one dreaded word had dominated Achaius's entire life. It was why he had spent his life in his room and had no color in his face. It was why the interior of the carriage was full of red silk cushions stuffed with cotton. It was why his servants were his only friends. Achaius heard Mr. Woodsworth bumbling around, swearing under his breath. He played with the curls on his auburn hair and soon grew bored. Achaius slapped his hands against the seat and stood up. "Mr. Woodsworth, I am going to come out and help."

"Wait Lord…"

Achaius opened the carriage door, stepped outside, and saw that the horses were dead. There were no wounds on their bodies or foam coming out of their mouths. They were just lying on the ground lifeless with their eyes staring at nothing, just as he remembered his fathers had been. Achaius stood in solemn silence. Mr. Woodsworth shook his head, got down from the driver's seat, and patted Achaius shoulders. "That's why I told you to stay inside."

Achaius wiped his tears away with his right sleeve. "What happened to them?"

"They just fell down and died. Poor buggers, I guess it was something they ate or maybe they were poisoned."

"Poisoned!"

Achaius jumped like he had a cricket in his trousers. Mr. Woodsworth nodded. "Yes, poisoned. You know there are people who stand to gain quite a lot if you don't come home."

Even though it was a warm and cloudless summer day, a cold shiver ran down Achaius's spine. "I don't wish to speak of these matters right now. I just want to know what we're going to do next."

"Well, look at where we are."

Achaius tore his gaze away from the carriage and saw they were on a dirt road in the middle of nowhere. There were lush green hills and gray rocky mountains that seemed to go on forever. The mountains were so tall that they appeared to touch the sky. There were small streams scattered here and there. Red squirrels were frolicking about as though they were in the Garden of Eden. This was the Scotland that for him, had only existed in his father's stories. Now he was seeing it for real, but Achaius just wished it were under far better circumstances. "This is a splendid place Mr. Woodsworth, but it's not good that we're stuck here, although I am sure if we wait someone will come down the road."

Mr. Woodsworth sighed. "Let me look around."

Mr. Woodsworth walked ahead of the carriage but made sure to stay in Achaius's line of vision. He was a big stocky man who had combed-over slick ebony colored hair to hide his bald spots. Achaius knew that Mr. Woodsworth was always trying to make himself look younger. After all, he had been telling everyone he was thirty-eight for the past eight years. Before coming into his father's service, Mr. Woodsworth had been in the Royal Navy. While there he picked up a wide variety of skills that had made him the ideal manservant. He worked as a cook, valet, tailor, butler, and bodyguard. There was nothing Achaius hadn't seen him do.

Mr. Woodsworth's time in the Navy had given him a deep scar that went from the top of his forehead down all the way to his right cheek. Achaius had met Mr. Woodsworth when he was a toddler and had asked

The Each-Uisge   Matthew McKiernan

him if he was pirate. Mr. Woodsworth just smiled and said that he wasn't a pirate, but he had hunted them down. Achaius knew there was no way he would ever be able to live a life like his. Mr. Woodsworth wore a brown shirt and pants along with a red vest with iron buttons. Achaius wore dark yellow pants with a matching shirt along with a white vest with ivory buttons. They both were wearing sturdy black boots.

Mr. Woodsworth wore a brass buckled belt. Tucked within it was a pistol and a naked dagger. Although the Highlands were no longer the lawless lands of days long gone, there were still ruffians about, and red deer were known to be aggressive during rutting season.

The young lord saw Mr. Woodsworth walking back to the carriage shaking his head. "I don't see anything for miles around except more road. Given your condition, Lord Sutherland, I think it's best you remain here while I go find help."

Achaius had never been alone before. Nannies, nurses, butlers, maids, and private tutors had always been just a command away. The idea of passing the night inside the carriage, even in a land as lovely as this, was inconceivable. Achaius just couldn't do it, even though he knew it was the safer choice. He yammered, "Please let me come with you Mr. Woodsworth. I know that there are days when I am weak, but today I am strong. I won't be a hindrance!"

"Lord Sutherland, I ..."

"I can't go through a night alone. I swear to God that the terror of it will kill me!"

Mr. Woodsworth looked at Achaius then gazed at the hills and carriage. "This won't be like strolling around your castle, Lord Sutherland. If you get hurt here, there will be no team of nurses and doctors to heal you. I have some skill in field medicine, but if you get injured there isn't much I can do. If you prick your finger on a thorn, or skin your knee on some grass, which are things most boys your age wouldn't even notice, you could bleed to death in my arms."

Achaius smiled. "Well, that's a risk I've taken since I left my mother's womb. I won't be a burden to you sir. I'll go get one of the trunks."

With a look of utter glee on his face, Achaius went to the back of the carriage where all the luggage was stored. He started tugging on one of the large trunks and Mr. Woodsworth stopped him. "I'll take that trunk and the other large one."

"I want to carry something."

Mr. Woodsworth sighed, "There are six trunks here and I know you can't safely carry any of them. I'm taking the two most important ones.

If you want to make yourself useful pick out a good camping spot when it's sunset because I highly doubt, we'll find a place to stay tonight."

Achaius nodded and let Mr. Woodsworth retrieve the two trunks. They walked down the road and Achaius strolled with a spring in his step. He realized that this was the only adventure he'd ever have in his entire life and wanted to make the most of it. Achaius waved an imaginary sword through the air and cut down many pretend foes. The sun shone high in the sky as the man and boy marched on. An idea crept into Achaius mind and he stopped goofing around as he put his hands in his pockets. "Hey, Mr. Woodsworth, would it be acceptable if we called each other by our first names like we used to, since no one else is around?"

Mr. Woodsworth tightened his grip on the trunks and grinned. "I won't tell if you won't, Achaius."

Achaius skipped around in glee. "Thank you, Wilson."

The two of them walked on until Achaius spotted something on a distant hill. It was just a black speck at first. Then as it got closer, it appeared to have the form of a man rushing down the hill like an avalanche. Achaius blinked several times to make sure his eyes weren't deceiving him on how fast that man was moving. Achaius pointed at the hills. "Wilson, something is headed right towards us."

Wilson's eyes landed on the running man. He dropped the wooden trunks to the ground. "Good God, he's a fast fellow. Achaius, get behind me."

Achaius obeyed and the man descended towards them as though he was running on lightning. The man reached them and stood just six feet away. The stranger wore a robe made of black stitched leather that pooled around his feet, completely concealing them. He carried a tree branch walking staff in his right hand. His face was one that could either be young or old. He had rowdy eyes and a scruffy beard, although it was his hair that shocked Achaius the most. The wild man's long brown hair had pieces of seaweed embedded in it. Indeed, the stranger smelled of the sea and Achaius assumed he must have just gone swimming in a nearby loch.

However, that didn't explain how he had gotten his hair filled with seaweed or why he hadn't tried to brush it out. Although, Achaius had the feeling that this salty stranger had never touched a comb in his life. The stranger spoke, and to Achaius it sounded like every word he said was a whimper. "I don't often see people like you in the Highlands."

Wilson made sure the man saw the hilts of his dagger and pistol as he responded. "We're just passing through. Forgive me, but I will not

The Each-Uisge — Matthew McKiernan

say more or let the boy speak to you until you tell us more about yourself, starting with your name."

The man giggled like a drunk horse. "I'll keep my story to myself and you can do the same. It's irrelevant in the grand scheme of things, but I can figure that you're lost, aren't you?"

"We're not where we want to be." Wilson stated.

The stranger tapped his staff against the ground then pointed it at the road. "Wandering down that on foot is not a wise decision. It will take you at least two days to find a spot with human habitation. But if you follow me, I can lead you to a nice little village where you can get horses."

The man's eyes seemed to be rolling around in his skull like marbles. Wilson looked the man over and then briefly looked at the road. "Where's this short cut?"

The wild man pointed east with his staff, towards a hill that led to a thick green forest. "Through those woods. If we start now, we can make it by midday."

Wilson tugged at his chin. "We'll travel with you if you agree to some terms."

"What are they?"

Wilson tossed the wild man one of the trunks. "You're going to carry that. Also, you're going to walk ahead of us, but stay where I can see you, even if you must relieve yourself. If you have a gang of hooligans in hiding, know that I'm a great shot and can have you dead before you are halfway through calling out to them."

The stranger picked up the trunk with his left hand. "I'm no thief. I have no comrades in hiding. I wander alone. I always have and I always will."

Achaius and Wilson followed the stranger who was humming to himself. Achaius had never heard someone hum like that before. It just didn't sound normal. He stuck close to Wilson and whispered to him, "Are you sure it's a wise idea to trust this stranger?"

"I think it's best we should return to civilization as soon as possible. Besides, I don't see this stranger as a threat. He's an odd fellow to be sure, but as your father always said, the Highland people have their own ways."

Achaius nodded. "I suppose so. It's just that this man…there's something really off about him."

After slowly descending the hill, they arrived at the entrance to the woods. Bright green moss covered the forest floor and every single tree. To Achaius it looked like the perfect place to settle down for a nap. He remembered napping a lot when he was small. His father used to tell him fairy and folk tales before he went to sleep, and Achaius felt as though he was at the start of one. The stranger led them through the forest. Even though there was no trail, he seemed to know where he was going. Achaius kept his eyes peeled for low hanging branches and also made sure to be on the lookout for sharp rocks and thorny bushes. He noticed that not a single leaf or twig graced the forest floor.

The stranger's cloak got caught on some gigantic roots. He sighed and tugged at his cloak setting it free. For a single second Achaius saw the wild man's feet. They were hooves. Achaius froze in place. He rubbed his eyes and blinked several times. Achaius told himself he must have imagined that. Then he looked at Wilson, whose face was paler than when he had told Achaius of his father's passing. Achaius uttered, "You saw it too, didn't you? He has hoofs."

"The stress of the day is making us see things."

"How can two people imagine the same thing? From what I've read, hallucinations don't work that way."

Wilson put his trunk down and called out, "Get behind me. Stranger, stop and turn around!"

The wild man turned around and placed his trunk on the forest floor. He leaned on his walking stick with his arms crossed. "You two look like you've seen the Devil himself, although I assure you, he isn't around these parts."

Wilson pulled out his firearm. "Show us your feet!"

The stranger raised his bushy eyebrows. "I beg your pardon?"

Wilson wildly waved his pistol. "Your feet man. Show us your bloody feet! Or I'll put you down!"

The stranger rubbed the back of his head while muttering, "The feet! It's always the feet. Why can't I ever get them right."

Wilson aimed his gun at the man's head. "What are you babbling about?"

The seaweed haired man sighed and grasped his staff. "I can't have my meal here. I was going to escort you to the loch, but I guess I'll have to drag you there."

Achaius shivered as he stammered. "The loch…meal…? What are…are…you going to eat?"

The stranger's eyes became as black as an eclipse. His hair became as green as the seaweed inside it. His jaw expanded as he smiled a mouth full of hundreds of sharp pointy teeth. He spread out his arms. "I plan to devour you two fools! Except for your livers, those can go to the worms!"

The Each-Uisge   Matthew McKiernan

Wilson fired his gun and the monster moved so rapidly that the bullet only managed to knock a few strands of his hair off. It lunged at Wilson as he drew his dagger and used it to block the monster's staff. "Run, Achaius, run!" Wilson shouted.

Achaius ran, he didn't even bother to look where he was going. He rushed through the trees bashing branches aside. His feet barely touched the earth beneath him as he sped across the mossy ground. The slow strolls he had taken around his castle hadn't prepared his body for this. Every breath felt like a weight crushing his chest. Achaius tripped over a root and fell on his hands. He couldn't stand. He needed to breathe. After catching his breath, he checked his hands. Luckily, they were undamaged.

Achaius managed to stand again. His legs shook and he leaned against a tree to steady himself. He glanced around and saw no sign that he was being chased as the forest was as silent as a graveyard, although Achaius could hear the blood pumping in his ears. For some reason he was now thinking of his father's stories. They were flashing through his mind like the drawings of a picture book. One of them had something to do with a man with hoofs, but there was more to it Achaius remembered the story had been so terrifying that he had either asked his father to stop or had done his best to forget about it.

If he could remember, he would know what that monster was and have some idea on what to do next. The bushes rustled. Achaius couldn't move. All he could do is put his hand over his racing heart. Wilson burst from the bushes. His clothes had tears all over and he had many bloody slashes on his face and arms. Wilson's pistol was gone, but he still held his dagger in his right hand. It was dripping blood. Wilson grabbed Achaius's shoulder with his free hand. "Are you all right, Achaius? Did you injure yourself at all?"

"I'm...fine, I think. That hoofed man, did you kill him?"

Wilson's hands started shaking. "No, I stabbed him in the chest and then he became something else. Oh God I feel like I'm trapped in a nightmare!"

The fact that Wilson was afraid made Achaius want to cry. "What did he turn into?"

The sound of flapping wings filled the forest. It was so powerful that it blasted the leaves off the trees. Wilson turned as white as a ghost. "It's here, Achaius. We've got to run and no matter what, don't look up!"

Wilson grabbed Achaius's hand and they fled across the woods. The wind was blowing through Achaius's clothes and it almost knocked him down. The speeding air stung his eyes forcing Achaius to close them. He still kept going as he heard a shriek that sounded like the cawing of a thousand crows. The violent wind stopped blowing against his face and despite Wilson's warning, Achaius looked up. A bird was flying above them. It was the size of an elephant. Its feathers were light gray. A huge parrot-like beak graced its face, and its talons were as large as it's body.

Achaius screamed as the behemoth descended upon him and Wilson. It snatched them up. Wilson tossed Achaius his dagger and Achaius caught it on instinct. "Stab it!" Wilson shouted.

Achaius thrust the dagger upwards and drove it into the creature's foot. It cried out in pain and dropped him. Fortunately, he was only about a foot off the ground and landed on his feet while his entire body wobbled as he held onto the dagger with an ironclad grip. The bird fluttered away and Achaius found himself chasing after it. He had no idea what he was going to do, but somehow, some way, he would make the bird let go of Wilson. He had to!

The behemoth avian flew higher and higher until it only became a speck in the sky. Then it released Wilson. Achaius watched him fall. As he got lower, Achaius heard his screams and Wilson disappeared into the thicket of the trees. The bird was gone, and Achaius didn't even give it a second's thought as he rushed to where Wilson had fallen. He found him lying on the mossy forest floor. His body was twisted at an odd angle and his limbs were bent like twigs. His head had smashed against an embedded stone and the right side of his skull had completely shattered.

Blood, brain matter and flakes of bone were everywhere. The dagger slipped from Achaius's palm as he fell on his knees and wept. He dug his hands into the ground and tore out chunks of moss as he wailed. "I should have stayed in the carriage. God, forgive me! This is all my fault. I just didn't want to spend the night alone. I'm so sorry, Wilson. It should be me lying there, not you!"

Achaius cried some more and finally collapsed on the ground. A weariness overcame him, and he just wanted to lie on the soft mossy ground and never get back up. But Wilson had given him his dagger and given his life for him. Achaius owed it to him to find a way out of this forest. If he was going to do that, he was going to have to keep the dagger with him, but he would need something to hold it. Achaius got up and crouched by Wilson's corpse. He grasped the bloody belt. "I know you really liked this belt, but I need it now. Listen, I'm going to get out of here and hopefully find a town nearby. I'll send people to get

The Each-Uisge   Matthew McKiernan

you and make sure you receive a proper Christian burial. This belt will be buried with you, I promise."

Achaius tugged the belt off Wilson's midriff and slid it down his legs. He yanked the belt off, unbuckled it, and put it around his waist. It was a big belt, and it took Achaius awhile to tightened it, but he managed to do it. Achaius stuffed the dagger into the belt and walked away from the body of his servant and best friend. He wished he had a compass to guide his way. Even if it took a while, Achaius knew that all forests ended. He walked on and kept his eyes peeled for the hoofed man or giant bird.

Achaius found himself free from a dense growth of trees. Grass, the blue sky, and the open country surrounded him once more. However, there wasn't any sign of a road. Achaius sighed and strolled on. He drank water from a small brook, and when he was finished, his stomach rumbled. He spotted a raspberry bush filled with the plumpest berries he had ever seen, but the bush was covered in thorns. Achaius's hands trembled over the berry bush. Could he take the risk? He grasped the hilt of the dagger and thought about using it to cut the thorns.

Suddenly, the sound of whinnying filled the air. Achaius turned to see a large dark horse. The horse had a white mane and eyes as black as coal. It had no saddle on its back, or shoes on its hooves. Yet for some reason Achaius wanted to ride it. He had never ridden a horse before or even a pony. Still he found himself walking towards the beast. The horse locked eyes with him and Achaius rubbed the horse's nose. "There, there you're a good…"

Achaius quickly ducked down and checked beneath the horse's legs. "Boy, yeah you're a good boy."

Achaius resumed petting the horse while he looked for its owner. Although the horse seemed wild, he knew there was no way a wild horse would be this friendly. There was no one else around. This horse was his to ride, but did he really want to do something so foolhardy? Even a minor fall could prove fatal. Nonetheless, Achaius had to get on the back of that horse. He slowly climbed onto the horse and luckily, it stayed perfectly still. He wrapped his arms around the horse's thick neck while hooking his legs around it. The horse didn't even flinch. Achaius smiled. "Okay, take me out of here."

The horse galloped. It moved with a speed that made everything around Achaius into one big green blur. He didn't know where he was going. He just knew that the horse had its own destination in mind. Achaius wanted to give the horse a good pat to signal it to slow down, but he could not move his hands or his feet. They stuck to the horse as though they were covered in tar. No matter how hard Achaius tugged, he could not get them free. "Stop, stop, stop!" he begged.

The horse did not respond to his pleas. Then Achaius saw a humongous loch in the distance. A dark gray mountain towered over it. The loch grew closer and closer. Achaius shrieked, because now he remembered his father's story and realized the truth. He had never escaped the horror that had haunted him. The wild man, the giant bird, and this horse were the same creature, The Each-Uisge. A monstrous water spirit that uses those guises to lure unsuspecting humans into the Scottish lochs, where it takes its true form and devours all of them. Except for their livers, whose taste it despises. His liver, that would be all that remained of Achaius when The Each-Uisge was done with him.

Achaius cursed, cried, and screamed. The Each-Uisge twisted its head to gaze at him. Its eyes were leaking black fluid and its teeth had become like those of an eel. It laughed the sickest and most twisted laughter that had ever inflected Achaius's ears. He tried with all his might to pry his hands free. He just needed to get one hand free, it had to be his right one. Achaius tugged and tugged at his right hand. It hurt; his skin was fused to the beast. He didn't let that stop him. Achaius yanked his right arm back with all his strength just as The Each-Uisge jumped into the loch.

Achaius's body slammed against The Each-Uisge so hard, that he got the wind knocked out of him. It took every ounce of his will to remain conscious. The Each-Uisge began to change. Its legs vanished and its skin became rubbery. Its mane turned to fins and its head grew even larger, as did its teeth. With one last painful tug, Achaius managed to free his right hand. He drew his dagger and pried his left hand loose. Achaius didn't bother to try to free his legs. Instead, he stabbed The Each-Uisge in its neck. Its blood filled the loch and blinded Achaius, but he kept stabbing it.

After a dozen stabs, he buried the dagger so deep he couldn't pull it free. Maybe it was the blood loss or the pain, but finally The Each-Uisge relented and let Achaius go. It sank into the depths while Achaius jerked upwards. Although he had never swum before, Wilson had told him how it was done. Achaius franticly kicked his legs and waved his arms. Somehow through all his flailing, he managed to make it back to shore and lie down on the muddy banks. He raised his arms and looked at his shaking hands. The flesh on his palms was torn and he had sliced two of the fingers on his left hand. The blood flooded from the deep gashes and Achaius knew no matter how much pressure he put on them, the bleeding would not stop.

The Each-Uisge — Matthew McKiernan

"No, no, oh God, no please!" he cried.

Achaius got up and pressed his bloody hands against his knees. "I've got to think of something! Come on brain, think, think, think!"

He glanced at a small branch on the shore and picked it up. "Fire! If I find some dry sticks and a piece of flint or something, I can make a fire and cauterize my wounds. I have to be quick."

Achaius scrounged around and managed to find some twigs and dry grass, but he didn't find any flint. The young lord realized that he didn't have time to look for any flame-starting rocks. He would have to just rub the sticks together even though they were already soaked with blood. Achaius would not let that stop him. He furiously stroked them together, praying with everything he had for just one spark. Finally, the pile burst into flames as though God himself had struck it. Achaius looked to the heavens in thanks and slowly put his hands on the fire.

It burned; the pain was much worse than what Achaius had feared. But he kept his hands over the flames, then flipped them over and saw that his palms were burnt like roasted meat, but they no longer bled, and the gashes on his fingers had been burnt closed. Achaius knew it was in his best interest to find a doctor as soon as possible. Just as he was about to leave the loch, he noticed that the dagger had appeared upon the shore. He quickly snatched it up and tucked it back into his belt. He smiled at the sky. "Are you watching me from up there, Wilson? Tell father I say hello and that I am thankful beyond words for every tale he ever told me."

Achaius scurried away from the loch as the warm sun dried his soggy clothes. The Each-Uisge was now at the bottom of the loch and probably wouldn't emerge until the next poor soul wandered into its territory. Achaius now knew that as long as he was extra careful, he would make it back to civilization, that is, if he didn't run into any more creatures from his father's stories. With all the danger he had faced today, Achaius realized that one never knows what they could encounter in the Highlands.

Matthew McKiernan resides in Yardley Pennsylvania. He graduated from LaSalle University in 2013 with a BA in English and History. He received his MFA in Creative writing at Rosemont College in May 2016. His first short story, "A Leap of Faith" was published in "Skive Magazine" in November 2013. He has since published over thirteen short stories in various genres, most of which are available on Amazon.

Dead Next Door

by Jabe Stafford

They're letting the dog out before sunset.
Now I'll get a solid report on the dead.
The screen door clangs shut behind Mother and Daughter. Both are still dressed in their school clothes. I curl atop the couch's headrest and watch out the living room window as Daughter skips down the sidewalk, Pete's leash in her hand. Golden Pete sniffs the grass and tugs her toward intriguing smells along our road.

Squirrel crap. A hydrant. Ten translucent human feet at the edge of the driveway.

I already accounted for the five dead, stuck for now in the dissolving sunlight dripping from the trees across the street. The darker it gets, the more their most distinctive feature returns. Menacing green eyes on one. Dreadlocks on another. Features I ignore except as a countdown.

Mother and Daughter round the corner and I lose them in the afternoon's last sunbeam. One last free heat source to savor. Golden Pete's on the scent now. Purrs rumble up from my chest and I shut my eyes.

Then I sneeze. Dust. Would that that was our only worry.

I uncurl and get up, ignoring the easy chair, the idiot box, and the bookshelves near the windows. No lamps are on yet, and kibble-crunching noises come from the shadows under the carpeted tiers of Feline Tower. Arching my back and stretching, I set to grooming paws, claws, shoulders, and back. Clean orange fur makes it look like the dead don't faze me.

First rule of order. Look like you're prepared for them.

The munching ceases. Paws thump down the Tower's carpet, then along the living room carpet onto the couch. Whump. Thump. Flump.

Shina lands beside me, her light, wispy fur announcing her presence and hiding muscles beneath. "Fall's 'bout to be over."

"And you have never seen a winter."

"What'll we do about the dead then?"

"Go without advance warning."

"You said Mother and Father get sad faster in the dark season. And that was the last kibble I scarfed."

"Those are the dark season's consequences, Shina. They think we get cabin fever, and we know they get seasonal depression. No more yowling. There are five dead at the end of the driveway. That makes the kitchen my initial post."

"I'll take the livin' room. We've got the Tower window and the couch window in here. Plus it gets Daughter gigglin' when I pounce between 'em."

Shina's poison-yellow irises expand. The sunbeam at my back fades.

Dead feet begin to shudder and un-stick themselves from the light at the end of the driveway.

I hiss, "Seems dark season starts tonight. Where is Golden Pete?"

A tail flick from Shina. "He's at th' other street corner."

We whip our heads away from the five dead and see the golden retriever's head straining against his leash. The end is in Mother's hands now. Mother passes Daughter a ring of metal fangs and she skips to the car in the driveway. She notices absolutely nothing about the presence of the dead that she just skipped through.

Translucent bodies rush the house. I leap off the couch, grip the carpet with my claws, and sprint into the kitchen.

Golden Pete scratches at the screen door, barking and whining.

Mother opens the outer door. Her crooning voice drifts over Pete's through the screen door mesh. "Calm down, Pete. There's no one in there but Shelly and Shina."

I ignore the chairs and spring from the kitchen floor to the table. Two of the five dead have already forced their ghostly bodies partway through the kitchen window.

Dashing the salt and pepper shakers aside, I skid to a halt and swat the nearest dead once, twice, three times. It soars across the block and ebbs from sight.

"Shelly, did we let a mosquito in?" Mother has entered the kitchen, smiling in her teacher's clothing.

Ethereal hands claw through the wall, reaching for her throat.

Ignoring Mother, I swat the second dead. The third shoves its hands through the kitchen windows. I beat it back with both paws and catch Mother's dangling hair. Both dead tumble twenty yards away from the house and vanish.

Dead Next Door — Jabe Stafford

"What's got into you?"

The fourth dead launches itself headfirst through the kitchen stove. It seizes Mother with both hands and bites her chest with incorporeal fangs.

I leap for the counter, claws tearing the dead silhouette from her body. The spirit vanishes and Mother yelps. "Stop that. You'll scratch me."

Daughter whips the kitchen door open at the same second. My paws scrabble at the countertop and I tumble to the tiles, twisting to land on four paws.

The fifth dead is not in sight.

"Here's your keys, Mom," says Daughter, closing the kitchen door and trailing in scents of autumn leaves. She carries a new picture frame and blankets, thick and soft with snuggle potential. She passes Mother the ring of metal keys, keeping her eyes on the frame.

A pale silhouette seizes Daughter's arms and plunges its teeth into her. Water wells up in her eyes.

I scrabble at the floor tiles, pouncing and swiping.

Daughter's lip trembles.

Both paws whip through the fifth dead, banishing it moments too late.

Daughter sobs. "She was my best friend, Mom. Why do people shoot people?"

The dead's phantom jaws amplify Mother's and Daughter's anguish with each mouthful of will and happiness they consume. Mother's gaze drops to the floor. A tear falls as she raises her head again. "I miss her too. It's terrible, I know, honey. *Someone* must not care at all if they're letting this kind of thing continue. We're doing what we can at school to make it more safe." She looks at me and winks. "And I bet Shelly's mad she missed that mosquito."

Daughter glances at me and a grin shadows her face.

I drag my tongue over one paw, then rub at my ears. Their verve has returned.

"Cats're always perfect," Daughter says. "I bet she got it. Is Dad still bringing an animal from the zoo tonight?"

Mother smiles wide. "Sure is. He thought that would be perfect to cheer you up a little."

They bustle around between kitchen and living room with blankets and book bags and smartphones. I block out the rest of their chat. I'd failed to protect Mother and Daughter for the first time since Shina joined us in her kittenhood. Their news about the zoo animal sends a frisson of hope along my spine. We could be getting a bigger cat than me to help repel the dead.

A whuff from behind sends me rushing back into the living room. Mother or Daughter had turned the lamps on while I wasted time brooding. My eyes adjust immediately, catching the picture frame Daughter was carrying. It is now atop the corner bookshelf.

Golden Pete pads past the door frame, his low barks drawing Shina down from Feline Tower as well. We cross to the couch and leap first on the cushions, then to the top so we may keep watch out the biggest window.

Dusk has fallen. Leaves atop the trees in the yards shimmer with sun rays, then darken. They are our neighborhood's skeleton giants. Hordes of dead lurk among the trunks. They will charge the house at any moment.

Golden Pete stands on the cushions and pokes his honey-gold head over the headrests between me and Shina to give us an extra set of eyes.

"Are the dead livin' it up out there, Pete?" Shina asks.

Pete pants, drooling on the couch. "More than a hundred. Out there. I barked. From far away. They fled."

"That's because you're a fearsome beast."

"And they're confused. With them other families. Comin' home. Plenty. Of prey. For them. To choose from."

"They'll stop playin' with their food once everything's settled. Thank ya, Pete."

"Mother mentioned a possible ally coming from the zoo," I say.

"Was that why you face-planted a minute ago?"

"Cut the comedy," I hiss. "One got Mother before I could stop it, and another got Daughter. It is hardly past sundown."

Pete hops down from the couch and paces the living room, tags jingling. "Am I. Back to. Snore duty?"

I flick my tail to make sure Shina is paying attention. "It *is* the dark season. The dead get more time unstuck. You can protect an entire room without moving. Thank you."

"No problem. Shelly. If they kick me off. The bed. I'll lay. Where I. Can see the dead."

"Excellent. Bark if any dead make it through and I will end them."

Pete chuffs and Shina rolls onto her back. "Do you watch action movies on the idiot box just for the lines, or do you really think cinema will teach you more 'bout the dead?"

I scowl at Pete and Shina. "If you are referencing my previous statement, I mean only to take the dead seriously. Remember who

Daughter lost. There are many reasons for that, and we will handle our responsibilities so the family can handle theirs."

Pete whines and shrinks to his knees. "I will protect them. Until sunrise."

"Cool," Shina purrs. "What new human reference wordies did you learn, Pete?"

"Teacher's pet," he replies, his panting slowing down. "And keys."

"I heard that one too," I say, watching the headlit cars turn into driveways along the street. People emerge, dragging sundry items into their homes with them. "Is that referring to the metal fangs on a ring I saw earlier?"

"Ring Of Fangs. Yes. Isn't that. Mother's favorite song?"

Shina flails with laughter and plunges to the couch cushions. Mother and Daughter are not in the room, so she lands flat on her back and squirms. "Peeete. It's Ring Of Fire."

"We each have strengths. Scouting and bark technique. Are mine. Music is not."

I shake my head. "Worry not. We all must learn human words on our own unl—"

My fur shoots upward and I tense, crouching for a pounce without knowing why. I place both front paws on the window, the better to devour the outdoors with my eyes. The only visible dead are two houses away at the abandoned house surrounding another dead with curling, ginger hair. They loiter there, not knowing the neighbors won't return. Daughter used to visit them and play with their pet snake, as Pete reported it.

Every hair along my tail bushes out and I hear it. A penetrating shriek. And with it, a pack of the dead pursuing Father's black van into the driveway.

Our ally.

"The zoo animal must be dangerous to them," I hiss. "Look how the dead work to overtake Father."

"Let's go, doggo," Shina shouts.

We spring from the couch with claws drawn, Shina ahead of me and Pete behind. Another leap and we are hustling along the kitchen. Barks shake the tiles beneath our paws. Shina bounds from floor to counter to refrigerator, knocking a cereal box into the sink.

Dead gush inside through doors, walls, and windows.

I jump to the stovetop and swat them as they pour in. One. Two. Threefourfive.

Headlights wash against the garage outside the window in the kitchen door.

Shina rends pair after pair of the dead from her high perch, seeming to climb the space between wall and ceiling with her blows.

The van doors open, slam closed.

Pete eyes us, watching for moments when we need to regain balance. He barks louder and harder during those seconds. Dozens of dead splash backward out of the house with each booming burst.

And are summoned back with each ear-shredding screech that comes closer.

Father opens the kitchen door, his unburdened arm reaching through the swirling dead he cannot see. "Down, Pete. Stop or you're gonna scare Daisy."

He marches in hefting a large birdcage. Squawks slice my hearing like serrated claws and I hunker down, still swinging at the invading dead. Between translucent predators and Father's bulk, I only make out feathered white wings.

Shina tumbles from the fridge to the floor, yowling and landing on four feet.

Pete staggers backward, but barks and barks despite his voice cracking.

"Cut that out, Pete," Father bellows.

I stand firm and swat at the dead twice as quick. "Keep going, Pete."

For every ten dead the dog banishes, the bird's shrieking brings twenty more. Deceased mouths clamp down on Father's back, chest, and head. Dead rush past into the living room.

Mother appears in the archway between rooms. "He's happy to see you. Give him pets." She sees the birdcage but not the ghostly maws that have begun champing at her skin. "Oh, you can't. Let me he—"

"Because I have this," Father roars, stepping to the kitchen table and setting the cage atop it. The squawking stops. "Didn't I tell you to lock the animals in the bedroom till we got the cockatoo settled?"

"When I got home we started to get ready—"

"And the cats spilled cereal and salt."

More dead leak through the kitchen walls and latch onto Father. He swears as loud as the bird screeched seconds ago. His face purples with each bite they take until Pete barks up at him, tail wagging.

Gobs of dead spray away from him like a bursting water balloon. Stillness coats the room until Mother speaks. "It still hurts to think of the neighbors. I wanted to cry and forgot to clean up what the cat spilled."

With the bird silent, the dead stay gone. Father steps forward and embraces Mother. "Sorry I lost my temper. Work was crappy and I just wanted to get Daisy settled."

Daughter skids into the kitchen on socked feet, kicking salt, pepper, and cereal dust into my nose. I sneeze once. Twice. It does not stop. Retreating under the table, I miss the conversation and their movements around the house.

The blanket Daughter acquired was to provide covers for Daisy's cage. The same way they were used for Shina's kennel when she joined the family almost a year ago. Father and Mother will need hours of bite-free time for their joy and drive to fully return. They may have more outbursts during that bite-free time, but we can provide a no-bite night even under the horrible circumstances.

I scamper away from the kitchen, into the living room, bounding up the stairs in the middle of the house to the second floor. Daughter has closed the doors to all rooms including Mother's and Father's. I gaze down upon my domain and refocus on it between sneezes and wheezes. Pete's claws clack on the kitchen tiles a floor below and a room to the left, out of my sightline. If any dead haunt the house at this moment, I cannot see them.

There are no immediate threats unless the bird decides to make our jobs harder.

Shina paws up the stairs to sit at my side. "Is it cliché to say I wanna eat that bird?"

I hiss through stinging nostrils. "This is not one of Daughter's cartoons. If we cannot communicate with it, then terrifying it into silence is a better plan."

"An' if that doesn't work?"

"Then we adapt. We run, observe, act, and revise."

"R.O.A.R." She licks a paw and eyes me sidelong between claws. "It's sassy. You sure there ain't a sense of humor in there somewhere?"

"We cannot relax, Shina. Dark season is here. This bird will have us chasing dead all night."

"That feathered thing's getting my blankets too. If it chews a hole in there and wrecks the cuddle potential, it's dinner."

"Humor and hunting live prey are luxuries we must do without." I sit tall and watch as below, Father crosses the living room and places the cage atop Feline Tower. It blocks the room's second window. "We must deal with losing the Tower window as well. Any view out that way will be obstructed at best, off-limits at worst."

"What's the plan, boss-o?"

"We cannot plan around what we do not know. If we fail to protect the family—"

"Then we eat the bird."

"Then they send us to the humane society if we are fortunate."

"Got it. Learn how birdbrains work. Time to earn that kibble."

Shina bounds down the stairs, slithers between Daughter's feet, and leaps to the bottom tier of Feline Tower.

The structure shudders.

Shriek after shriek bursts from the bird's beak.

I descend and weave between Mother and Daughter toward the couch. Two more leaps and I'm atop the headrests.

Dead hands claw through the window faster than I can keep up with. I send eight packing with heavy swipes, but many more swarm in, drawn by the bird's cries.

Pete steps up behind me and barks in a rhythm, banishing dead that I miss. Amid the chaos, I catch none of the family's agitated words. Father chases Shina away from Feline Tower and she joins me on the couch. When she is a good distance from the birdcage, the squawking stops. Pete ceases barking when it's no longer needed to repel the dead.

No bites this time. Our first triumph of the evening.

As the night advances, Father talks to Daisy. He murmurs rhythmic phrases and feeds her seeds. Training her, I assume, since the words he speaks are one syllable. Her responses range from shrill gibberish to word mimicry, and the dead seem able to tell the difference.

The bird's english words provoke no response from the dead. Even her smallest cheeps lure the dead like mice to peanut butter. Each wave requires all three of us to act swiftly, jumping from floor to couch to Tower when we can reach it between Father's scoldings. Several dead seep through, tearing at our humans with phantom mandibles while we strike at their too-numerous companions.

The family argues during dinner. Anger and anxiety saturate the kitchen. The bird's racket interrupts every positive event in our home as it happens. Shina and I scramble in circles around the kitchen, banishing dead amid the family's conversation about funeral arrangements and providing a home for exotic animals who no longer have a habitat.

After dining, the family observes the idiot box in the living room, leaving a space next to Daughter empty on the couch. The lost friend's seat. I use it to ascend to the window behind the couch and beat the dead away from them. When Pete barks, Father waves at him with firearm magazines, his own hand, and a bedroom slipper when snore duty draws closer. Golden Pete's persistence shows how much he deserves that name.

An hours-long panic mode sweeps us through the evening. In a good hour, Daughter bubbles with laughter at Shina's acrobatics and the family reminisces over the neighbors' exotic snake. During a bad hour, Father locks both Shina and Pete in his and Mother's upstairs bedroom, leaving me to face hordes of dead alone while he trains Daisy.

Strangely, the bird makes less noise and draws fewer dead during this hour. I feel its beady black eyeballs tracking me, a constant pressure along my spine. It is the hyperawareness of an intelligent predator salivating over future prey. My bobbing and slinking among rooms is not enough to halt the invasion, but fewer and fewer dead answer the bird's twittering summons. The dead get in, but they bite no one before I banish them. They must have found more appealing families elsewhere along the block.

When snore duty arrives, I get my first moment alone with the cockatoo. Mother and Daughter retire upstairs to prepare for sleep. Father lets Shina out and takes Pete outdoors to urinate. I observe from the top of the couch. Where Pete marks, the dead stick until morning.

Shina has frozen at the top of the stairs. I flick my tail, signaling her to pay attention.

She mewls, "Save me a drumstick."

I ignore her and prowl along the couch's top toward a bookshelf in the far corner. Crouching low, I spring higher than I have in years and scrabble for a foothold atop the shelf. My back claws hook on the shelf edge and I gain purchase at the pinnacle. From here, I see Mother cross into hers and Father's room for sleep, leading Pete in behind them.

No noise from the bird. She swivels away from the Tower window she'd been gazing into and fluffs those chalk-white feathers at me. A sweat-soaked straw odor hits my nose and I sneeze. Crawling along the top of the bookshelf, I pass photographs of the family. One is of them hugging the former neighbors. One is of me, Shina, and Golden Pete. The new one is of Daughter and her red-haired friend and pet snake.

I try to make my first words to Daisy more authoritative than my approach was. "My name is Shelly. I protect this place with Shina and Golden Pete." Indicating their general directions with a tail-point, I add, "You bring the dead into my family's home. How do you explain your behavior?"

Her predatory gaze from earlier is gone, replaced with a hollow-eyed distance. "Caged and dying. Dying and caged. Burning empty, burning full."

Madness? Had this creature been traumatized and reduced to chanting, unaware of its actions? "Do you know what the dead are? Your noisemaking attracts them. It would help to quiet down. Working together is ideal."

"Were together, now it's razed."

"What's razed? Look, this home is not usually chaotic. The dark season is upon us and we need—"

"Don't you think it's bull, it's bull?"

Hissing, I creep closer. "Either you are faking insanity or you are only capable of repetition. Which is it?"

Daisy shies away from the bars. "One year old. One year old."

"You can see the dead stampeding inside every time you squawk, can't you?"

Her oily eyes peer at me, the Tower window, the window behind the couch, then at me again. A vigorous nod.

I pad backward. Father and his fellow zoo keepers must be developing Daisy's cognition. I peer at Shina, shaking my head once.

This newcomer is as Shina was when she first arrived. We may be able to help, or at least teach her a balance between mimicking human speech and silence for the family's sake.

"Young one, I hope you are eager to learn. We all need that."

"Eager to learn," she repeats.

"In my ancestors' days, cats moused. If too many mice got in, the master kicked us out or worse. The dead are our generation's mice, only ghosts don't fill the belly. Kibble does."

A vigorous nod from Daisy.

"When too many dead come through the walls, the family's too sad to remember kibble. While you're here, the idiot box will call that depression. Mother will say it's bad memories and pain. Father has referred to it as post-traumatic stress.

"They are right. The dead magnify those things and always have. Where dead linger, willpower and happiness are their dinner. We simply urge them to move on, by paw and claw and bark."

I peer at the cockatoo's beady eye and tilt my head. "Does this help you understand, Daisy? When the dead are allowed their prey, it makes the humans commit unspeakable acts. Is it not similar at your zoo or in your old habitat?"

"Unspeakable," Daisy replies. "Were together, now it's razed. Want peace. Can't have."

Silence from the bird. It seems she heard. I shall observe to make sure her cognition develops as Father wants. The work of keeping this

Dead Next Door — Jabe Stafford

house free of the dead will be tougher, but not necessarily permanent. Other zoo animals have grown and left our home with a sense of duty to repel the dead.

Difficult times are not improved by unnecessary infighting.

Warning arfs burst from the master bedroom.

Dead. Inside.

I spring from bookshelf to couch and leap up the stairs. Something tumbles to the floor behind me. Wriggling through the cracked-open bedroom door, I find a dozen dead surrounding Mother's side of the bed.

I lower myself for a pounce at the nearest one, but Pete's muted whuff slings all the dead on Mother's side out through the walls. He scoots his head toward Father's side where more have slithered through the walls.

Pete lets loose another whisper woof. The bark crashes into the clawing dead and flings them outside.

Mother mumbles. "Pete makin' that noise?"

"He must be having doggie dreams," Father groans muzzily.

Pete's next baby bark catches the last dead clawing through the window. It soars away.

One of Golden Pete's eyes glints at me in the gloom, then goes dark. A wink. Mother and Father noticed nothing. They roll to the side and sleep on.

Clever dog.

Emptiness claws my stomach while I slink from the bedroom to the top of the stairs in the hall. Uncountable dead flood the living room, their hollow eyes fixated on Daisy at the top of Feline Tower. Chill scents emanate from the un-living. Either the bird summoned them while I was with Pete, or they are gathering to see the source that has drawn them here in such massive numbers for the first time.

Daisy's cage has been left uncovered.

My fur bushes outward and I hiss. "Shina. The dead. They heard the bird."

Shina's paws thump to the carpet from behind me. She'd been in Daughter's room, abandoning her post and enjoying a new blanket's worth of cuddles. Undisciplined. I twist to find her preparing to fly down the stairs at our enemy.

With a swat, I stop her. "No. Wake Daughter and get her out here."

Glistening ghosts glide from the bird toward the stairs. A slithering snake circles in the grass outside the biggest window, lit by the dead stuck in Pete's trap.

"She was sad from missing her friend again," Shina hisses. "I just cuddled—"

"The blankets," I spit. "Daughter has them. They will silence the bird."

Her eyes bulge and she scampers back down the hall into Daughter's room.

Dead pour up at me with grasping hands.

I bare my fangs and leap to the left. Straight at the wall.

The first two dead that try to reach Daughter's room meet my claws. They splatter backward into the drywall even as I push off it and twist in the air.

Four dead have gotten their torsos around the corner toward Mother's room. I slash at their backs and legs on the rebound. All four plummet skyward and vanish.

Mad mewling from Daughter's room hits my ears when I land. Raucous squawking stabs out from the bird's direction. The tide comes again.

I spring, rebound, and swipe, a dervish whirling against the dead. Each blow launches dozens from the house. Packs of them rush above me each time I touch down. A spin and a slash catches their knees and they scream skyward without a sound. None pass.

Ever there are more with each squawking summons. Their ethereal forms overlap each other, many occupying the space of a single dead. Clusters make it through to both bedrooms.

Shina's cries and Pete's renewed barks announce their arrival in the upstairs hall. My crew has reached my side. Lights in the hallway flash on amid the chaos and Daisy's frantic wailing.

We cats leap at the dead in the air, eyes adjusting fast. Golden Pete barks at the endless horde. They re-gain ground with each screech from the bird.

"Stop climbing the walls each night," Mother yells, awake and storming out of the bedroom. "You'll wreck the paint."

She pushes us back toward her bedroom. Dead rip at her arms, shoulders, chest.

Father emerges, face purpling again from rage. Shades paw and bite at him from every angle. I scream and launch at his back, batting swarms of them away. Most are gone by the time he grips the fur at the back of my neck. I withdraw my claws and slump in his hand.

He drops me limply to the carpet, then bellows, "Where are the goddamn blankets?"

Dead Next Door   Jabe Stafford

I see Daughter's pajama'd form stumble from her room, blankets folded in her arms. She is crying openly. With Pete barking and Shina yowling, I tear between everyone's feet and lash at any dead in my path. One, two, three leaps and I'm down the stairs and atop Feline Tower.

Next to the problem.

"Daisy," I snarl between the cage bars. "Your actions paint you red."

"Now it's razed," she rants. "Razed, razed."

I twist to glance at the stairs. Pete's barking has cleared the dead away, and Daisy is talking.

"We offer kindness and forgiveness," I continue, "but you summon the dead regardless."

"Their own medicine, own medicine."

Mad mimicry means no dead reappear.

Father reaches the living room with the blankets.

I snarl, "What do you get from putting our family through hell?"

"Actions paint humans red, paint them red—"

Thick blankets drop onto the cage and clip me. I flop off the Tower's top and roll my back, landing on four paws and sprinting for the top of the stairs. No dead can hear the bird's muted screams from outside and Pete's been barking, so my journey is clear. When I reach Shina and Pete waiting for me atop the stairs, the house is silent except for Daisy's now-useless ruckus and the family's sobs as they hug together in the middle of the living room.

Their words of mourning for Daughter's lost friend turn to a full frustrated break down. No dead are in sight. We've failed. They will not sleep this night, and we will not eat.

The face of a lone dead lunges through the window behind Daisy. Red hair curls around its translucent cheeks.

"It feels like Katie's still here, mom," Daughter says between hiccups.

The three of us descend to the living room once more and I yowl at the familiar form.

The noise is lost in Mother's sobs. "I feel the same way, honey. It's going to be okay. She's always here with you."

Katie's ghost unhinges her jaw and swoops toward Daughter.

Pete's bark slows the geist down, but it keeps coming.

"The man that shot her should die," Daughter shrieks.

With a whine, Pete snuggles Daughter's legs, standing tall.

The family doesn't notice when I leap from the carpet onto Pete's back, then launch myself at the dead girl with twenty stabbing claws.

They sink in and Katie's spirit tumbles down through the floor out of sight.

I land atop the firearm magazine and skid to a halt. Whipping around, I see Father's gaze lock onto the handgun featured on the cover. Vengeful hunger slithers behind his eyes.

Pete whines and Shelly loops herself between Father's and Mother's legs.

"It wouldn't bring her back to us," Mother breathes. "That man might deserve that, but your friend deserves the best we can give her. That's what matters right now. Remembering her."

"Aw, Pete," Daughter says, kneeling and burying her face in his fur. "You know we're sad don't you? He misses her too."

Father puts his back to the magazine, hugging Pete along with the family.

Rage crackles through my fur. Rage at the terror and pain the world has dragged into our home. My stomach squirms and grumbles. Their pain will be softened by more cuddles later, and by action now. We still might have a shot at some kibble.

I whip around, expecting more dead in my domain. I scour the lingering dead from every bedroom with claw and fang before re-claiming the stairtop, my crew falling in once again.

Mother is holding Father and Daughter in the middle of the living room. She clutches a gold-plated picture frame in one hand. The photograph of Daughter and her red-haired friend Katie, the former neighbor with the snake. I will deny that I knocked it off its shelf in my haste.

We watch Father break from the hug, then brace Daisy's cage to the Tower with cords. I catch the words, "We'll get through this," and, "They told me Daisy was rough to train, but we've had zoo animals before and so have the cats."

"You made home. Safe again," Pete says, panting with the effort of banishing so many dead. "Shina told me. Your plan."

"It's a patch-up if ya ask me," Shina says, wriggling on her back. "But what're we gonna do, get an exorcist?"

"Shina said. She had the blanket idea. First. You just. Acted on it. Before she. Shared it."

"Thought dogs were s'posed to be loyal."

"That is. Different from. Secret-keeping."

"She did have the thought of stopping the bird first," I admitted.

Pete freezes mid-pant and Shina licks a paw as though she doesn't care.

I add, "She wanted to eat it."

Tongue flopping out again, Pete rolls his brown eyes. "How am I. The grown-up here?"

Mother takes Daughter's hand and leads her back up the stairs toward us. Shina flips back to her feet and hurries to her post atop the couch un-asked.

I meet Shina's poison-yellow eyes when she looks back, seeing the future leader within them. If she could balance the laugh-at-everything attitude with the ability to think and act that I saw today, we might survive this dark season. Another thought I would deny telling her I had if she asked.

There will be many opportunities to show her who she could be.

I see Father pick up the firearm magazine and head upstairs next. No sound from the birdcage reaches the street, because no dead flock to feed on our family. Pete's tail wags and I follow him into Mother's room so he can resume snore duty. I bat at his flappy tail, memories of the days when I'd been a different cat warming me.

Clawing from my empty stomach centers me again. "Pete," I say, "did the neighbor's snake say anything when you visited with Daughter a couple months ago?"

He hops onto Mother's bed and turns round and around. "When Daughter held him. Yes. I forget. His name. I think it was. A chant."

Chants. Mimicry. Since when are snakes and birds part of the same club? I spring up next to him. "What was he chanting?"

"'Smoked out habitats. Smoked out habitats.' That's all. That he said. That I remember."

"Have you seen it on any of your walks recently?"

"They're scouting excursions. Not walks. No snake."

I flick my tail and jump off the bed. "Thanks Pete. Keep that memory sharp."

"You got it. Shelly."

I leave him to snore duty and curl up against the wall at the top of the stairs. Thoughts stalk my mind the way the ancestors hunted in their time. Daisy had searched out the windows frequently this night. The dead's attack patterns had not remained consistent, but had ebbed and crashed upon the house. I lose track of whether it is the ancestors' growls or my stomach's that rumble on and on into sleep.

When I wake from my hunger-induced nap, I find the house dark and see Shina rigid at her post at the living room's biggest window, batting dead back in ones and twos. Her fur sticks up in patches and she stumbles, but recovers and fights all the harder. The family must have said their goodnights and gone to bed.

Hunger was no excuse to neglect duty, yet I had. Shina had noticed and covered for me. When I was a younger cat, I could have ground it out. Thanking her and doing more later became top priorities.

Daisy's long-winded squawks have died out. Her cage rests alone atop Feline Tower.

Murmurs slip from beneath the door to Mother's and Father's room.

"Love, we forgot the kibble."

"Ooh, right. Gotta feed those fuzzy protectors."

"They keep us safe from the mosquitos."

"Maybe we should put them in charge of the world?"

Giggles bubble out from Mother's and Father's bedroom. I crack one eye and pretend to sleep, my back against the stairtop wall.

Father's slippered feet emerge and descend the stairs in the dark. A bag crinkles in his hands. My mouth waters.

The sound of kibble filling metal bowls sings joyously through the house, a clarion bell that will ring again and again so long as we run, observe, act, and revise.

Harder than the things coming for us.

Jabe Stafford's adventures around the Midwest have taken him to UW-Madison where he earned a BA in English Literature. He's taught Tae Kwon Do, volunteered at renaissance faires, and made some great friends with his cheesy British accent. Twitter: @OculusWriter

The Genie of the Ring

by Clarissa Gosling

Summoning number 1273

I am summoned to the world again, appearing in a cloud of smoke. "I am the genie of the ring. Your wish is my command."

I don't know how long has passed or where I am. All I can do is keep track of how many times I am summoned.

My bow is full of flourishes. In front of me is a scrawny youth cowering away from me. My ring, with its large ruby and fine gold setting, adorns one finger and is the only thing of any value I see on him. His clothes are rags and his feet are bare on the sandy soil.

While I wait for him to instruct me, I look around. We are in an enormous underground cavern piled high with jewels and gold. I can't even count the amount of treasure lying at our feet. Beyond what I see, I feel the magics around us. They bind us to this place, neither in nor out of this world. This is a magus' treasure trove. The spells guarding it are beyond my power to disarm.

I peer through the gloom deeper into the cave, trying to determine which way the entrance is. The walls are undulating, with a sandy floor. All directions are equal, so it appears wherever the doorway is it has been closed behind this poor fool. There is no movement in the air, and my purple silks lie still against my skin.

What does this boy want with me? How did he end up owning my ring? And how did he get himself trapped in this place?

"Oh my master, what do you wish?" I ask again. This is my life now. I am tied to the ring, appearing as demanded to fulfil its owner's commands.

"Who... who are you? Where did you come from?"

I bow again. "I am the genie of the ring, oh master." I point at the ring on his finger. "What is your command?"

How long have I been away from this world? Once a command is completed, I am forced back into the ruby, to sleep once more until I am summoned again. In this cavern, it is impossible to tell how long ago I last walked on its earth. And his rags tell me nothing about fashions or location.

My previous master, Iharad Qadir, was a cruel magus obsessed with the accumulation of power. I can't believe he gave his ring away, or that the ring was stolen from him. So how does this youth now hold it? The only answer that makes sense is enough time having passed that the magus' bones are dust. The power of my ring forgotten along with him.

My new master pulled at his hair and wailed. "I am lost and trapped here by my uncle. At least he claimed he was my uncle. And now I am imprisoned here with nothing to eat and no way out."

"You must be explicit and use the form 'I wish...' for me to be able to help you." I motion with my hands to encourage him. "For example 'I wish for a cushion.'"

He stares at me, swallows, and then tries. "I wish for some food and something to drink."

I snap my fingers and a range of dishes appear to one side. Each one piled with succulent meats, breads, baklava, and fruits. I snap my fingers a second time and jugs of the freshest water and the finest wines stand next to them.

"Refresh yourself and gain strength. I hope there is something here that suits your palate. I had to guess what you might prefer."

His eyes grow wide as he looks from one dish to another. After a minute, he kneels next to the closest dish and stuffs as much as he can in his mouth. As his rate of consumption slows, he looks up at me.

"You have some too." His voice is muffled as he speaks with his mouth open.

I bow, oddly disconcerted. "I have no need of your sustenance. But your offer is appreciated." No one has ever suggested I share in what I provided for them before. I'm uncertain how to respond. "Do you have another wish, my master? If not I will return to the ring until you need me again."

He shoots up, his face pale. "No, don't leave. I wish you to talk to me. Tell me about the ring and how it works. What can you do?"

I take a deep breath. "I am the genie of the ring. I serve whoever holds the ring within the limits of my power. Rub the stone and I will

The Genie of the Ring Clarissa Gosling

appear to fulfill your wish. Once I complete my task, I return to the ring until I am required again."

He looked at the ring on his hand, holding it in different ways in the light. "You live in here?"

I smile and nod. This master is unlike any master I've had before.

"It's not very big."

I shrug. "It doesn't have to be. I am not a powerful genie, so I only need a small receptacle." I consider him. "Tell me who you are and how you came to get the ring."

"Oh, yes. I am Ala al-Din from Baghdad." He bows his head to me "A few days ago, I was hanging about in the market when a rich man came over and claimed he was my long-lost uncle. He showered my mother and I with gold and fine clothes. Then he brought me on a journey with him. He said he was going to show me wonders like I'd never seen, but he marched me deep into the desert. Then he shouted strange words and threw a powder into the sand. At his feet a steep tunnel opened. He insisted I enter alone to find him a lamp, as he was too old for the climb down." The youth shrugs. "I was worried he would disappear and leave me there, so he gave me the ring as a reassurance he wasn't going to run off. And he said I could keep as much of this treasure as I could carry, as long as I gave him the lamp." His eyes widen at the mention of treasure. "But as I returned to him, he wanted me to throw the lamp up first. I had tucked it down into my back and couldn't get it easily while I climbed out. When I refused to stop to take it out and pass it up first he cursed me, saying he'd wait for me to die and return with another gullible fool. Then the opening shut on me. I must have rubbed your ring without realising it."

OK, so Ala al-Din was given the ring without knowing what it was. Could his uncle be my previous master? He was searching for a lamp said to contain the greatest genie ever. Could it be here? Did I dare hope? At least he hadn't found it yet. That would be a catastrophe. Though one I hoped for in a way. The lamp had been lost for decades, and with it my dreams.

"Why he didn't buy one in the market I don't know, as there are far finer ones there than this dirty old lamp."

I gasp as I recognise the lamp he waves round his finger. My head falls to hide the tears in my eyes.

The youth shrugs. "I guess I'll never know." He looks up at me. "So, I wish you to take me out of this cavern and return me home."

I consider his wish and the lamp he holds.

"Providing you with food is simple. But the magic in this cave is strong, while I am weak."

He sighs. "Well, it was too much to hope for. At least I won't starve." He sits down and looks at the jewels around us. "If only my mother could have but one of these she would be happier than ever I have made her." He puts his head in his hands and weeps.

"Master, I might not be able to break out of here. But if that lamp is the one I believe it is, then it contains a genie far stronger than I. He could transport you wherever in the world you wished." Pasha Hamza had almost no limits as a human, so as a genie he would be formidable. This cavern would be nothing to him.

The youth looked at the lamp. "Really?"

"Polish one side of it and the genie will appear." I cross my toes, hoping for a glimpse of my love.

Ala al-Din raises one eyebrow. "Well, here goes nothing. Thank you."

His hand goes back and forth on the side of the lamp and a flash of smoke spurts out. As it clears, I see his form, the one for whom I chose this life of servitude. But I am sucked back into my ring before he notices me.

All I keep is the image of him there, bands of gold on his wrists and ankles to match mine, and wrapped in turquoise silk. To once more share a master fulfills the greatest wish of my heart. It's almost like being together again.

Summoning number 1274

I am summoned to the world again. I leave my cramped ruby and stretch out into the sky.

"I am the genie of the ring. Your wish is my command."

Trapped in my ring, I am in stasis, only blinks passing between each summoning. Every time it surprises me when time has passed and my masters are visibly older. I can recognise the poor barefoot youth I last saw in the man who stands before me. But instead of rags he wears the finest silken clothes, and instead of the face of youth, his is now worn with cares and laughter. He is not yet an old man, but it has been some years since I last saw him, and years that have treated him kindly, it seems.

"Oh, genie. The most dire calamity has befallen me. You must help. My bride and my palace have disappeared and I don't know where. And her father, the Sultan, swears he will take my head if I don't return with her within forty days."

The Genie of the Ring — Clarissa Gosling

I smile at him. "Hello again, my master. What do you wish for first?"

He takes a deep breath. "I wish you to bring my palace back. And all the people inside."

I examine our surroundings. Trenches score the ground. Paths cut off clean at the edge of them, as if there had previously been a building there. I inhale and fill my lungs with the scents of a magic filled with cedarwood and cumin. My stomach clenches as I recognise it. I haven't felt his magic for aeons. Despite both becoming genies hundreds of years before, we have barely interacted since I followed him into servitude. He was tricked into bondage, but I followed willingly, unable to give him up.

"The genie of the lamp did this."

My master nods. "I left the lamp here with Princess Badoura, my wife. I don't understand how it could be used to do this. Or why she would want to leave."

I bow my head before him. "My powers are not great enough to undo what he has wrought."

"Then I am lost." He sinks to the ground, pulling at his hair.

My heart races. Will he follow my direction? "I apologise I cannot bring the palace back here, but I am able to follow where it has gone." Will this allow me to see my love for more than a glimpse? Do I dare hope?

He looks up at me, blinks, then jumps up. "Well, let's go then. I wish for us to follow where my palace has been taken."

I reach for his hand and with my other hand, I click my fingers. The central town square is exchanged for a barren landscape. Only here a beautiful ornate palace rises from the sands. It looks like a mirage, the sunlight gleaming off the precious stones and metalwork.

My master gasps and pulls forward.

I hold his hand tight, stopping him running into the building.

He faces me. "I need to get my wife. Why are you stopping me?"

"We don't know who else is here, my master. Or why your palace was brought here. Let us be a little cautious before we run in and are captured too. Let me scout for you." That way I can search for the lamp and who holds it as well.

He sinks in on himself and nods. "Please."

I continue looking at him, waiting.

"Oh, yes. I wish for you to scout round and find out what is inside."

"Wait here for me." With a thrumming heart I head towards the palace and the new master of the lamp.

The building is tasteful and full of wonders. I can see my love's hand in its construction and appointment. He always had an eye for architecture and design. But I can't find any sign of the lamp. After some time, I find a group of five ladies. I stop to listen. They're unable to see me and I can't interact with them. But I hope to learn more about what has happened.

They all wear matching silk dresses, in a variety of pastel shades.

"Your highness, don't despair." One lady kneels next to a chaise lounge, holding the hand of another lady lying back. "There must be a way to escape."

One by the door comes running. "He's on his way."

The ladies position themselves around the reclining lady, who wipes her tears and sits straighter. As she sits up, I see the diadem on her brow. This must be the princess, my master's wife.

The door bursts open. With a shock I recognise Iharad Qadir, my previous master. His black hair is threaded with grey, but he is as arrogant as ever.

His lip curls. "Well, my lady. No more stalling. Agree to marry me and we will return to your father's city where we will rule together."

"I am already married. I can't break the vows I made." Thankfully, wishing for someone to fall in love with you was impossible for any genies to fulfill.

He snorts. "Forget about him. He is nothing. And very soon he will be gone."

She raises her eyebrow. "Would you have me forget about you so quickly, too?"

His grin is cruel and shows off his golden tooth and the scar through his eyebrow. "You will never need to, my lady. I will give you everything you desire. With me you shall want for nothing."

She stands and faces him. "I want to be left alone. Can you give me that?"

He frowns and clenches his fists. I study his lavish decorated robes. As he puts his hand on his hips, he pushes back his outer robe, revealing the lamp hanging from his tied belt.

I gasp. My old master now has the lamp. He can't be allowed to control that power. He will bring the world to its knees. Now more than ever I know I need to help my new master.

My old master turns, as if he heard me, but his eyes skate over me.

"Well, your refusal will have consequences, my lady." He smirks. "Adieu. I will not return until you call me. And call me you shall."

The Genie of the Ring   Clarissa Gosling

I follow my old master as he leaves the ladies alone. He makes his way to the central chamber of the palace. Once there, he lounges on an ostentatious throne, studded with precious stones. It clashes with the other décor, so it obviously wasn't part of the original fittings.

I need a plan to recover the lamp from his power and return it to Ala al-Din. At least he will be pleased to hear that his wife is well, I hope. How far can I stretch the intention behind his last wish? He didn't explicitly wish for me to do anything beyond searching for what is here. So I am limited in how much I can interact with my surroundings.

He claps his hands and a servant boy appears in the doorway, bowing.

"Bring me a jug of iced mint tea with honey and lime. And see that the ladies are served only bread and water from now on."

The servant bows again and disappears into the darkness beyond the door.

While he waits, my old master studies the lamp, turning it over in his hands.

I follow the servant, and with one breath I infuse poppy seeds into the drink. I can't do too much, or my old master will notice, but I hope this will make him sleep.

The servant notices nothing. He places the jug and a glass on a silver tray. I loiter behind him and watch as my old master takes his first sip. He doesn't seem to notice anything wrong, so I return to my new master.

He paces out of sight of the palace. As soon as he sees me, he runs up. "Did you see her? Is she alright?"

"The man who I think gave you my ring is here. He has the lamp and wants your wife to marry him and to rule her father's lands together." Though whether that would be sufficient for him is another question.

Ala al-Din puts his hands over his face. "What can we do? It's hopeless."

I smile. "I placed a soporific in his drink. He should be asleep now."

"But what good will that do?"

"Well, once you take the lamp back you can return the palace to its proper place." I smile at him. "Come on."

He blinks and follows me. We find my old master snoring on the throne, the lamp lying on the floor at his side.

My new master unhooks the lamp from his belt and smiles, his confidence returned. Without waiting, or thanking me, he rubs the lamp.

Again, I am sucked back into my ring as my love arrives. This time, our eyes meet for a second. I see his shock as he recognises me. I trust him to fix everything. And I am left in the darkness again with my memory of his smile and recognition. That will need to keep me going until next time I am brought out into the world.

Summoning number 1275

I am summoned to the world again. It is a relief to stretch and I look about in order to determine where I am and how long has passed since I was last summoned.

"I am the genie of the ring. Your wish is my command."

This time it is a lady who holds my ring. Her grey hair is braided and though her fingers are bent, her eyes are sharp. Her clothes are fine, though the muted colours tell of a recent grief. There is no surprise on her face at my appearance, which is unusual when I first meet a new master.

We stand in a garden, full of blooming flowers, including multiple types of roses, irises and amaryllis. A lush paradise at odds with the dry air and harsh sun.

"I know this is the first time we have met, but I owe you my husband and my happiness." She smiles sadly. "Before Ala al-Din died, he told me the truth of where all his wealth came from. The story of how much you helped him, and how you saved his life and mine. Now I would like to repay that gift."

I bow again. "There is nothing to repay, Queen Badoura." As that was who this had to be. "I do as my master wishes, as long as it is in my power. So, please make a wish."

She stretches out her hand, with my ring lying in her palm. "I wish you to be free."

The golden bands round my wrists and ankles break, and the ruby in the ring cracks. I will never again reside in there, waiting to be summoned. My first lungful of free air tastes sweeter than ever. I have no idea what to do next, or where to go. I am stuck. Should I rejoice at my freedom or despair at losing the only link I had left to my love? I will now grow old as he continues forever young, but enslaved.

In the other hand, she offers the battered, tarnished lamp that holds my heart.

My mouth dries, uncertain what she is doing. Will I now be subject to his power, or is she getting rid of me, as she doesn't need both of us?

"While you helped my husband, and saved his life, the genie of the lamp performed only what was requested of him and no more. So we give him to your judgment. Have him serve you, free him, or give the lamp away. I want nothing more to do with it."

My hands reach out for the lamp of their own accord, and I am unable to articulate my thanks.

I cradle the lamp and consider my options. The lady leaves and I continue to stare at the metal, tracing every bump and mark. How long has passed since we last saw each other and talked? What will he think of my deal to follow him into the chains of life as a genie? I learnt more about power and the frailties of people over the centuries trapped inside my ring than I ever thought possible before then.

Dare I summon him to find out? Yet if I don't do it now, will I ever gain the courage to do so? Before I can find more excuses, I wipe my hand on the side of the lamp and wait for the smoke to appear.

"I am the genie of the lamp. Your wish is my command."

He appears, clad in the same turquoise silks and golden bands I had glimpsed before. My eyes drink him in, the bronzed muscles and dark eyes that were my only consolation for years uncounted.

"Hello, my lover. How have the years treated you?"

His mouth drops. "But...how? Is this a dream?"

I grin and reach out to him. His face feels just the same as I remember. "I wish for you to rebuild our cottage, fully furnished and with enough gold to keep us comfortably for the rest of our natural lives."

He frowns at me, but has to do as I ask. He claps his hands and we appear where our story started. Time has not been kind to our old home. Abandoned and unkempt, it is almost unrecognisable.

Another clap transforms the dilapidated cottage. Fresh thatch and a fresh coat of paint, with a handful of goats and chickens running round the fenced off area in front. Through the windows I can see the inside is clean and appointed in a more modern style than it had been centuries before, when we had last lived here.

"As you desired, my master." He is uncertain, shuffling from foot to foot.

My worries fade as I study my perfect house. The one we had only dreamt of having before we were tangled up in the thirst for more and more power.

"Would you be happy to remain here with me? To continue where we left off before we were tempted away with stories of magic and power?" I wait for his answer. My heart races and I daren't look at him, just in case he refuses.

"I... This..." He sighs. "I don't deserve it. I don't know how you are here, or if this is real. I want to agree, but will that just be more torture when it is taken from me?" Tears form at the corner of his eyes. "I thought I saw you in bondage as I am, and I grieved for you. I know not what power has kept you, or how you stand before me." His hand shakes, the silk he wears waving in the breeze.

I see the hesitation in his eyes. They speak of scars and ordeals that I know nothing of. The genie of the lamp was said to have stopped wars, to have devastated cities, and to have brought ruin on nations. No doubt he was forced to do much more that was never spoken of.

I hold the lamp out between us. "I wish for you to be free." How can I expect him to choose when there is no choice as he is.

The golden bands round his wrists and ankles break, and the lamp cracks in half. He drops to his knees, tears welling up in his eyes.

I crouch next to him and take his hand. "I wish for you to live here with me, to finish the life that we once had." I pause, sweat trickling down my back. "Will you?" Would he? What would I do if he declined?

One hand reaches for my cheek and he touches his forehead to mine. "You were my lodestone, my memory of all that was good and right. I am not the same person I was then, but for you I will try to be better."

I cling to him. "Neither of us are who we were, but together we can be what we should have been."

With that we enter our cottage and the start of our new life.

Clarissa Gosling has always lived more in the world of daydream and fiction than in reality. In her writing she explores purpose and belonging across worlds. Having never found her own portal to faeryland, she is resigned to writing about fantastical worlds instead.

The Brightening
by R.A. Clarke

"Okay, I'll see you later!" I shouted, stretching up the gritty edge of the dry river. My parents told me when I was little that the *Big Ones* liked to call the river's near-black surface a 'pavement' or a 'bike path'. I remember giggling at the silly sounding names.

"Where are you going?" Yolanda asked, her scrunched face tightening even more in bewilderment. Yolanda had been my best friend since we were tiny hatchlings—practically inseparable. We even made burrows next door to each other once we'd hit adulthood, finally big enough to move out on our own.

"Across the dry river to see Nate. I told him I'd visit next time it rained."

"Across the river? Now?"

"Well, yeah... when else?" I laughed, looking up to the beautifully thick blanket of clouds looming overhead. A fat raindrop crashed onto my head, its bulbous form splitting and scattering about. I giggled and stretched up, undeterred. Like most worms, I loved the rain.

"It's been raining for a while already, Wanda. The clouds could dry up soon. I wonder if you should just wait until the next shower. Nate can wait." Yolanda slid beside the pavement, looking at me from below.

Such a worrier. She hadn't adapted well to our evolving friendship arrangement, either. Always trying to keep me around as much as possible. I mean, it was true, since I got a boyfriend, we hadn't been able to spend as much time together. But wasn't that the cycle of life? Change was simply something we'd both have to get used to.

"I promised him." Reaching the flat top of the river, I paused and met her gaze. "I really don't want to disappoint Nate. Plus, I think he wants to make it official this trip."

"Official, like *mate*?"

My pointed face twisted in a girlish grin as I nodded. "I think so." My lower half curled with glee.

"Wow, so you really love him…"

"I do, very much," I replied, unable to keep the elation from my voice. Soon, I'd have a cocoon growing, percolating little hatchlings of my own. My heart swelled just thinking of that possibility. Nate would make such a great dad, always patient and kind. I knew he'd be eagerly waiting for me on the other side. I could think of nobody better to share a burrow with. Perhaps we'd even move across the fence, put down some roots in a whole new yard.

How wonderful that would be.

Yolanda sighed with a bittersweet smile. "That is amazing. I'm so happy for you."

I leveled my gaze, recognizing the conflict broiling within her. "Listen, we'll always be best friends, no matter what. You know that, right?"

"I know. It's just strange, that's all. It's always been *just us* until now." Then she shook her head, abruptly snapping a brighter smile into place. "Don't worry, I'll get used to it, eventually. I truly am happy for you."

"Thanks, Yolanda." I smiled back. "I really appreciate your support. When I get back after the next rain, I hope Nate will come back with me. Maybe to stay! Then you two can finally get to know each other better. Won't that be great?"

Her facial features softened, smoothing supportively. "Pretty great."

"You'll like him." I beamed, feeling like a swooning teenager. "Now, I better get moving." Rolling my accordion-like body over the top of the ledge, I paused to peer back down.

"Okay, well, get across as fast as you can. No dawdling."

"Yes, mother." I scoffed with a laugh.

Her hairline brows furrowed in response. "I'm serious though. You don't know how much time you've got."

"Oh, I have plenty of time," I said, my slender head turning skyward once more. "The rain won't be going anywhere for a while yet. Look at those clouds? They're dark and thick for as far as the eye can see." *Well, as far as my eyes can see, anyway.* All worms had miniscule eyes, which resulted in poor long-distance vision. The farther, the blurrier.

"Well, just be careful. And watch for birds!" If Yolanda had hands like the Big Ones did, I knew she'd be wringing them.

The Brightening   R.A. Clarke

"It'll be fine," I assured with a nod. "Enjoy the rest of the rain. Oh, and I heard the Nightcrawlers were having a big party by the compost heap. You should go." I shot her a wink and a teasing grin. "Maybe you'll meet your Mr. Right."

She chuckled at my sing-song tone. "Ugh, not likely, but we'll see. None of the worms around here are my type." Yolanda waved farewell with her tail.

I waved back, and with that, I pushed away, setting forth on my journey across the dry river. Cool liquid pooled and rippled atop the hardened plateau, creating a perfectly slick surface for me to slip across. Reflective droplets splattered all around me, landing hard and steady.

I couldn't have asked for a better day to travel.

As my tail end gripped the pavement, I strained every muscle to elongate and stretch forward. Then, like a closing slinky, the countless rings lining my body compressed, pulling in my rear to start fresh with another launch. Repeating that motion over and over, I worked my way across. I was making pretty good time, too. I spied other earthworms cruising across just like me, scattered about and travelling in all different directions. This river was always bustling when it rained. This landmark was the dividing line between town and country worms after all. A bridge between two very different worlds. On one side of the path stood the entirety of town, while on the other side, there lay fields, a bushy forest, and a farm.

Yolanda and I lived in town all our lives. Having both grown up there, we loved it. There was easy access to compost piles and gardens, and all kinds of other fungi to munch. Plenty of Big Ones to watch—they were fascinating creatures. Plus, our place was close to the dry river, making travel convenient. Not that I'd travelled very much yet—but I wanted to more. This was my first time crossing alone.

Nate, on the other hand, was a country worm, born and raised. He lived beneath what they called the 'cow farm'. That's where we'd met, actually. He and his buds had thrown a huge spring shaker a couple months ago. The invite had spread far and wide via the cricket telegram, telling worms to come as soon as the first big rain of the season fell. All were welcome.

Feeling a little stir-crazy after a long winter, me and Yolanda decided to be bold and go. Neither of us had ever been to the farm before. I remember being excited for a new adventure, and grew even more excited as soon as I saw Nate coiled up next to his friends. He noticed me right away—came and talked with me. We connected immediately, and I knew he was special. Since it was my first time on a farm, Nate took me on a special tour. It had appalled me to see all the huge horned beasts that lived and clomped around above ground. But then, he let me taste the manure… and I understood the appeal of calling such a place home. It was delicious.

Approaching the great yellow line that divided the pavement—an odd, broken trail that ran the entire length of the dry river—I grew increasingly excited for the visit ahead. The line itself was a welcome sight. Soon, I'd be sliding over it. Officially halfway there.

"Wanda!" A familiar voice called my name, the word echoing slightly.

My pinhole-sized eyes strained to see. The voice rang out again, and I zeroed in, trying to spot the source. I saw movement. My vision was a touch hazy at that distance, but it didn't matter. I knew exactly who I was looking at. A smile spread across my face.

"Nate!" His handsome, slender head had poked above the far edge of the river, waiting for me to arrive just as I'd hoped he would be. "I missed you so much! I'll be there soon!"

"I missed you too, babe," he called back, voice infused with excitement.

A swath of light flashed across the pavement. So fast I thought I'd imagined it. Glancing up, I saw nothing but grey clouds. "Huh…" Shaking my head, I pushed onward.

Moments later, another flash came, brighter this time. The quick heat warmed my back. *Now, I definitely didn't imagine that.* Again, I looked to the sky, this time seeing faint tendrils of blue breaking through the swiftly moving clouds. *Oh, muck.*

"Wanda, babe, you better hurry. The rain's letting up!" Nate shouted. He was right, of course. The previously steady shower of droplets eased as the clouds thinned.

Another band of light passed over, filling the width of the dry river, its glare sending up cries of alarm from all the worms still traversing across. I followed suit as tubular bodies strained, huffing and grunting to rush their movements.

It wasn't until the last raindrop fell, with no more to follow, that I accepted the truth. It was coming… and soon. My sense of urgency amplified and panic taking hold as I pushed ahead, my sole focus set on getting across. Perhaps I should've listened to Yolanda when she said it had been raining for quite a while already. One could never truly predict how long a shower might last. I kicked myself for going hillside, mud-slipping when the rain first started.

The Brightening   R.A. Clarke

The wind died down as the remaining shreds of the storm dissipated. Clouds grew lighter overhead, and the previously fluffy blanket covering the sky separated at the seams. A golden shine washed over me every few seconds, the world brightening around me. The light was so warm. It was horrible. Voices all around rose with concern. Some turned back, close enough to one side of the dry river. Unfortunately, I didn't have that luxury, having just crossed the centre line. Anyone stuck in the middle didn't have any choice. And all I could think of was getting to Nate.

The intermittent flickers of light strobed faster and faster until the shadows barely offered a reprieve. Nate shouted at me, his voice elevated, fearful. I even thought I heard the faint cry of Yolanda's voice from behind, but it was too far away for me to confirm. Worry rose like bile in my throat, but I swallowed it down. I couldn't let it control me now. In this moment, my focus had to remain concentrated on moving my body. It took a lot of effort to maneuver and coordinate my lengthy body, especially with increased speed.

Sweat broke out on my slanted brow. Hazy lines of warming air wavered up from the pavement in every direction I looked. The air grew thicker, heavier as the temperature rose.

This is not good.

Glowing light intensified above, shining hot and brighter than any of my nightmares. It no longer flickered amidst the clouds. It held steady now, like a Big One holding a flashlight in search of bugs. My skin tingled and tightened as countless tiny pores puckered in complaint of the searing heat. Screams of terror pierced the air. It was here.

The sun.

High above, that golden white ball of scorching firelight glowed without care or mercy. The death dealer. Wincing, I turned away and hurled my body forward. No time to waste. Being hot wasn't the worst of my problems. No, there was more to sunshine than just light and heat. The sun emitted terrifying rays.

Water had already evaporated from the river's surface—precious moisture greedily reclaimed by an ever-warming atmosphere. Soon only large puddles would remain, none of which was I lucky enough to be close to. I'd never felt so vulnerable before.

A searing bolt of photons slammed into the surface, slicing through the air with a *whirring* noise. Everywhere I looked, similar bursts collided with the surface. Like gamma-ray lasers, they burned anything they touched, relentless in their assault. Some were thin and razor sharp, and others were robust. How did the Big Ones remain impervious to the sun's violence? In fact, it didn't seem to bother *any* mammals. They walked around, blissfully unaware and unaffected. But us worms... we knew. We burned.

The first ray scorched my skin, and a scream erupted from my mouth, guttural and raw. Then another, and another, as my outer layers felt like they were being peeled apart and cauterized in the same instant. Unobstructed, the sun shone down without mercy. Grunting, I closed my eyes and pushed forward. *Come on Wanda. You can do this.*

"Wanda, I'm coming to get you!" Nate shouted through the din of pained voices.

My eyes sprung open again. I was three quarters of the way across the river now and could see him clearly. He was up on the pavement, taking his first long stretch toward me.

"No! Get back!" Another ray sliced into me. I shuddered, letting out a raw whimper.

"I can't just leave you out there!" he shouted back, groaning beneath the sun's glare.

"You have to. We can't both die. I won't allow it!"

"You will not die!" He surged forward, but was quickly cut down as a searing beam blasted into him, the largest I'd ever seen. As the light dissolved, its energy absorbed by the ground and Nate's motionless body, I screamed.

"Nate!" Panic overtook me. I'd been trying so hard to keep my fear under control and focus on the task at hand, telling myself to keep completing one slide after another. If I could just do that, I'd eventually hobble my way to safety. But what if that didn't happen? No longer could I ignore the starkness of reality, how many worms had lost their lives to the sun's devastation. Not only was my determination rapidly dwindling, but so was my hope.

Tears welled in my eyes as I remembered my parents. They'd been caught in The Great Sun Attack of July 2018. Vivid images flashed, bringing me back. The air had been moist that day, the clouds stormy and ripe for rain. It poured for nearly half an hour straight, and all the worms came up for air, to socialize or conduct necessary business. My parents had been waiting for a solid rain so they could go visit an old family friend. I'd stayed with my aunt, still too young to travel the dry river. I remember waving along the river's shore, watching them go. They made it halfway across before the clouds blew over. It happened so suddenly, faster than anybody could have predicted; the rain chased away by an expanding blue sky. There hadn't been enough moisture, and the sun blazed overhead.

The Brightening — R.A. Clarke

My folks hadn't stood a chance.

And now I might share their fate. All five of my already racing hearts hammered a jungle beat in my chest. Left and right worms faltered—shrivelling, their screams deafening. The few who managed to slip into the safety of a puddle watched the chaos in fear, knowing the end would eventually come for them too. Puddles didn't last forever.

Movement registered from the corner of my eye.

A worm appeared over the far edge of the river. *It was Tom—Nate's best friend.* I watched as the crazy worm braved the elements to latch onto Nate's rear end. With a powerful heave, he dragged my boyfriend backward, disappearing from view. A tired smile split my pointed face in two. My hearts filled with relief. He was going to be okay.

But that wasn't good enough. I needed to see it with my own eyes.

Gathering what remained of my strength and my tattered body, I pushed my muscles to the limits. Latching the ground and stretching forward, I inched forward again and again. I couldn't give up now.

Bolts continued to rain down, hitting me; the repeated impact growing more devastating by the second. My strength ebbed. It was so hot. My skin ached and burned unlike anything I'd ever felt before. If I had a nose, I could only imagine what kind of putrid smell would fill it. Sure, every worm could tell you a tale of being caught in the sun at some point in their lives. But they usually ended by a harrowing description of seeking refuge, burrowing into the earth. Unfortunately, that wasn't an option for me. I had no relief. No salvation.

The edge of the river seemed so close, yet not close enough.

I collapsed; the weight of my tubular body too great. I couldn't drag it any further. Exhaustion and pain gnawed at me from the inside out, invading and multiplying like a deadly virus. It was debilitating and eviscerated any hope I had left. My mouth was dry. *Everything* was dry, dehydrating and shrivelling beneath the onslaught of a hateful sun.

As I trembled, a grim realization hit me. I could not make it.

"Don't give up! Please, don't give up!" Yolanda's voice rang out, a distant echo.

Releasing an involuntary moan, I tried to hoist myself up one last time, but sagged dejectedly, with nothing left to give. My voice was hoarse, barely a whisper. "I should've listened to you, my friend. I'm sorry."

The screams dwindled, fading away. Looking to my right, I locked eyes with a nearby worm as a large bolt of firelight wracked her body. I knew her. Her name was Marny, and she wasn't much older than me. The poor girl was in terrible shape, her body deathly pale, blackened by the sun's searing scars. I was certain I looked much the same. Charred. We didn't know each other well, but at that moment, we shared a tremulous smile.

Marny's pained expression morphed into one of resignation. As she rested her head and closed her eyes, I broke down into sobs. *No, I'm not ready to die. I have so much more to do.* To grow old with Nate and make tons of babies together. To fulfill my dream of exploring the world.

A bolt of light jack hammered my head into the pavement, the driving impact leaving me dizzy. It branded my skin. The edges of my vision dimmed, and my once frantic heart rate slowed. Apathy crept in, pushing panic aside. It was over and there was nothing I could do to stop it. Acceptance took hold like tree roots, anchoring my fears. It was time to move on to wherever worms go. Some said a great compost heap awaited us worms in the afterlife, where everybody is moist and well fed. Happy. I used to scoff, but now I hoped it was true.

The ache in my body dulled even as more attacks wracked my listless form. It felt dangerously close to relief, and I welcomed it. Like Marny, I gave in to the reality of my situation and closed my eyes.

I thought of Nate as the world gave way to silence.

#

"Aw, poor little wormy," a booming voice thundered, reverberating in my receptors.

The ground trembled beneath me. With great effort, I pried open an eye. How long had I been out for? Had I made it to the compost heap?

An imposing shadow fell upon me, blocking the scorch of the Sun. Peering up I saw a juvenile Big One, her form short and chubby, with blonde ringlets that fell beside her ears. She was soaked, slick with water, and wore clunky coverings on her tall walking limbs—the kind my parents warned me about. *Rubber boots. Worm crushers.* With great effort, I opened my other eye. Looking past the Big One, I saw the blurry outline of two more—older ones, both splashing in puddles further down the dry river.

"I'm gonna save you before my brothers come and squish you!"

Did she say save? A spark of optimism ignited. *Are Big One's capable of such mercy?*

Her giant hand reached down to pick me up and placed me gently inside her palm. She repeated the process, collecting as many worms as she could, piling them around and on top of me. The weight grew uncomfortable, but nothing compared to what I'd already been through. I was too depleted to care. Looking around, I spied weary faces daring to smile with hope. Unfortunately, I also shared this salty palm with worms who weren't so lucky. If I had any moisture left, I would've cried.

My stomach lurched as the great hand swept across the dry river and lowered us into the grass.

"There you go. Good luck little wormy's," the voice boomed again. A toothy smile lit up her gargantuan face, and I couldn't help but smile back. She spread us out on the grass, then returned to the pavement to collect more.

I trembled with relief as the Big One's sheltering shadow retreated. The grass was cool and wet, the black dirt moist and heavenly. Not exactly sure where I was, I scanned for Nate. Not seeing him anywhere, an immediate sense of self-preservation took over.

There's no time to look for him.

I didn't pause to talk with other survivors, certain that they would be thinking and doing exactly the same thing as me. Getting into the dirt, hydrating, and healing was all that mattered now. Worms could only survive being parched for so long. This was life or death.

Mustering whatever strength I still possessed, which wasn't much, I burrowed.

My thoughts returned to Nate as I worked, each ribbed section of my body working together to carve a worm-size tunnel into the earth. Where was he? Did he survive? Hopefully, he was okay. I wanted so desperately to find him—to see him—but it would have to wait. My haggard form wouldn't get far in its current condition. No, I had to regain some strength first.

Instead, I screamed, hoping he might hear. "I'm okay, Nate!" my voice rasped, feeble and lethargic. Sadly, I was too far away for Yolanda to hear. I couldn't assure her I'd made it to the other side. She'd be worried sick until I could contract a cricket to send a message. Though I felt bad, it was the reality of our world. Sometimes I felt so jealous of ants, spiders, and butterflies. Free to travel wherever they want—and quickly, they had no limitations. Letting out a deep sigh, I continued burrowing. All I could do now was hope she saw the Big One scoop me up.

Nearly submerged, with only my head remaining above ground, I watched the blonde-haired Big One successfully gather more handfuls of worms before her brothers came stomping by. *Stomping.* I cringed as their slapping rubber boots finished the job the Sun started. The girl yelled at them, telling them to stop, but it was too late. So many more lives… lost.

A deep ache swelled within.

That could've been me. If the sun hadn't finished me off, those boots certainly would have. Had the blonde one not intervened to pick me up, my story would be over now. Yet, that didn't happen. I was given a second chance. Despite the sorrow of the situation, I conjured a smile for my unexpected saviour as she chased off after her not-so-nice kin.

"Thank you," I whispered, then ducked beneath the wet earth, breathing it in. It didn't matter that she couldn't hear my words; I just needed to say it. Her simple act of compassion would never be forgotten. She saved my life.

R.A. Clarke is a former police officer turned stay-at-home mom living with her family in Portage la Prairie, MB. She enjoys plotting fantastical novels and multi-genre short fiction. R.A was a 2021 Futurescapes Award finalist, and has won the Writer's Games and Writers Weekly international competitions.

Follow her at: www.rachaelclarkewrites.com.

Some Things Remain
by R. A. Meenan

Someone screamed. Jaden Azure looked up from his tools and perked a white, catlike ear. The battery-powered lantern he used to see while he worked flickered ominously, casting thick, dark shadows on the walls of his blacked-out shed. The dragon-shaped Defender communicator pendant he was working on gently hummed, the only other sound his sensitive hearing picked up. Screams in the night were common these days - war caused a lot of nightmares - but if it was followed by anything else...

A full minute passed. Jaden turned on his modified broadcast radio, hoping to catch any walkie-talkie chatter. Nothing.

Then something that sounded like a gunshot echoed through the night. But quiet. Suppressed.

Raiders.

"Damnit." Jaden grabbed his satchel off the desk, shoved his radio, tools, and pendant haphazardly inside, then grabbed his fist-sized, white Gem and activated a magic shield around him and the shed, leaving the door unshielded in case anyone needed a place to hide.

Damn these raiders. He should have been safe here. Atlas was supposed to be perfect. Miles away from the nearby city of El Dorado, absent from all maps of the area, and devoid of any electronic communication, save Jaden's pendant and his pathetic radio. A ghost town in the California desert, hiding away thousands of anthropomorphic zyfaunos all trying to dodge the US military's aggressive draft campaign.

While the US would never openly admit it, it was widely believed zyfaunos were receiving less training than humans, yet being put on the front lines as bullet sponges while their human counterparts got better training and less dangerous assignments. Draft dodging had become commonplace.

But so had communities housing said dodgers. And competition for resources was fierce. Communities raided other communities to stay afloat. And Atlas had become a prime target in recent months.

The shed door opened and his wife Alexina stuck her head in. The cream-colored fur over her snout and between her eyes glowed bright in the lantern light, a stark contrast against the black of the rest of her fur. She stared at him, quills shaking, her deep orange eyes wide with worry. "Jaden."

"I heard it," Jaden said. He turned off the lantern and shoved that in his satchel too. "Where's Embrik?"

"Here." The red, black-streaked quilar appeared next to Alexina, flicking his thin tail, his amber eyes glowing in the dim moonlight. He already held their grab-and-go bags.

"Any idea where it came from?"

"Military checkpoint," Embrik said. "Point Mesa, half a kilometer away. Likely a suppressed rifle."

"I thought so too," Jaden said. "Shit." He snatched his black jacket and balaclava off the wall. Suppressed fire meant stealth. Definitely raiders, and they were getting bold. Atlas was in trouble.

Jaden tossed two more jackets and balaclavas to Embrik and Alexina. "Get these on."

Alexina pulled the balaclava over her face. "Plan Defender?"

"Too late for that," Jaden said. "We're already compromised. Plan Guardian. Alexina, get Kyrie in the air to warn the community. Evacuate the area. Snuff all lights."

Alexina nodded. She waved a hand and in a flurry of snow, a barn owl materialized beside Alexina, bringing the vibrant scent of deep winter with her. Kyrie, the ice phoenix of the Order of Phonar, was one of Alexina's two summons. The other one, Archángeli, had been missing for years and they all felt the absence.

The phoenix summon looked like any normal barn owl, aside from the abnormally long tail feathers and the scattered, white and blue peacock feathers among them. Her eyes were also a rich, thoughtful green, though she had no pupils. She sized up the three of them, then flew off into the night.

Two small snowflakes landed on Jaden's nose. *Protect the Archon and the Prinkípissa.* The summons communicated telepathically through their elemental magic, and Kyrie's voice normally had the soft, singsong sounds of gentle snowfall. Comforting, familiar. Something to keep the zyfaunos here calm.

Now her words had a sharp edge to them.

Archon Embrik and Prinkípissa Alexina, his wife and best friend, and his only friends in the lonely years here. Both were royalty of Athánatos, exiled just like Jaden. He wrinkled his snout, glancing at his companions. As if they needed protection. They had stronger magic than he did.

But not the training you do, Guardian, Kyrie reminded him. She melted into the darkness.

Jaden bit his lip and flicked an ear back. Not like that training helped him much. They lost zyfaunos with every raid.

And nothing compared to the losses he faced during the attack on Sol so many years ago. He lost everything that day. His first wife. His kids. His best friend. His sister-in-law. Her fiancé.

Though for all he knew, that fiancé started the whole problem. It was just a little strange that he disappeared the night before the attack that obliterated the island of Sol. And stranger still since it was that fiancé's kin that led the attack.

"Jaden," Embrik said, gripping his shoulder. "Stay with us."

Jaden sighed. It was harder to do these days. Living in this war now brought a constant memory flow of the wars he had previously survived, along with all the memories of his life before the genocide on the island of Sol.

Especially his life on Zyearth. His true home. A place he'd never see again, unless he got that damn pendant communicator fixed. Nearly fifty years on this backwater planet and the technology was finally catching up enough that he might have a shot at repairing it. No luck so far though.

"Jaden," Alexina whispered.

"I know, I know," Jaden said. "Sorry." He shook himself and pulled the balaclava over his head, hiding his white fur. He passed each of them a handgun with a suppressor. "Follow the sounds of the gunshot. Wide circle, elemental signals. Guns for emergency only. Try to avoid killing any of them – we can't interrogate them if they're dead."

Alexina and Embrik nodded to him.

They headed out.

#

Jaden hugged the cliffside on the outskirts of the community, ears perked, scanning the moonlit horizon for the raiders. Silence. No movement. Where did they go?

Something snapped. Jaden pressed himself against the cliff.

There. A human in full military fatigues moving between the community's huts, holding a rifle. Suppressed, like Embrik suggested.

Jaden frowned. A soldier? Had the US military finally caught them? He scanned the soldier for any identifiers – an insignia, a flag, even the type of uniform might give him some clue of where this person came from. But there was none that he could see, and the uniform was made up of pieces from several countries. Stolen clothing, perhaps?

The raider paused, waved a hand, and two new raiders appeared, each in similar mishmashed uniforms. They whispered with each other in some unrecognizable language, then ran deeper into the huts.

Shit. Jaden followed behind.

One of the raiders shouted and pointed. Jaden followed his gaze. A zyfaunos, wolf by the looks of it, ran for the safety of an evacuation zone, hands over their head. All three raiders raised their rifles.

Jaden snarled. Not on his watch. He held his hands out.

Thick, sharp ice spikes grew from the ground in front of the soldiers, blocking their rifles. They leapt back in surprise, shrieking in their unusual language.

Don't kill them if you don't have to. Jaden waved a hand and surrounded the soldiers with more ice, trapping them. His heart pounded, and in his haste to trap them, his ice magic came out wonky – some pieces were far thicker than others. Draso's horns, that is not what he needed right now. *Just stay put—*

One of the raiders screamed and fired her weapon at the ice spikes.

The stream of bullets bit each ice spike differently. One stream cut through a spike, dropping on one of the raiders, impaling him through the chest. Another large piece fell and pinned a raider's hips and legs. Bullets hit thicker ice and ricocheted off, some rounds escaping their frozen prison and others bouncing around before finding their mark in the body of the shooter. She fell to the ground, convulsed for a second, then stopped moving.

Damn it! Jaden rushed forward and waved the ice away. The shooter was dead, as was the man impaled. Jaden turned to the crushed raider. Like he thought, the man had a full military uniform and military issued rifle. But was he US military? And if he was, why would they attack in the middle of the night like common raiders instead of rounding them up for military service?

The man stared up at him with wild, terrified eyes, gasping for breath, trembling. Blood dripped down his mouth.

Jaden furrowed his brow. Literal decades of life as a soldier and he still couldn't stomach watching an enemy die. He couldn't save him. He'd have to end his suffering. It'd be a terrible thing to let the man bleed out here, alone and in pain.

But maybe he could get something out of him first. "Where did you come from?"

The man blinked at him, clearly confused. He tried to speak, but spat up blood instead.

Jaden flicked his ears back. The man was done. Jaden reached out and pressed his hand to the man's head. "This will be painless."

The man shut his eyes.

Jaden pressed gentle ice magic into the man's head, freezing his brain. He stopped moving. Quick. Unaware. He sighed and prayed last rites over the three raiders.

But then someone groaned.

Jaden shot his gaze up. The zyfaunos who had been trying to run. Jaden rushed to him. *Draso, let me save him!* He leaned down and checked the wolf over. Blood pooled under him. Jaden put a hand to his back checking for breath. But… nothing. He checked a pulse. Nothing. He was gone.

Jaden slammed a fist into the ground, ice spikes shooting up around his hand. Damn it all!

A tiny flicker of flame lit up the night sky, catching Jaden's attention. Embrik. He said a quick prayer of last rites over the dead wolf and rushed for the embers.

Alexina and Embrik hovered over a captured raider with a shock of red hair. He glared at the zyfaunos. Four other raiders lay dead around them, scarred by elemental magic.

Jaden flicked his ears back and met Embrik's eyes.

Embrik shook his head. "They attacked the Frosttail family," he said. "No survivors."

Jaden's heart turned to ice. No survivors. The Frosttails had three kids. He glared back at the remaining raider. "You kill *children* now?"

"*Va te faire foutre,*" the man snarled. The language was French, though he didn't know what it meant. The message was quite clear though. French soldiers attacking a draft dodging camp. Was France a US ally or enemy? He couldn't recall. Too many players in this disgusting war.

Jaden gripped the man by the collar. "Who are you working for?"

The man spat at Jaden, but Jaden blocked it with a shield. *"Meurs, d'animal,"* he said. He bit down hard, cracked something in the back of his mouth, and started gagging and foaming at the mouth.

Jaden jumped back. Suicide pill. Definitely not a raider. Something bigger was going on here.

After a second, the man stopped moving. Jaden sighed. Embrik looked away and Alexina rubbed the fur on her arm.

Kyrie appeared above them and dropped snow on their heads. *The village is evacuated and the enemies vanquished,* she said. *But not without casualties.*

Jaden flattened his ears. "Better meet up with Aaron."

#

"Twelve Atlas residents died in this raid," Aaron said. He flicked his black tipped weasel tail. "Including the entire Frosttail family." Jaden winced. The loss punched him in the gut. Aaron snorted. "That's the fifth attack this month. We can't afford this, people."

Jaden leaned against the wall of the shallow cave the leadership team evacuated to in these incidents. The light from his lantern licked the cave walls. Embrik stood by his side, his usual stoic expression cracking in the wake of the incident. Alexina had opted to tend to the wounded.

Twenty wounded. Twelve dead. Including children. Aaron was right. This was unacceptable. Jaden lowered his head, kicking himself. He should have been quicker. He should have been *better*.

Jaden, Alexina, and Embrik had arrived in Atlas about a year ago. The community had been quite a mess. Poorly organized, weak leadership, victims of dozens of attacks from surrounding dodger communities and raids, and they had very little in the way of defense.

Then the mages had arrived. Earth didn't have many natural mages. The majority of Earth natives, human and zyfaunos alike, didn't even believe in it. It still shocked Jaden that the residents of Atlas chose to keep them here instead of chasing them away for witchcraft. But when choosing between shattering an established worldview to believe in magic, or dying horrifically at the hands of vicious raiders, most would choose the former.

With Jaden's ice magic, Embrik's fire magic, and Alexina's control over every element, plus Kyrie, Atlas finally had a chance at survival. Jaden hadn't intended for their visit to make them Atlas' protectors, but he needed a safe, secluded place to make repairs on his pendant with the new technology he had swiped and he thought Atlas was it. Just had to lay low.

But as they got to know the residents here, all hiding from a war no one wanted to be a part of, Jaden found it harder and harder to convince himself to leave. These zyfaunos needed his help. He vowed to stay with them, at least until the war ended and they wouldn't have to fight off raids anymore.

He had failed Sol. He wouldn't fail Atlas.

Ezrah, a hyena, leaned back in her chair. "I still say we cut the heads off the damn invaders and line a row of pikes with 'em instead of burying them. That'd scare 'em off."

Jaden flicked an ear back. "We aren't barbarians, Ezrah. We show respect to the dead."

Ezrah rolled her eyes. "Don't worry, Jaden, I'm only half joking."

Jaden eyed her. "Half joking."

"Half." She grinned at him.

Embrik shifted his weight. "To my knowledge, burying of the dead happens infrequently. These people are trying to survive just as we are. We *need* to show them respect even as we defend ourselves."

"What we need," Levi said, flicking his puma tail. "Is better communication and more aggressive patrols."

Ezrah threw her hands up. "Not this again."

"Just *listen* for once," Levi said. "We're getting hit harder and more frequently because we can't see them coming. I know Jaden has said we'll be discovered if we use radios—"

"And I'm *right*," Jaden said.

"—But we're *already* being discovered," Levi said, glaring at Jaden. "We can't hide anymore. And while Kyrie is helpful, she's just too slow to get us out in time."

"Kyrie can traverse the entirety of the community in under five minutes," Embrik said, irritation in his voice. "And her method of communication is subtle, undetectable with electronic instruments, and fast."

"But not fast *enough*," Levi said. "Alexina can't assign her to anyone else, so if we're raided when you aren't on patrol, there's no way to warn everyone in time."

Jaden narrowed his gaze. "But if we use radios—"

"We'll get the message out far faster," Levi said. "And then it won't matter who's on patrol."

Embrik's tail swished in anger. "If we wish to continue hiding—"

"*We can't keep hiding*," Levi smashed a fist to the table. "We should take the offensive. Armed patrols. Kill anyone who comes near. If we just—"

"If we start killing anyone and everyone who gets even a whiff of our location, the US will have troops on us immediately," Jaden said.

"If that were true, why hasn't it happened already?" Levi challenged.

Jaden flattened his ears. That was a good point. Why hadn't it?

Levi flicked his tail. "You don't have a clue, do you?" He breathed out a low growl. "For all we know, this is all *your* fault."

Jaden bared his teeth and Embrik formed fists, but Ezrah beat them to it. She stood and placed a clawed hand on the table, flexing her fingers in a display of aggression that made even Jaden's fur stand on end. She spoke with a quiet, barely contained rage. "Too. Far. Levi."

Levi bristled his fur. "Is it? Don't you think it's a little suspicious that Jaden and his band of magicians show up just before we start seeing a huge increase in raids?"

Ezrah curled her black lips up in a snarl. "Jaden and his team saved us from extinction, you damn pussy cat."

"What proof do we really have of that?" Levi shouted. "I think—"

"*Enough,* Levi," Aaron snapped. "I won't have you slandering Jaden and his pack. I better not hear another word. Do I make myself clear?"

Levi flicked his ears back and furrowed his brow. He turned on Jaden and Embrik instead. "Nothing to say in your own defense?"

Jaden exchanged a glance with Embrik, then leaned against the wall again. "We prefer to let our actions speak for us."

"Oh, they're speaking loud and clear," Levi said.

"Levi, *drop it,*" Aaron said. "Or I'll have you removed from the council. This isn't about Jaden. It's about Atlas." Levi let out one more low growl before sitting down. Aaron sighed. "Despite your prejudiced little outburst, you make a good point. As useful as Kyrie is, she is the only method of mass communication for the entire camp. It's not fast enough. Jaden, even you have to admit that."

Jaden wrinkled his snout, but nodded. Embrik splayed his ears, silent.

"Levi also makes a good point about hiding," Aaron said. "We aren't doing so effectively anymore. I don't think that means we need to kill every human that we find," he added when Jaden moved to protest. "But it's clear we need more patrols. Armed patrols. Just in case the raiders get too close. We don't even have to kill them – just scare them."

"Do you really think that'll work?" Jaden said.

"I think it's better than sitting here waiting for the mages to save us, as Levi put it," Aaron said. He gave Jaden a sympathetic glance. "You guys have been tremendously helpful. I agree with Ezrah that you likely saved us from extinction. But your magic alone isn't working anymore. We're too big and too much of a target for resources."

"We could always move," Jaden said, though he already knew the response he'd get.

"Out of the question," Aaron said. "Even if we could get all three thousand of us out of here without drawing massive attention to ourselves, where would we go? No, we have to stand our ground here. We only have to outlast the war, then we can go back to our normal lives."

"The war could last decades, Aaron," Jaden said.

"Then we better batten down the hatches," Aaron said. He pointed to Levi. "Get together anyone willing to go on patrol who has some knowledge of firearms. We'll start planning new routes tomorrow morning. And let's get the radios off the bodies of the humans before we bury them." Ezrah snorted, but said nothing. Aaron continued. "Maybe we could set it to a specific frequency that others won't pick up. You could do that, couldn't you Jaden?"

Jaden furrowed his brow. "Uh, maybe. But even if I did—"

"Just do what you can," Aaron said. "I know this will put us on their radar, but if we get those radios set up right, we can mitigate the damage. Alright?"

Jaden crossed his arms, but nodded. "Yeah, sure."

"Alright everyone," Aaron said. "We've got our jobs. Let's get to it." He dismissed the group.

Jaden wandered out of the cave with Embrik, ignoring Levi's sneer. That did not go well. They hadn't even brought up the fact that these guys looked military. And now they wanted radios? This was a really bad idea. No matter what he did to the radios, someone outside their camp would pick up the traffic. There was no escaping it.

Unless… He patted the side of his satchel. Maybe they had one shot after all. He ran to his shed to get to work.

#

It took a solid month of work, but Jaden finally got the radios working the way he wanted.

Much as he hated to admit it, Levi had a point. They weren't getting warnings out fast enough, and that cost lives. But at the same time, using radios would practically paint a ten-meter-tall neon sign with the words "Look At Me" over their heads. They needed a signal that Earth technology couldn't pick up.

So he reworked all of them to run on a Zyearth frequency. Specifically, a Defender military frequency, similar to the one his Defender pendant used. He had to sacrifice some of his precious tools and technology that he planned to use to fix that pendant, but it was worth it. He had a long life to lead. The residents of Atlas did not, if he didn't protect them.

It wasn't perfect. After all, he only had one pendant to go by, and electronics weren't his specialty, but for their purposes, it worked well enough. He brought the radios to Aaron and explained his plan.

Aaron grinned. "Fantastic, Jaden. Exactly what we need." But he paused, frowning. "Weren't there eight raiders with walkie-talkies? We only have seven radios here."

Jaden flicked an ear back. He hadn't even thought to count the radios. "You're right. That doesn't bode well. Did a raider escape?"

"Maybe," Aaron said. He twitched his whiskers. "Though I don't think it's likely. You counted the dead yourself, all killed by your magic. Not like they could survive that." He shrugged. "Levi picked these off the dead. I'll ask him about it. Maybe one of the radios broke."

Jaden narrowed his gaze. Levi. Of course. He probably stole one for himself, that bastard. He could ruin everything. "Make sure he didn't steal it."

Aaron sighed. "I'll do that. Thanks, Jaden."

Jaden monitored the radio and pendant chatter night and day for weeks after they started the aggressive patrols.

As he anticipated, the broadcast radio couldn't pick up their modified walkie-talkies, but the pendant's communicator could. It seemed they were undetectable. It also gave him hope – if the pendant's communication worked short range, he could hopefully get it to work long range and get back in contact with planet Zyearth.

Oh, to be home again… Away from Earth. Away from these memories. The scars. What a luxury that would be.

The new patrols went without a hitch as the militia either killed or scared off any curious raiders. No casualties on their end. And if Levi had stolen a radio, he clearly wasn't using it, and if a soldier really had gotten away with the missing radio, it's not likely they could use it against Atlas. The relief was palpable. Months of monitoring and testing proved that his Defender frequencies were working. Thank Draso.

Maybe now he could stop worrying so much about protecting Atlas and get back to fixing the pendant.

He had the broadcast radio on constantly now, but hadn't picked up chatter for weeks, either from the enemy or from their own radios.

It was more of a formality at this point. Background noise while he worked.

Alexina entered his shed one night while he fiddled with the pendant. "It's nearly dawn, love," she said. "Come to bed."

"In a minute," Jaden said. "I'm so damn close..." His eyes drooped.

Alexina chuckled. "My angel, you will never finish if you fall asleep at your desk."

Jaden sighed. "Okay, good point." He checked the time. "The next patrol shift starts in two minutes. I'll head to bed then."

Alexina nodded to the silent broadcast radio. "The radios seem to be working well."

"They are, thank Draso," Jaden said.

"Mmm," Alexina said.

Jaden paused and looked up at her. "Something wrong?"

"Levi is speaking out against you again," Alexina said. "I heard him at the well. He claims that the reason the raids have stopped is because he caught you in the act and called you out in front of the council. He believes you had to stop or lose everyone's confidence."

Jaden waved a hand. "Let him play his political games."

"He is trying to discredit you, Jaden," Alexina said. "Turn the population against you so they turn to him for protection instead."

"As long as Atlas is protected, I really don't care how, or who's doing it," Jaden said. "Levi can do whatever the hell he wants."

Alexina flicked an ear back. "You are sure you are okay with it?"

Jaden dropped his tools on the desk. He sighed. "Honestly, no, but in the long run, it doesn't matter. I'm not a resident here - I'm a visiting mage. Once the war is over, once I get this pendant fixed, it's time to go home. Then maybe I could get my life back together again. Escape this hell hole. Start over again."

Alexina moved into the shed and wrapped her arms around Jaden's shoulders. He wanted to shrug her off, get back to the pendant but...

"You'll come with me, won't you?" Jaden asked.

Alexina laughed. "We have been married for decades and you just now ask me this?"

Jaden stared at the floor. "I... I wasn't sure I'd be able to until now. I'm still not sure, but since the pendant is communicating short range, hopefully I can get it to work long range. If I can..."

She kissed the top of his head and nuzzled his quills. "Of course I will come with you. I married you knowing I would." He sighed relief. But one more thing bit at him.

"Will Embrik?"

A long pause. "He is committed to Athánatos," Alexina said. "Even if he will never see it again. I cannot see him leaving for a new planet."

"Mmm." Jaden flicked his ears back. Leaving Embrik would be… hard. He had been a solid rock when Jaden had lost so much at Sol. And he had introduced Jaden to Alexina. He couldn't imagine trying to go through life without him. He gently gripped Alexina's arms as she hugged him. "I'd think he'd want to get away from it. He puts a lot of blame on himself for what happened."

"As you do with Sol," Alexina said. "And yet neither of you hold fault."

Jaden shrugged, but didn't counter her. Maybe not Sol… but his family. Aurora, his wife. His kids, Matt and Charlotte. Aurora's sister Solana… all lost, because he wasn't strong enough.

"My love," Alexina said. "Their deaths are not your fault."

He gripped his knees. Damn it all… this again. "I know it's not."

"You say you know it," Alexina said. "And yet you refuse to forgive yourself for it."

Fire and ice. If only she knew. He pinched the bridge of his snout.

Static blipped on the radio. Jaden glanced at it, eyebrow raised. He hadn't heard so much as a ping in ages. What the hell?

Then one calm word came through.

"Fire."

A massive explosion shocked its way across the community, violently shaking the shed and knocking both him and Alexina to the floor. The door blew wide open. Jaden scrambled to his feet then pulled Alexina up. He shielded them both. "Get Kyrie, find Embrik now!" He grabbed his tools, Gem, and pendant and shoved them in his pockets.

Alexina summoned Kyrie as a second explosion rocked the village. Screams and cries filled the air and the flicker of firelight danced its way through the shed's open door. Jaden and Alexina rushed out.

Everything was chaos.

All the lower huts and camps were bathed in flame, towering high into the sky. Jaden froze. This wasn't a raid. They wouldn't destroy resources. Was this the military? Why would they do this?

"Take out the fires!" Aaron shouted. Jaden turned. The weasel rushed toward them. "The fires, get them out!"

Jaden turned toward the flames, forcing his mind to focus. He held out his hands and waved ice and snow over the burning huts. Alexina followed him, using ice, snow, and water. The flames greedily ate their magic, hissing and spitting, spewing steam in great clouds, but nothing calmed the blaze. Buildings fell, cutting off screams and wails, drowning everything in ash.

It was too much. Too much!

"Jaden!" Embrik rushed through the flames, pushing them aside with his magic, with Kyrie leading the way. Five others followed him, Levi among them. The patrol.

Jaden relaxed, though barely. At least Embrik was safe.

Levi snarled at him. "You—!"

Someone shouted in French.

"Watch out!" Aaron shouted. A shot rang out, hit him in the head, and he fell. He didn't move.

Jaden's legs turned to jelly, and every adrenaline gland fired at once. "Go for the caves, go, go!" Jaden shielded them all and they ran. But it wasn't enough. It never would be. If a missile hit them…

A flash of red screamed past him. The smell of burning. The wails of the dying. He had faced this all before on Sol. Hot magic stung his nose, children screaming, the taste of ash. Was this Atlas or Sol? Was this happening now or in his head? Where the hell was he? He pulled his ears over his head. "No, no, *no.*"

"Stay with us, Jaden," Embrik said, gripping his shoulder. "We—"

Bullets rained over them. Jaden strengthened the magic shield, but it wasn't enough. The bullets shredded parts of his shield and their five companions fell. Levi lay flat on the hard dirt, his eyes unfocused, his bleeding mouth open.

Why did everyone fall so quickly when they got shot?

Embrik tugged on him. "Jaden—"

Jaden fell to his knees. He failed. Again. Damn it, it was never enough!

Embrik pulled harder. "Jaden—!"

"I can't, I can't, *I can't,*" Jaden said. "I can't, Embrik*, I can't,* they're dying, they're *gone*—"

"Jaden!" Alexina said. "You help no one but the enemy if you stay here."

"*I'm not helping anyone anyway, am I?*" Jaden said, his voice shaking. "Not Zyearth, not Sol, not Atlas. Why the hell am I even here? Why didn't I die when the Omnirs took Sol? Why do I continue to live when everyone I know keeps *dying?*" He sobbed. "What good am I to *anyone?*"

Alexina leaned down and met his eyes. "You helped me. You helped Embrik. You gave us our lives back, Jaden, after we lost everything on Athánatos. We would have fallen into despair without you and your drive to make things better."

Jaden glanced up at her, her face blurry in his tears.

She forced a smile, a strange sight among the white fires blazing around them. "You will help many more besides. It is in your nature, Guardian. Your very blood. But you have to survive."

Jaden stared at her, his ears flat against his head. His ears rang with the sounds of fire and screaming and death.

But she was right.

Embrik helped him up. "We will save who we can. Come, my brother." They ran into the fray.

#

The morning light revealed the damage.

Jaden glanced out over the remains of the camp, trying and failing to keep his mouth shut. He was already breathing too many ashes of the dead. He didn't want to taste them too.

There was nothing left. If anyone survived, they hadn't been able to find them, even with Kyrie searching and killing fires. All the huts, the tents, the sheds, the equipment, food, water, clothing… everything gone in a smear of black ash on the desert floor.

Jaden could only stare.

He should have died with the rest. Hell, he should have died on Sol. But he didn't.

He formed a fist.

He was tired of hiding. Tired of sitting aside, protecting pockets of the helpless until cruel things took them from him. It was time to meet cruelty head on.

#

Locating the enemy's camp was easy. With the combined power of Kyrie, Jaden's broadcast radio, and the brazen trail left by the enemy, they found it just as the sun set. But it was what that camp held that shocked them.

Ten humans. Only ten. All wearing those strange uniforms. And all speaking… English. Jaden remembered the one word on the radio. Fire. In English. Weren't they speaking French on the battlefield? They weren't raiders. Their simple camp suggested they weren't draft dodgers. Just who were these people?

Only one answer. Military. US military, despite the fact that they spoke French on the battlefield, trying to throw them off.

Worse yet... one of them was the red-haired suicide raider they had found on the last raid. Not raider. Soldier. Alive and laughing, making animal ears with his hands in the light of their fire. A walkie-talkie sat on his lap.

That was where the missing radio had gone. Did he use the radio to monitor Atlas? How had he done that when Jaden has been so thorough? He should never have agreed to using the radios.

Jaden watched the whole scene behind a clump of Joshua trees, with Embrik and Alexina on either side of him. He ran a finger down the Defender pendant, now slung around his neck, as a reminder. *You are a Guardian. A Defender. It's your job to take out dangerous individuals.* And they deserved it too, damnit.

Then why was he so reluctant?

Embrik gripped his shoulder. "You are sure you want to do this?"

Jaden nodded with more confidence than he felt.

Alexina sighed. "Make it quick."

He shouldn't. After the way they ripped through Atlas, killing everyone in sight, burning adults and children... they deserved to feel the same death they thrust on the citizens of Atlas.

But that wouldn't bring them back. And he wasn't a Defender to torture. He was a Defender to make the world safer.

It would be better to freeze their brains. He took a deep breath. He had learned the technique from Alexina many years ago. The Athánatos used it to end the suffering of the dying, those who couldn't be saved - quick, painless, compassionate. Typically, it had to be done while holding the head of the intended target, but Jaden didn't have that luxury.

Time to test his magic.

He tapped the Gem in his pocket, held out a hand, aimed at the red-haired soldier, and called on his magic.

The red-haired soldier stopped midsentence, his eyes wide. Then he fell.

The other soldiers blinked. One walked up to him and checked a pulse. "He's dead."

"What?" another asked.

Jaden reached for a second soldier. He fell down dead too.

One soldier screamed. The remaining pack snatched their weapons and glanced around, trying to find their strange attacker. Jaden pushed faster, harder, trying to get each one before they discovered him. It made him sloppy and the magic leaked. One soldier's eyes frosted over.

Another had icicles form in his nose. A third had their hair completely frozen. But one by one, they fell to Jaden's power.

By the time he finished, Jaden was spent. Too much magic. Too much death. And nothing made up for the loss of Atlas. But the deed was done. Looking around… he wasn't sure why he did it. It wouldn't bring Atlas back. He shook his head. Maybe it'd at least keep them from doing it to anyone else.

He and the others walked out from behind the trees. Jaden picked up a rifle – wouldn't do to be unarmed, especially with his magic spent, but he intended to do last rites. *We respect the dead.*

"Well, well," a voice said. "That was quite a show there."

Jaden whipped the rifle up.

A tall, sandy-haired man in uniform stood near them, rifle in hand, with two other soldiers beside him, zyfaunos, one fruit bat and one quilar.

Jaden's blood pressure shot up seeing the quilar - he was bright red with black streaks through his fur and quills, similar to the quilar that had destroyed Sol. *But they all died. There are no more Omnirs.* He forced himself to calm before he did something he'd regret. Too much killing.

Unlike the soldiers he had just killed, these soldiers wore standard US military uniforms, complete with identifying insignia and flags on the arms. Clearly different from this ragtag band.

Though that didn't make them trustworthy. Jaden aimed the rifle between the man's eyes. "Who are you?"

The man lifted his hands respectfully. His fellow soldiers did the same. "Brigadier Ackerson of the United States Marine Corps," he said. "My team were hunting these renegades after we got reports of missile fire in the area. Seems you beat us to it."

Jaden narrowed his gaze.

"You from that razed commune to the east?" Ackerson asked.

Jaden flicked his ears back. "Yes."

"Any other survivors?"

"No."

Ackerson moved his hands down, but Jaden waved his rifle and the hands went back up. "You're angry."

"The US military just destroyed a camp of innocents," Jaden said. "Of course I'm angry."

Ackerson nudged one of the dead soldiers with his foot. "They don't look like US military to me."

Jaden squeezed the trigger, ever so slightly. "People can disguise themselves."

Ackerson took a deep breath. "You're angry," he repeated. "Rightfully so. They killed your people."

"Get to the point," Jaden snapped.

"Channel that anger," Ackerson said. "Come with me and get revenge."

\#

"You want us to work for you?" Jaden said, incredulous.

Ackerson's team brought them to a small military camp just outside one of the rural civilian towns. They were in an air-conditioned tent all alone with the Brigadier and the fruit bat from before, in as private a situation as one could probably get in an outpost military base.

Jaden gripped his Gem, letting tiny ice crystals work their way through his fur in agitation. Alexina had Kyrie hovering outside the tent in case things went sour, and Jaden could smell the metallic scent of Embrik's suppressed magic.

The Brigadier had a veritable feast set out for them – roast chicken, baked apples, loaded salads, hot, buttered bread, and three types of potatoes. The smell wafted by Jaden's nose, making his mouth water, but he wouldn't touch it. He didn't trust this man.

"You'd run black ops," Ackerson said. "Undercover, completely oblivious. No cameras, no press, nothing. Just you taking out targets in ways the world won't understand. Well, the rest of this world, anyway."

Embrik flicked an ear back. "Be clear, human."

Ackerson laughed. "Fair." He leaned forward, grabbed a bread roll, and began buttering it. "Those soldiers you took out. Not a mark on them. No sign of physical trauma. But I watched them drop, one by one." He smiled at Jaden. "You used magic."

Jaden's eyes widened. "You know about magic?"

"I have a wide variety of people on my team, Mr. Azure," Ackerson said. "You are not the only ones with magic." He nodded to Jaden's Gem. "Nor are you the only one with a Lexi Gem."

Jaden could hardly believe what he was hearing. More zyfaunos with Gems? With magic? Where did they come from? How did they know how to use them?

"These people, like you, are angry," Ackerson said. "I've given them a chance to get revenge on the people who used them for so long." He waved a hand. "I'm offering you and your team the same chance. Work for me. Use those powers to do some good in this world."

Jaden kept a straight face, but his mind raced. He was a soldier. But what was a soldier without an army? By himself, he couldn't do much. But with this man here...

But it could be a trap. What was to stop him using them like pawns to push some agenda, just like the soldiers who destroyed Atlas? Besides that, why stay here? He knew the pendant worked now. He could get the right technology, fix the pendant, and contact Zyearth. He could go home. He glanced around, until he met the eyes of the zyfaunos fruit bat. His mind wandered.

You are a Guardian, a tiny voice said. *Your title demands you do good. There's still good to do on this planet. Stay. Do good. Zyearth can wait.*

He glanced at Embrik and Alexina. Both of them looked uncomfortable, though Embrik nodded to him, once again giving him the power to choose for them. Jaden took a deep breath. As much as he wanted to go home... they were still needed here. He turned to Ackerson.

"How long?"

Ackerson raised an eyebrow and smile. "Asking the smart questions." He waved a hand. "We're at war. War forces people to do terrible things. But you can leave at any time. No contract."

Jaden raised an eyebrow. "No contract."

"No paper trail," Ackerson said, grinning. "It's a lot harder to be ghosts if they leave evidence. Do we have a deal?"

Jaden formed a fist. He didn't trust this man. But he still had a job to do. For Sol. For Atlas. For all the potential good he could have done had he had the right resources. For his oath as a Guardian. He nodded. "We do."

Ackerson smiled, just slightly crooked. "Excellent," he said. "Then welcome to Mage."

R. A. Meenan lives in her own private world of elemental magic and dragon A.I.s, cultivating a love of the weird, the wild, and the whimsical. When she's not sailing through space, she teaches college English students, hoping to rekindle the love of the written word.

Play it Again, Sem

by Marsheila Rockwell

Lanny Pantera sat in the back of the courtroom watching his quarry. The bailiff—an androgynous brick wall named 'Pete'—held the door for her as she entered. Lanny didn't deign to stand during the imperious "All rise!"

He studied the judge as she took her seat behind the bench, her black robes a stark contrast to the wisps of blue and purple hair escaping her RBGesque bun. She seemed young for the office, but that didn't surprise him—all of his targets looked perennially youthful, because they were. It sort of came with the territory.

When he'd first zeroed in on Lemmon, AZ, he'd been focused on the County Attorney. The ballbuster lawyer seemed a likely contender, as she was known to take particular delight in emasculating men and appeared to have a personal vendetta against every sex offender who had ever dared walk her city's streets. Not that Lanny blamed her for that—he himself had never been one to use force or trickery as forms of foreplay, unlike some of those who'd displaced his generation. And after what had been done to his daughter, Aura…no. If the County Attorney wanted to castrate rapists on the evening news, he'd be the first to donate to her reelection campaign.

But that was just the problem. She would be happy to do just that, and bask in the press she received for it, positive or negative. Which meant even though she seemed like a prime candidate for the Ambrosial Abstinence Club, she wasn't who he was looking for, after all.

This judge, on the other hand. Despite the multi-hued hair, she kept a low profile. But Lanny had used his P.I. cover to dig into her past a little, and what he found had intrigued him.

She'd just appeared on the scene here five years ago, with impeccable credentials. Before that, she'd been in the Midwest, then back east, and then…it got murky. Well, murki*er*.

She was a judge, but he couldn't find record of her having run for or been appointed to that position in any of the jurisdictions in which she'd worked. Colleagues from her previous stints on the bench barely remembered her, and if they could recall her, they all seemed to think she'd studied law overseas somewhere. Probably Oxford, maybe Cambridge. No one really knew, of course, and perusals of student records had yielded no clues.

Not that she would necessarily have kept the same name even if she had been a student there. Just because she was going by Chris Athans now didn't mean she'd been using that identity a century ago, or whenever it was she had supposedly earned her Latin Legum Baccalaureus, or Juris Doctor, or whatever degree written in fancy calligraphy he probably *wouldn't* find framed on the walls of her office. (Not for want of trying; the fact that he couldn't pick the mundane-seeming lock also confirmed he was on the right track.)

Last up on the judge's docket for the day was a routine sentencing hearing for a homicide that had been the result of domestic violence. A bit surprising, since his quarry had never cared overly much for domesticity or its trappings, but he supposed she couldn't cherry-pick all her cases.

Today's sacrificial lamb had drowned his wife in their bathtub in the midst of a drunken rampage—what the defense called an "alcohol-induced blackout"—and by the time he'd sobered up enough to call 911, it was too late to save her. He'd been charged with criminally negligent homicide. The man's public defender had blamed his client's actions on a decades-long struggle with untreated alcoholism, as if bacchanalia were some sort of disease and not an acceptable excuse for the occasional murder. But justice had never been Lanny's purview even when his kind *were* in power, and it wasn't his to dispense now, either, at least not to mortals. No, he was more in the business of meting out punishment these days, thanks to his mother. Who was really everyone's mother, he supposed, or at least the Mother of Everything Beautiful. (His aunt Nyx had had children, too, of course, but 'beautiful' was not among the many words he could use to describe that lot.)

The victim's own mother, herself the survivor of an abusive marriage, had given a fierce and poignant statement, as had the woman's adult daughter from a previous marriage. All the while, the defendant had hung his head in a fairly credible show of grief and shame, not responding to any of the invective hurled his way.

And then Judge Athans asked him if he wanted to address the victim's family and, over the objections of his lawyer, the man said that he did.

There was silence in the courtroom as he made his way from the defendant's table to the witness stand, was sworn in, and sat. When his lawyer asked him to describe what had happened in his own words, the man seemed to have difficulty answering. Judge Athans motioned for Bailiff Pete to pour him a glass of water from a gold-toned pitcher on her bench. The man gulped it down gratefully, then looked over at the judge.

"Are you ready now?" she asked, almost gentle. At his nod, she gestured for him to proceed. "Then, please. Tell us your truth."

The man began to speak, and a look of surprise washed over his features, rapidly morphing into horror. He tried to clap his hands over his mouth to stem the damning tide of words, but to no avail.

"Yeah, I was drunk, but I wasn't *that* drunk. I knew what I was doin' the whole time and I ain't sorry I killed that bitch. She had it coming."

The room erupted into total chaos at that point, with the public defender screaming for a mistrial (which Lanny didn't think was actually a possibility at this stage of the game), the press screaming for soundbites, the family screaming for blood. And through it all, Judge Athans sat in her chair, fingers laced beneath her chin, a small smile playing about her lips. She made no move toward her gavel to quell the commotion.

If this was a routine day in her court, Lanny would hate to see a crazy one.

#

Lanny caught up to her outside on the courthouse colonnade. She'd doffed her robe, revealing a blouse with a bright floral print, navy slacks, and matching pumps. She'd unknotted her hair, and it flowed down her back, the blues and purples he could see before joined now by greens and pinks and golds.

The clothes and the dye job gave him momentary pause, but his target *was* the goddess of wild things, so perhaps her choice of disguise wasn't all that out of character.

He got quite a bit closer than he expected he'd be able to before addressing her.

"Judge Athans?"

She whirled, and he saw why she'd been so easy to approach. She'd been busy texting Pete. Lanny wondered if she were having a relationship with the bailiff. Not unheard-of for a virgin goddess, he supposed, but certainly not what that lot were known for.

"Yes? Can I help you?"

"I certainly hope so," he said, lunging forward to grab her arm before she could react, biting down on his fake tooth and breathing out a fine mist of corrupted ambrosia as he did so. Her surprised gasp did the rest, drawing the poison into her system, even as his touch exposed her for who—and what—she truly was.

Except…it didn't.

When one of Chaos's offspring touched another, their true nature was revealed to the world for a matter of moments before whatever guise they had adopted to survive in mankind's modern world fell back into place.

Lanny had been expecting to see the Virgin Huntress standing before him, clothed in a short chiton with a crescent moon circlet on her brow and her signature bow and quiver strapped to her back. The same Olympian goddess who'd arranged for the rape of Lanny's daughter Aura—her own cousin—just because Aura had claimed to be the prettier of the two.

But Judge Athans's appearance didn't waver. Which meant….

"You're…*not* Artemis?" Lanny wasn't even sure if it was a question or an exclamation of disbelief. "Shit."

"What? No, of course—" the judge began, then stopped, a look of recognition dawning on her face. He wondered how he looked to her—hooded, in tight black leathers, a sleek black crossbow slung over one shoulder? Like the hunter he'd been, or the assassin he'd become? Whatever she saw, it was no doubt a far cry from the jeans, cowboy boots, and western snap shirt stretched over a nascent pot belly that he wore for the benefit of the mortals. "Lelantos?"

He chuckled ruefully and inclined his head.

"Titan of Air and Stealth—mostly Stealth, these days—at your service. But I go by Lanny Pantera here."

"That's funny," she replied flatly, clearly unamused. "I thought you went by 'God Hunter.' Or is it 'Killer?' So hard to keep all your epithets straight."

He shrugged. There was no point in trying to deny it.

"Both. And you are?"

"Really? The hair's kind of a dead giveaway."

Then it clicked.

Play it Again, Sem — Marsheila Rockwell

"Iris?" *Of course.* "Chris Athans. 'Chris' for *chrysopteros*, the golden-winged, and 'Athans' for...oh, right. Immortal. Clever."

She did a double finger-gun gesture, one hand framing each side of a decidedly sarcastic smile.

"Clever Goddess of the Rainbow, that's me. Former midwife-by-proxy to your sister Leto and messenger girl for Zeus's lofty proclamations, now delivering verdicts for myself. At your service."

And then talons the likes of which Lanny hadn't seen in millennia wrapped around his throat and he was yanked backward, almost off his feet.

"Shall I kill him for you, sister?"

And then that clicked, too.

Pete. Ocypete, the harpy.

"Not just yet," Iris replied, and the viselike grip on Lanny's neck loosened. Marginally. "He's hunting Artemis, a choice bit of information we may be able to use for bartering with the Twelve. But slightly more pressing at the moment is finding out what in Tartarus he breathed into my face a minute ago—" she held up a hand to forestall the bailiff/harpy's criticism, "—my fault, yes, I know; I should have been paying better attention. Whatever it was, I'm guessing it's not going to give me rosy skin and glossy hair or make me look ten years younger."

She folded her arms and glared at Lanny expectantly.

He grimaced.

"Yeah...no. Just the opposite, actually."

The grip around Lanny's throat tightened again.

"Spill," Iris demanded. "Everything. And then tell me how you plan on fixing it."

#

Lanny sat at the bar at Nectar, Iris and Pete flanking him on either side. The harpy drummed her long, blood-red nails on the scarred wooden countertop, an unsubtle warning to him not to try anything sketchy. It was too late for that, of course, but what she didn't know couldn't hurt him.

He hoped.

Nectar was an underground establishment for immortals where his kind were decidedly unwelcome; Titans had no need of the philters served here, and as a rule, chose not to mingle with those who did. But Iris had spoken with the bouncer, an Oread whose name Lanny didn't catch, and after a quiet but heated exchange, the mountain nymph had reluctantly vouchsafed his entry, glaring daggers at him as he passed.

He'd told Iris that the antidote to his poison needed to be mixed with ambrosia, and Nectar was the only place in a 500-mile radius where that elixir of the gods could be obtained, though out of necessity, it was so watered down as to be hardly worthy of either the name or the cost. Still, he supposed immortal beggars couldn't be choosers. Not if they wanted to *stay* immortal, anyway.

In truth, no matter how diluted it was, the ambrosia itself was the only remedy needed, its purity the cure for his airborne toxin. The small vial he'd brought to the bar with him contained plain olive oil. Extra virgin, to be sure, but still just olive oil, and not even from Greece, but made locally in Arizona. It was just for show.

But he'd no more let Iris know how easily her decline into mortal decay could be reversed than he would hand her his crossbow and offer to pose with an apple on his head. After all, she was just as guilty as any of the Twelve of letting humanity's crimes against Gaea go unpunished, their divine attention having turned long ago from protecting the Mother of Everything Beautiful to keeping themselves alive and relevant in a swiftly changing world. But Gaea's only directive when she had released Lelantos and his sibling Titans from Tartarus had been to make the Olympians pay for allowing her to be so abused at the hands of humankind. The fates of lesser deities, he assumed, were left to Titanic discretion.

Iris ordered them drinks from the bartender, whom Lanny recognized as Thyone, Dionysius's once-mortal mother. As a goddess, she had presided over her son's drunken frenzies, which had eventually driven her mad. Here, she went by her mortal name, Semele—'Sem'—and was disguised as a stereotypical biker chick with a patch over her left eye. She'd lifted it to peer at him suspiciously before fetching their drinks, revealing the lightning-shaped scar that sealed the socket shut, a little memento of Zeus's displeasure.

Sem brought out two shot glasses full of honey-colored liquid for the goddess and the harpy and then dropped a dented and dusty can of Natural Light down in front of Lanny with a wicked smile. Known among gods and mortals alike as one of the world's worst-tasting beers, it was probably more watery than the ambrosia, if that were possible. It was also surprisingly popular among poor college students just looking for a cheap buzz, so Lanny wasn't too surprised that Sem kept a supply on hand, even if it had long since expired. The city *was* home to one of the state's largest universities, and immortals were known for hitting on

Play it Again, Sem — Marsheila Rockwell

liberal arts students who they thought would be impressed by their command of the classics.

Lanny popped the tab, took a big swig of the centaur piss masquerading as alcohol, then set the can back down on the countertop, wiping his mouth with the back of his hand. His expression didn't change, and his gaze never strayed from Sem's good eye. Her smile widened and she inclined her head slightly in acknowledgement, then went to take care of a couple of satyrs at the far end of the bar.

Turning his attention back to his companions, Lanny pulled the vial of oil out of his shirt pocket and unscrewed the dropper.

"Not so fast," Pete said, reaching for her own shirt pocket. She brought out a piece of plain green cloth that Lanny recognized immediately. Known as Achlys's Veil, the fine mesh fabric had been woven from strands of the Goddess of Misery's hair. Achlys was the Patroness of Poisons, and when her severed hair was exposed to a toxin in any form, it would immediately begin to shimmer and undulate, as if trying to return to its mistress's deadly head. Then it would dissipate into death-mist, and any nearby mortals who breathed it in would die within moments, their eyes clouding over with a thick chartreuse film.

Lanny was impressed. Veils were even harder to come by than ambrosia. Though unlike the nectar of the gods (which was a finite resource now, climate change having long since destroyed the habitats of the mystical flowers from which doves had once collected it), Achlys's hair could be replaced—if one were brave or stupid enough to attempt its harvest.

Pete snatched the vial dropper from Lanny's hand and squeezed several drops of oil onto the green cloth. There was, unsurprisingly, no reaction. The harpy snorted in disapproval, glaring down her beak-like nose at him, her beady eyes hard as flint. But she handed the dropper back to Lanny without comment before secreting the Veil back in her pocket.

"Well, it wasn't like I was going to poison her *again*," Lanny said. He gestured toward Iris's glass. "If I may?"

The goddess nodded. He squeezed several drops of the supposed antidote into her drink, and they all watched as the oil separated into tiny balls of liquid before dissolving completely, leaving the ambrosia looking no different than it had before.

"Here's looking at you, kid," Iris said, lifting the shot glass and downing the drink in one long draught. Then she set the glass upside down on the bar with authority and called out, "Play it again, Sem!" as she motioned for another round.

"Isn't the line actually—" Lanny began, but she interrupted him.

"Doesn't matter. That's what people *think* the line is, and perception is nine-tenths of the truth."

He couldn't very well argue with that.

Lanny nursed his Natty, making no move to finish it as he watched Iris and Pete try to drink each other under the table. The sisters had switched from ambrosia to straight ouzo after Iris's *Casablanca* tribute, the anise-flavored liquor being one of the few things that could give immortals anything resembling a buzz. As they drank, he tried to casually pump the rainbow-haired goddess for any information that might lead him to Artemis and the rest of the Twelve.

"So, a judge. Seems like a big change. I'd've thought maybe…," he almost said 'circus performer,' and thought better of it at the last minute; Pete's claws were still a little too close for comfort. "I don't know. CEO of FedEx?"

Iris snorted. She waved at Sem again, who brought over a bowl of cheese popcorn and some dubious-looking napkins.

"Please. I got tired of playing DeusEx employee a *long* time ago. At the beck and call of gods more powerful than me, a delivery girl to bring their messages to mortals? Unable to interfere with the outcomes that resulted from those messages, few of which were good and none of which were just?" She shook her head. "No thanks. As soon as mankind's numbers started to rise and it was obvious Zeus's power was waning, I took the fastest rainbow out of town and set up shop for myself, doing something where I could finally actually make a difference."

"Punishing mortal criminals?"

"Well, just the guilty ones."

Lanny's curiosity perked up at that.

"How do you know if they're guilty or not? You're not a goddess of truth."

The rainbow goddess's answering smile was radiant, her human disguise unable to suppress the full beauty of her delight. Lanny felt an unexpected thrill at the sight, though he chose not to examine its cause too closely.

"No, but I don't need to be. Not when I have Zeus's ewer."

Of course. The golden pitcher Lanny had seen in the courtroom. It hadn't contained just any water, but water drawn from the River Styx, which would cause a perjurer to die if he should drink from it—unless, of course, he immediately recanted, and told the truth.

Clever Goddess of the Rainbow, indeed.

But Lanny was more interested in the fact that the Stygian water from Zeus's ewer worked just as well on immortals as it did on mortals. Meaning it could be very useful in tracking down the Twelve, since once he found one Olympian, that one would then be forced to give up the locations of any of the others he or she might know.

"Nice. But what about Zephyrus?" The God of the West Wind had been Iris's consort, before. Lanny needed to know if the god was still in the picture. He told himself it was purely to understand how many potential obstacles might lie between him and getting the ewer from Iris.

She frowned, taken off guard by the seeming change of subject.

"What about him?"

"What does he think about you hiding out in the desert, disguised as a do-gooder judge?"

She let out a ringing peal of laughter and Lanny felt another thrill. Like the first, he tried to ignore it, though with less success this time.

"I have no idea, and I wouldn't care even if I did. He chose not to come with me when I left." She gave a sort of half-shrug. "Good riddance. He always was a bit flighty."

Lanny laughed at her quip, and Iris smiled warmly at him, and that was when Pete put her talon down.

"This has been super not-fun, but we got the antidote, we don't have any information for you about the Twelve—not that we'd give it to you if we did—and we've got cases on the docket in the morning. So this party is officially over, kids." She stared at him, hard, as though she could will him away from her sister with the force of her animosity alone. "And if we never see you again, it'll be too soon. Take as much offense to that as you need."

She was clearly trying to dismiss him, but Lanny wasn't about to let that happen. He had to get his hands on that ewer. And if there were other reasons he didn't want to end his association with the goddess of the rainbow just yet, well, he'd sort them out later. Right now, he had to secure at least one more meeting.

"Oh, but we'll *have* to see each other again," he said, feigning surprise at the harpy's words. "Didn't I make that clear?"

"Make *what* clear?" Pete replied, her voice gone low and dangerous. Lanny flashed back to the feeling of her talons squeezing his throat shut and he tried not to swallow nervously.

"One dose of the antidote won't be enough. I'm not sure how much of the poison Iris inhaled, but she's going to need at least one more, maybe even two or three. And they have to be spaced out to prevent overloading her system and actually making what's left of the toxin spread faster. Once a month would probably work fine." He looked expectantly at Iris, trying unsuccessfully to ignore Pete's murderous expression and the deadly rhythm of her hands clenching and unclenching. "Should I call you?"

Iris nodded, doing her best to hide a smile from her sister. She scribbled a number on one of the wet napkins and pushed it toward him. "That's my cell," she said, and winked. Lanny thought he heard Pete choke back a growl on the other side of him, but he was honestly too afraid to look.

Then Iris stood and raised her glass to him in a toast.

"Lanny, I think this is the beginning of a beautiful friendship," she said. Then she drained the glass and tossed it down, motioning for her impatient sister to join her. And as Lanny watched them walk out of Nectar, he had just one thought.

I sure hope so.

Marsheila (Marcy) Rockwell is a Rhysling Award-nominated poet and the author of twelve books and dozens of poems and short stories. A disabled pediatric cancer and mental health awareness advocate and reconnecting Chippewa/Métis, she lives in the desert with her family, buried under books. Find out more here: www.marsheilarockwell.com or on Twitter: @MarcyRockwell.

Thank you…

Thank you for taking the time to read our collection. We enjoyed all the stories contained within and hope you found at least a few to enjoy yourself. If you did, we'd be honored if you would leave a review on Amazon, Goodreads, and anywhere else reviews are posted.

You can also subscribe to our email list via our website, Https://www.cloakedpress.com

Follow us on Facebook http://www.facebook.com/Cloakedpress

Tweet to us https://twitter.com/CloakedPress

We are also on Instagram http://www.instagram.com/Cloakedpress

If you'd like to check out our other publications, you can find them on our website above. Click the "Check Our Catalog" button on the homepage for more great collections and novels from the Cloaked Press Family.

Made in United States
North Haven, CT
27 October 2021